The Hard Seed

Also by Mary Pomfret and published by Ginninderra Press
Writing in Virginia's Shadow
Cleaning Out the Closet

Mary Pomfret

The Hard Seed

You have to be a hard seed to survive in a desert

For Rose

The Hard Seed
ISBN 978 1 76041 607 2
Copyright © text Mary Pomfret 2018
Cover image: Kathryn Harrison, 2018, used with kind permission of the artist
Internal illustrations: Julie Andrews, 2018, used with kind permission of the artist

First published 2018 by
GINNINDERRA PRESS
PO Box 3461 Port Adelaide 5015
www.ginninderrapress.com.au

Bridport & Brown

Barristers and Solicitors

Ms Mia Sweeney

Editorial Services

Dear Ms Sweeney,

I act for the estate of the late Iris Bloom (DOD 10 August 2006). Further to our recent discussion, I have forwarded what appears to be an unpublished manuscript which my late client, Iris Bloom, left at my office shortly before her death.

In the final interview, Ms Bloom amended her will, setting aside an adequate sum for her writing to be put in order so that it might be forwarded to potential publishers.

Immediate family members have made strong but legally unsubstantiated objections to the publication of Ms Bloom's work.

The work is dedicated to someone by the name of 'Rose'. However, my investigations have failed to reveal any family member, friend or associate of that name.

Please note that I have included handwritten letters which may or not be part of the literary work. I will leave this to your discretion.

Kindly forward your account when convenient, and please keep me informed of your progress.

I remain,

    Yours sincerely,

        William Bridport

Prologue

It's never wise to reveal too much too soon.

Mr Bridport had rung days earlier to let Mia know the job was on the way, but just because you are expecting something doesn't mean you are ready for it. The law was full of euphemisms. Just exactly what did the term 'misadventure' mean? An accident perhaps? Whatever the case, Iris Bloom was dead. And Mia had never worked for a dead woman before; her clients had always been – even if not completely healthy – at least alive. In the past, there had been a few alcoholic writers who'd engaged her services and one or two heavy dope smokers, and then there had been the young man who was convinced he was Hemingway's reincarnation. But Mr Bridport's was probably the most peculiar request she had ever had.

The envelope sat on the kitchen bench for a week before she could face opening it.

'It's not a bomb,' George said, after dinner one night. 'Open it. Go on. You'll be paid for this work.'

Finally, Mia slid a knife through the top of the buff-coloured envelope. After all, they had bills to pay and she needed all the work she could get. For some reason, Mia had expected a brown-paper parcel tied with knotted string. She had pictured a frail sunspotted hand pulling the string tight over the paper, patting it and smoothing out the creases, wishing it well on its journey. But instead the manuscript came in a standard business envelope.

Mia flicked through the pages – some had been typed and others were handwritten on lined paper, possibly torn from a school exercise book.

'It looks like a mixture of old letters mixed up with what seems to be a novel,' Mia said, placing the solicitor's letter in the top drawer of her desk.

'Documentary evidence?' asked George, leaning back in the chair and stretching out his long legs.

Mia wished her husband would go away. He didn't have enough work to do, that was his trouble. He was at his most annoying when he was in-between projects.

'Do you know the difference between facts and evidence, Mia?'

Mia ignored him. He went on to explain that evidence could be destroyed and a fact was only so if it could be proved but, once established as a fact, is always a truth.

Mia sometimes wondered what life would be like when he retired, when he would be in the house all the time. But she would have to worry about that when the time came. Perhaps one of them would die before it happened. Either way, it would be a relief not to have him prattling on all the time.

'Well, I wonder which will be more interesting – the facts or the fiction?' George said.

A fine line, Mia thought, reluctant to discuss this one with George. He wasn't a historian for nothing. Facts were his core business: facts, documents, evidence and research. George had no time for imagination and he would argue his case for hours.

'I see the novel is dedicated to someone called Rose, whoever she may be,' Mia said, swivelling her chair towards the window, looking out and hoping George would soon leave the room. Eventually, she heard the door close behind her and breathed a sigh of relief. This was going to be a big job. And so she began her task.

In the days that followed, Mia worked on the manuscript whenever she could. Now the university semester had begun again, George had lectures to prepare. Having something to occupy him stopped him from coming into her office and trying to make conversation about whatever he happened to be thinking about at the time. Anything from the amount of junk mail they seemed to be getting, to the neighbour's barking dog, anything at all. But she couldn't blame George any more – ever since the semester had begun he was hard at work designing his lectures for the new students. Even though now her study was still and silent, the days working on this manuscript had started bleeding into weeks.

Papers were scattered across the scarred and scratched surface of her old desk. A certain smell came to Mia every time she began reading Iris's handwritten pages. The scent of sorrow? 'But you can't smell sorrow,' she could imagine George saying. But the more Mia read Iris's pages, the more she came to realise what a strange and haunted woman she must have been. Perplexing and mystifying too that Iris's family objected so much to her writing. Maybe she might discover the reason hidden deep in Iris's maze of stories, her web of words.

Roisin

5 July 2001

Dear Rose,

Well, here I am, again. Back on this island, I feel cast away, adrift. I have arrived back at the place where I was born, the place where I began and where I will, undoubtedly, end my days.

Today the sky is grey, the buildings are grey and I am grey. I suppose I should be thankful my mother left the house to me. Her lavender perfume still hangs in the air.

Even Arnold noticed it. 'This house stinks of old people, Iris,' he said to me this morning.

I couldn't help it – I had to say, 'You mean it smells of us, Arnold?'

He just grunted and said, 'It smells of your mother.'

I guess she thought the house was so run down the rest of the family wouldn't want it. Seems she might have been right, because I haven't heard from any of them since we moved in. Most likely my brother Jim and sisters Bridie and Marie are happy with the cash and the business left to them. I wonder will I see any of them before I die.

I remember just before I left, all those years ago, one day when the snow covered the mountain almost down to the base and clouds gathered low, I said to my mother, 'The spirits are around today, Mum.'

She stopped whatever she was doing – probably peeling potatoes or chopping onions – and asked me what on earth I was talking about.

How could I tell a woman as practical as my mother was that I sometimes heard voices crying in the wind? Perhaps that's why I had to go – to escape an island so steeped in the suffering of a past which hides and shapeshifts in shadows, is sealed in sandstone walls and where its unrequited revenants go unheeded and unreconciled. But that wasn't the only reason I left this cold island and headed for the desert.

But now I have reached a certain age, I was thinking I should keep a journal of sorts. Not a memoir – most definitely not. I don't like memoirs. There always seems to be a trace of the narcissist about them, I feel. But I have decided my time would be better spent writing to you, Rose. Such a beautiful name.

Sometimes, I wonder about my own name. I think I would have liked something more glamorous. But I console myself with the notion that Iris was the messenger of the Greek gods who guided souls to the Elysian Fields. I hope my mother is there now, in the Elysian Fields.

The house hasn't changed much. The roses are still growing strong. Mum looked after them well enough, even though I don't think she ever loved them as I do. Luckily, I will have Arnold's help when he's up to it. The neighbour said to me the other day, 'Your mother worked in the garden right up until just before she died, you know.' I will have to ask her if she knows anyone who could use Mum's mirrors. I am not sure why she had so many. I have no need of mirrors. Memories will be my mirror.

Funny the things you remember once you begin this memory game, this summoning up of the past. Last night, I thought about the man who came to collect me from the Greyhound bus depot to take me to out to the cattle station to begin my job as governess. He wore a battered old Akubra and a dark blue shirt with the sleeves cut out and he smelled of horses and sweat when he reached over and put a cassette in the tape deck. It might have been Charlie Pride or maybe Slim Dusty. Can't recall, now. But, whoever it was, the country music helped me relax as we sped along the dirt road in the old, white ute, dust flying, blue heeler chained up in the back, all the way to the cattle station – thousands of acres of scorched, red earth.

I remember when we pulled up in front of the homestead, he said to me, 'How long do you think you'll last out here, girlie?'

It's a bit of a cliché, isn't it, marrying the station owner's son, but I didn't do that. I don't think the station owner even had a son. I married Arnold, the head stockman. Forty-five years this September. He was far too old to be riding horses, but Arnold is so stubborn, Always has been. It wasn't the first time a horse had thrown him, but it was the last. He's lucky to be alive. Lately, I've noticed his speech is getting a bit better and he's not limping as much.

But here, at least, he will get the treatment he needs and the cooler weather will be so much better for him. And the skies here aren't always grey. Sometimes, the sky here is so clear and blue even in the middle of winter and the sun is warm if you find a sheltered spot, like I did this morning. I had my coffee sitting on the low, brick fence in the back corner of the garden near the pomegranate tree, and I think my cheeks might have got a bit sunburnt.

Sometimes I go on and on to Arnold about how I miss our life on the station, but he never seems to hear me, and even if he did, what good would it do? I think one of the things I miss most is the rugged, ochre-coloured mountain ranges I used to look out at from my kitchen window. But now I have another mountain to gaze upon – dark and wild.

And to have made a start on my new novel is a wonderful thing. I must find a writing group, because Arnold is absolutely hopeless at anything like that. I can't talk to him about writing on any level. He wants a happy ending. He doesn't understand all writers do cruel things to the characters they love. I attempted to discuss my novel with him the other night. I told him, 'If my heroines had known what was in store for them, they might have made different choices.' But then I thought what a silly thing it was to say. I made the choices for them, didn't I? But nonetheless, we would probably all make different choices if we could see the road ahead. I'm sure I would have. I know I would have.

Now I must work on my stories. It seems all I have left. Stories and memories. I must be careful not to get them confused.

Iris

Baggage

Why hadn't she worn her flat shoes instead of the black leather stilettos? What a foolish, vain mistake. Her heel caught in a crack on the platform but she managed to steady herself. Breathless, she made it – but only just. Ten seconds later and she would have been left standing on the dark platform watching the last train heading out into the night. She climbed aboard just as the whistle blew. Well, she was on her way, for better or for worse.

Roisin lifted her small suitcase onto the luggage rack. She looked around the carriage, hoping she was not the only passenger. No problem finding a seat. No mothers with excited noisy kids ready for the zoo, or football fans going to watch the match, or commuters headed for a working day in the city.

The carriage was empty apart from an elderly woman with a plastic bag tied around her head – probably because it had been raining – and a forlorn-looking boy dressed in his school uniform. Roisin sat opposite them, these her fellow travellers, grateful she wasn't alone in the cold, dimly lit carriage that smelled of stale body odour and hot chips. She unfolded her newspaper and held it at a certain well-practised angle, close enough to observe the unsuspecting, and far enough away to appear uninterested.

The schoolboy's tie hung loosely around his neck and the cuffs of his blazer were stained. Perhaps he hadn't even been home from school. He looked no more than fourteen. A tattered copy of *King Lear* poked through the open zipper of his backpack. Motionless, he sat staring out of the window, his arms folded across his chest. Roisin noticed the chipped, black nail polish on his bitten fingernails. Was he running away? He had an aura of tragedy about him – alone so late at night, thin and vulnerable – poetic almost. But maybe he wasn't going far – perhaps he would just make a round trip and he'd go home on the early morning train. His mother would surely be worried sick about him.

Roisin looked again at the old woman, whose face was heavily etched with lines, especially around her mouth. A smoker most likely, with false teeth.

'What time does this train get in?' rasped the woman, the bag still on her head and tied tightly under her chin.

Roisin wondered if she should mention the bag on her head but she decided against it. People don't always respond well, even if you are trying to be helpful.

'Midnight,' replied the boy.

It was a shock to hear him speak, even if it was just one word.

'Had your tea, love?' the woman asked him.

He didn't reply and continued to stare out of the window. He did have a pale, hungry look about him.

Roisin followed his gaze into the night. Sometimes, it's all any of us can do – stare out of the window. Wasn't that what Virginia Woolf said, or was it someone else? Roisin watched the flickering images – station signs, empty platforms, peeling billboards, graffiti – as the train sped on through the thick night. Isn't this how life is, she thought, imposing upon us as we move onwards through the hours and the years? What choices do we really have? she wondered, glancing down at her hands. More age spots, every day it seemed. She had given up calling them freckles.

Two days ago, her sister Bridget's phone call had been an imposition of a kind, something that demanded a decision that, either way, was thorny. It was an invitation, if you could call it that. It would have been nice to receive the invitation in good time, with lots of notice. But the invitation to their parents' anniversary party had come to her in the same strange yet predictable way she received most invitations to family functions. Never a simple card in the mail. Nothing that straightforward. It was usually a last-minute thing, often through a third party. The kind of invitation that was just a face-saving exercise by someone wanting to be seen to do the right thing. It was difficult to go, difficult to stay away. Either way, she would lose.

Short notice serves its own purpose. Just like the invitation to her brother Pat's wedding which he made the day before, even though she was living in Darwin at the time and the wedding was in Melbourne. She'd even been stupid enough to send him a present. But maybe one dishonest act deserves another.

So nothing much had changed. The golden anniversary party had all been arranged. All Roisin had to do was show up. Most people with any sense just wouldn't go.

'Going somewhere nice, love?' croaked the old woman.

'Well, I'm not sure. I hope so. A family get-together. A garden party for my parents' fiftieth wedding anniversary,' Roisin said, wondering if a lie would have been easier.

'Well, you never can tell with those affairs. Fifty years is a long time. A lot of water has flowed under the bridge in that time,' the woman said. She made a sound that could have been a laugh or a moan.

Maybe I should be grateful for at least some kind of family, Roisin thought. This woman probably has no one at all. Perhaps there was a daughter somewhere who had invited her at the last minute to attend a child's christening and who would say, 'Mum, you didn't have to come.'

Would anyone say to her tomorrow, 'Roisin, you didn't have to come'? Probably not. Not outright, anyway. But there are many ways of making someone feel unwelcome. Bridget was expert at it. The irony of it was, usually Bridget was the one who got the word to her.

Roisin folded her newspaper and put it on the empty seat. She looked at her watch. The train pulled in at a station and no one got on. Still quite a way to go. She found herself thinking about the last time she had seen her family. At least a few Christmases back, it would have been. Oh yes, there'd been that argument. She couldn't remember now if it had been with Bridget or little Mary. She always thought of her youngest sister, Mary, as little. Strange, as she was far from little now. Most probably the argument had been with Bridget. Yes, it was Bridget, but Mary had been there. It had been all about the fruit salad and their mother had cried, as usual.

'Roisin, you get out of here,' her father had yelled at her, 'and take your sour grapes with you. Don't you come here upsetting your mother and your sisters with your nastiness and spite. You're just lucky your brother's not here.'

An uneasiness began to descend on her, but there was no turning back now. The train travelled into the darkness and, just for a moment, Roisin dozed off.

When she opened her eyes again, the boy seemed hardly to have moved. His face was still turned towards the window, his arms still folded.

The old woman had begun rummaging in a grubby-looking handbag and pulled out a pack of tobacco. 'Won't be long now, thank goodness,' the woman said. 'Dying for a smoke.'

The train finally slowed to a halt at the city platform. Now, her friends the schoolboy and the plastic-bag lady walked past her seat and began to disappear from her life, like pages of a lost manuscript blowing away in the wind. In her mind, Roisin had become close to them, she had begun to know them well. She would miss them, her friends the tragic boy and the bag lady.

Roisin was the last one to get off the carriage. A solitary conductor stood at the turnstile, all the station shops were closed, the windows dark. The sound of her heels on the hard platform echoed in the silence. She showed the conductor her ticket and passed through. Well, at least if nothing else, she had arrived and she was here for the big day, for the party tomorrow. That's the thing about arrivals – they are non-negotiable. When you have arrived, you are there.

23 September 2001

Dear Rose,

I think I have been a bit of a misery these last few weeks because Arnold said to me a few nights back, 'Time you cheered up, Iris.'

Well, I have to admit I am feeling a lot better since I have found a writing group. So thrilled they have let me join them. Just a chance encounter at the library – but life is often like that, isn't it? I went for the first time last night. Writers young and old were there. Oddly, I had the feeling I have with so many people that I had met some of them before. Most likely, our paths had never crossed, but it's strange how some people have a sense of familiarity about them that's hard to define.

The meeting was at a man named Hugh's house. His wife is called Sally. Such a sweet and harmless name.

Hugh had a bottle of red on the go and he offered me a glass. He asked me what it was like.

I said, 'Not a poisoned chalice,' and he looked at me as if I were crazy. Not sure why I made such a comment, but I often say things without knowing why.

A young writer called Eric kicked us off. He read with such conviction – something about a spaceship landing in the outback with an almost endless descriptive passage about how the aliens could not find their way out of the forest. No forest in the outback when I lived there. I couldn't help but wonder if he had a girlfriend or wife. Most probably not. Most likely he lived alone in a cream-brick unit and visited his mother every Sunday night for tea. His mother might be a nervy little woman who rarely left the house, whose grey roots always needed retouching, but perhaps not. She might be nothing like that at all.

I think my constant imaginings about people irritate Arnold intensely and, in a way, I can understand why. But for me, it is my research method. Imagination, not facts. Sometimes I think one of the best jobs for a writer would be a taxi driver. Innocent bystanders, they must witness so many fragments of life's mini-tragedies, never seeing the end or the beginning, just a few passing scenes.

When Eric had finished his reading, Hugh said to him, 'Yes, well, perhaps it might pay to research the geography of the Australian inland a little more.' I think he meant it kindly.

When it was my turn, I read my little poem. I dashed it off the other day. It needs something. It's unfinished, but some things are better left that way, don't you think?

Silk
sachets
pale ribbon
tied
lavender-filled
mother's
favourite flower
her scent
wafts
ghostly.

I don't think I will use it in my novel. A little too sentimental.

Arnold seems to be settling in okay but he gets very restless at times. He picked me a yellow rose today. 'This is for you, Iris,' he said, and he actually smiled at me.

Last night, when I got into bed, the sheets didn't feel quite so cold.

Iris

All Alone In a Big Bed

'In town for a visit?' said the driver, not even looking over his shoulder.

'Yes, you could say that – a family party, actually.'

'Family party, huh? My family, back in Athens, never made it out here. My kids never knew their grandparents. Can't have everything in life but, can you?'

'No, you can't have everything.'

Bridget hadn't offered her a bed, so a hotel it was. Still it was better than sitting in the travellers' lounge all night with the bag lady, or on a cold seat on the station platform with the tragic boy.

Now, Roisin was wondering why she had even come at all. But how can you not go to your parents' fiftieth wedding anniversary? A garden party, 1930s style – a fully catered affair with the best champagne and cucumber sandwiches, all paid for by Patrick, her younger brother, the golden boy. Just how Pat had made all his money was never discussed, but he had lots of it and it just wasn't possible to make all that money from a career in the navy.

She could have just said no. But she had come; she would show up. Tomorrow, her parents would celebrate fifty years together and their loving progeny would look on in awe, pay homage, play their parts, the roles they had been given. Roisin knew that to contest or resist a role could be dangerous. You might be forced to the edges, become the one who unsettles others merely with their presence, allocated a minor role and seen as a malcontent, a whiner even. Bridget said something similar a few days back when they had spoken on the phone, when she had issued the summons – or was it a refusal of entry?

'The party? What party? Am I invited?'

'Still wearing your crown of thorns, Roisin? Of course you're bloody well invited. I wouldn't be ringing you otherwise, would I? It's Mum and Dad's golden wedding anniversary. Surely you haven't forgotten.'

Roisin had become skilled at the practised smile, even had her teeth bleached and tried always to wear lipstick in the presence of her family. Tomorrow, she would smile till her jaw ached. But alone in the cold back seat of a taxi, there was no need to even try to smile.

The taxi took her silently through the city streets. She gazed out at Friday-night crowds of partygoers, the end of the working-week revellers. A stranger to that kind of life now, the face she wore when she was alone settled on her, an unsmiling face that reflected back at her in the window, a face that once had wished for more, once had wished for love.

Roisin stared at the back of the cabbie's head. He'd fallen silent. He probably thought she was only another middle-aged woman, just another lost cause, living out the days like a ghost, with no man and no hope of ever finding one again. He probably had about five kids and was most likely a grandfather, even. His wife would be curled on the couch, asleep now, knowing her husband would be home in the early hours of the morning, and she would be there for him with coffee and eggs and bacon, news of the family comings and goings and a warm hug before he went to sleep for the day.

The taxi pulled up outside the hotel.

'Thanks,' she said as she paid the fare.

'Hey, lady, cheer up. It might never happen!' he called after her.

Not brave enough to face the emptiness of the hotel room immediately, she had her bags sent up to the seventeenth floor and headed straight for the piano bar. The late-night pianist was playing 'It Must Be Love'. She sat on a stool next to a man who seemed so familiar.

'In Melbourne for long? Glass of red?' he asked, not waiting for the answer.

Roisin sipped the wine. Last of the big spenders. House red – the worst.

A stranger, yet she had met versions of him many times before. He introduced himself as Nick, a salesman in town to promote a new mattress. He launched into a monologue about his ex-wife, his debts, his children, whom he hardly ever saw.

She stared into the mirror behind the bar, watching a tired-looking woman listen to a balding man, slumped over the bar, talking into his glass.

Nature never intended for a man and a woman to be together for a lifetime, Nick waxed on. He bought her drinks, and yet more drinks. 'Things change, people change. Life doesn't stay the same. People who think love is forever are fools,' he said.

Nick, a warrior poet, roaming the streets of Melbourne, selling inner-spring mattresses, knew a lot about nature's intent, it seemed.

'What about swans?' said Roisin.

'The Sydney Swans?'

'No, swans on a lake. You know, real swans. Don't they mate for life?'

'Fuck swans. They don't live long enough to get bored. What do you do for a crust?'

'I'm a writer.'

'A writer, huh? I knew a writer once. She ended up killing herself. No one ever found out why.'

Nick's maundering continued. He looked like he might be Greek. He wanted to go to Greece for the Olympics one day, he wished he had finished his degree and become an architect, his grandmother was dying from cancer, business had been tough lately and, finally, 'What's your name?'

'Roisin.'

'So what do you write about?'

'Oh, I write all sorts of stories…usually it's all about the character. I might write about you one day, Nick.'

'Feeling tired yet, Robyn?'

The bar was closing. It was three o'clock in the morning and yes, she was tired, too tired to spend any more time with him. But she was grateful for the haze of the wine and Nick's ravings. He'd been a diversion for a while. They went up in the elevator together. A short balding man and a nondescript older woman, they could have been husband and wife.

Nick got out at the fifth floor. 'Goodnight, Robyn.'

'Thanks for the drinks,' she called after him.

He raised his hand and walked away, without looking back.

Roisin opened the door of the hotel room. It smelled of citronella, other people and loneliness. She turned out the lights and stared out the window over Port Phillip Bay. She tried not to think of Dave. The sheets were cold. Cold sheets, alone in a big bed, everyone is a stranger. She lay her head on the hard hotel pillow and thought about what to wear tomorrow – the black floral strappy sundress, or the magenta linen shirt and denim skirt? No, maybe not the skirt. That could look frumpy with its elasticised waist. Bridget and Mary would look so elegant; they always did, with their perfect skin and designer clothes. Dave always liked her in the floral dress, Roisin remembered. She would try it on again in the morning. Hopefully, she could still squeeze into it.

Her head thick and her mouth dry, she awoke earlier than usual. Too much red last night with Nick. She looked through the hotel window. The sun was shining – a good omen if nothing else, but omens are not always to be trusted. The sun never shone more brightly than on her own wedding day and now the faded photographs and a stained white wedding dress were packed away in lavender tissue paper in a battered old case, at home, under her bed.

They never did get to celebrate even their tenth wedding anniversary, Dave and her. She could remember the soft plumpness of Dave's hand as he held hers at the altar on their wedding day. He hated the softness of his hands – he wanted the hard hands of a farmer's son. But no matter how hard he tried, his hands were always soft and fleshy. Yes, she could remember the physical sensation of his touch but she couldn't remember that feeling of love for him. She only knew she did feel it once.

Roisin stepped into the shower. Still she could never close her eyes in the shower. She let the water run over her for half an hour then stood dripping on the cold tiles. Looking down at herself, she wondered how she ever got so out of shape. Perhaps make-up would help. Strong eye make-up and lipstick. She applied it carefully, anxious not to look overdone. There must be a moment in the life of every woman when youth departs, silently, without notice and never returns.

'You'll just have to do,' she said aloud to herself. Roisin found comfort in talking to herself more and more. Sometimes she found herself talking to herself in the supermarket or even when she was gardening. She'd have to watch that, because people find it odd, people who don't live alone don't understand.

She slipped on the sundress and struggled with the zip. It fitted, but only just. She would wear her sandals for her beach walk. Now she was dressed, she liked herself a little better. Thankfully, her ankles were still thin.

She made coffee from the brown hotel sachets and took the standard white mug out to the balcony and took a sip. It tasted like a blend of cardboard and gravy. How she longed for a cigarette, so she took deep breaths instead.

Her stomach churned and she wasn't sure if it was from nerves or the house wine Nick had bought her last night. When she had been married to Dave and she had been away in a strange place, she had always called him. Even though it had been years since their divorce, whenever she was away from home and alone in hotel room, she felt the urge to ring him. 'How's the dog?' 'Is it raining there?' But no more solace in familiar small talk to stave off the soulnessness of a hotel room.

Roisin picked up the hotel phone. How foolish to be asking to be connected to man who probably wouldn't even know her in the morning light. He'd told her his room was number 531. Just why she remembered that detail she wasn't sure, any more than she was sure of the reason he had given it to her. He might have already checked out.

'What the… Who the fuck is this ringing me in the middle of the night?'

'It's me, Nick – Roisin. You remember we had drinks at the bar. I'm sorry. It's nearly nine o'clock and it's sunny. Nick, I'm scared about today – please say something deep and poetic about life and love.'

'How about this – if you're so screwed up about your parents' anniversary party, just don't go. Don't go. Now, I'm going back to sleep – catch ya.'

She stood silent for a few seconds.

The phone startled her with its ring. It was Nick. 'Hey, Robyn – have a good time.' The phone went dead again.

She looked into the phone the way people do when the other person hangs up on them. How easy that would be – just not to turn up. If only it were that simple. She would file Nick away in her memory. How few men there had been in her life. Perhaps she could pretend he had been one of them.

Three hours to go before it started, the gathering, the celebration, the ordeal. Midday, Bridget had said. A walk along the beach, breathe in the sea air, clear the head. Yes, that might help. She headed towards the pier. It was good to walk. She sat down and unbuckled her sandals and sank her feet into the rough grey sand. It was going to be a warm day but the breeze was still cool. Even though it was so early in the day, people were everywhere: reading newspapers at the outdoor cafés, sipping cappuccinos, walking dogs, roller blading, riding bikes and pushing children in prams. If she half closed her eyes, it could be an Impressionist's painting – Seurat's *A Sunday on La Grande Jatte*, maybe.

The sand was cold on the soles of her feet, the seawater lapped against her ankles and the stiff breeze blew sand hard against her bare legs.

Roisin thought about the day ahead. No Dave to shield her now. Now she would have to face them on her own. She would try to smile and to make herself useful, invisible, to be almost 'not there'. Like a ghost.

Slowly, Roisin made her way back toward the hotel. She walked into her room to see a message on hotel paper on the bedside table, handwritten by some unsuspecting hotel receptionist who probably was in a hurry to go to morning tea, and who had no idea of her ever-so minor role in the unfolding narrative.

Try not to be late. We want the family there before the others arrive. Bridget.

Roisin sat down on the edge of the bed and pulled on her black stilettos. Coarse sand was stuck to the soles of her feet and in-between her toes. She gave them a quick rub, but there was no time to soak her feet now. Time to go.

25 October 2001

Dear Rose,

I sometimes wonder what will happen to my writing when I go. What happens to all the thoughts you leave behind if they are not heard by someone? Do they just float like spectres and creep into the dreams of the unsuspecting?

Last night, I had my first dream in this house – I have had this dream so many times before. I have only just begun to dream again since the move. Perhaps the medication has been blocking my thoughts. This dream was a big one. No point telling Arnold about it. If I tell you about it, maybe it will make more sense to me.

Furniture casts shadows against grey featureless walls. Cavernous black fireplace overflows with powdery ash. At the touch of a match, the paper turns and twists back upon itself, at first as if in resistance, and furls and softens into grey blooms that blacken and die. Bits of newspaper, not entirely devoured by the flames, fragments with scorched curled-up edges, lie waiting for a well-meaning breeze. It's hard to recall the carpet. If there had been carpet, there would have been holes and the frayed hessian underlay would have shamed the stained and faded roses trodden on and muddied by heavy steel-capped boots and uncaring stilettos. But I'm not sure if there ever was carpet.

At least, in translating the images into words, in writing it, I feel at least I have told someone. I have told you. When I got up this morning after the dream, I put the kettle on and as it came to a boil I felt a sob rise from deep within me. I had to cry out loud to release it. Arnold came hobbling in to see what on earth the matter was. I burnt myself, I lied.

Iris

Garden Party

The taxi pulled in behind the Mercedes, silver and shining in the sun. It was Pat's, of course, or Patrick as her mother always called him. Her precious only son, who was just like his father, after all, wasn't he? Roisin walked slowly down the red-brick path lined with white geraniums, breathing deeply, trying to slow her heartbeat, and knocked softly on the door, already ajar. No answer. She walked in. And it hit her, that familiar smell – bacon fried hours earlier for breakfast, old roses, traces of her sisters' perfumes, her father's cigar smoke – the smell of her family. She could hear a soft buzz of voices coming from the garden. The lounge was as it always had been – dark and cluttered. The grey and pink birds of an uncertain species still adorned the wall, the African native head ornaments with rings through their noses sat on the mantelpiece and the silver ashtray stand still stood next to her father's chair, a green velvet recliner.

An anxious-looking woman wearing a strappy floral dress that was too tight stared back at her from the mirror that hung over the mantelpiece. For a moment, she thought it was her mother.

Against the wall was her father's library – an old dusty bookcase with a lifetime's collection of books, magazines and papers. She scanned the titles. Her mother always dusted everything in the house except the bookcase and the books. Strange. It was as if there was something she didn't want to disturb. *Bleak House* was lying face-up. Perhaps her father was engaging in a little literary vanity. He only went to school until he was twelve, but he loved everyone to know he was a self-made man.

'You don't have to go to university. Everything worth knowing is in books, except those romance books that Roisin's always writing,' he used to say when he was holding forth, and he was often holding forth. There weren't too many things Frank didn't have an opinion on.

Roisin wiped her finger over the dusty shelf. She didn't feel quite ready to face them all yet, her family. She needed to get her bearings, to set her compass, to hang in the shadows a little longer. Her palms were clammy and she had a lurching feeling in her stomach, but she would have to join them soon. There was no getting out of it now.

A faint smell of jasmine wafted down the passage. Her mother's statue of the Blessed Virgin had its own special place on the wooden sideboard and was draped with rosary beads. Today, her mother had placed a bunch of white roses in a crystal vase in front of the statue and had lit a votive candle. Staring into the flame, Roisin made a wish that all would be well. A wish is the same as a prayer, isn't it? It's just that prayers seem to carry more weight in the eyes of some, she thought.

'Who is that down there, hiding in the shadows? Is that you, Roisin, skulking around in the ashes?' It was the familiar voice of her father. 'Come out, girl, and show yourself.'

Roisin peered down the dark hallway and could see them all standing, crowded together in the courtyard. 'Yes, it's me, Dad,' she called back, walking toward them all.

'So, you made it, Roisin,' said Bridget. 'How nice.'

Her mother kissed her and said, 'Are you hungry, dear?' The catch cry of all mothers to their adult children who no longer need them.

'No thanks, Mum, I'm not hungry. Happy anniversary to you both.'

At that precise moment, it dawned on her she had come without a present. In the rush to get there, she'd completely forgotten.

As if reading her thoughts, Bridget said, 'Roisin, have you seen the silver goblets Mary, Pat and I bought for Mum and Dad? We had them engraved, but we thought you would do your own thing. You usually do.' Glinting a smile, she showed Roisin the elegant silver goblets lying side by side in a blue velvet box.

She read the engraving:

From your loving children
Bridget, Mary and Pat

'Yes, of course. Wonderfully tasteful, as always, Bridget. In the Tarot, goblets or cups always symbolise lovers. Beautiful choice. I didn't have time to buy a present. Do you think you could have my name engraved too?' Roisin said, forcing a smile.

'It might be a bit late for that, Roisin. Time for a glass of champagne. Time to wet the baby's head, so to speak. Come on, Mam's set up her best glasses,' said Pat.

How long had it been since she had seen him, her brother – four, maybe five years? Longer even. His years in the navy showed: crisp shirt taut across his muscular back; short tight hair; impeccable grooming and an unmistakable air of authority.

He pulled a bottle of Moët from the ice bucket, eased the cork out, and poured the sparkling wine into the tall glasses. 'Now, here's a toast to Mam and Dad – fifty years together and never a fight between you! Here's cheers to you both and may there be fifty more!' said Pat, beaming at them all.

'Thank you, Pat. What a wonderful son you are,' said Frank.

'Cheers!' they all chorused in response.

'Cheers!' Roisin made sure she clinked every glass. She didn't want to miss anyone. That would be bad luck, wouldn't it?

Frank kissed their mother's powdered pink cheek and put his arm around her shoulder. He raised his glass. 'To my beautiful Kathleen. My one and only.'

Pat, Mary and Bridget moved together and began speaking words into the air, in a language they all understood. But Roisin didn't know the code any more. Perhaps she did once, long ago, but she didn't understand it now. She'd forgotten the rules. She stood alone looking into her glass thinking of her last session with her counsellor.

'I can't find the words to describe how I feel when I see them laughing and joking and loving each other,' Roisin had said at her last appointment.

'Would the word "excluded" work for you, Roisin?'

'It might come close. But it's probably more about who I am. What

I am. Am I so worthless or unlovable that even my own family can't abide me?'

'How do these feelings serve you, Roisin?'

'They don't serve me at all. Not at all. Except…maybe…except for my writing.'

'That's your answer, Roisin. Your writing is your answer.'

'That's the thing about writing: it teaches you to be cold-blooded amidst all kinds of hilarity and tragedy. But it's not foolproof, though. Everyone comes unstuck sometimes.'

Roisin sat on the cracked, brick wall in the corner of the garden and tried to remember when she had last sat there. The old rosebush was still strong and heavy on the wooden arch and the jasmine smelled sweet and cloying in the warm summer air. Perhaps it would be easier to get through today if she paid attention to the externals, the details, and tried to stay detached and observant. Roisin told herself this would not be an auspicious day for reflecting on her own emotions. It was a day she needed to get through as best she could.

She took a sip of her champagne and looked up. A dark shape filled the rose arbour.

'Well, look who it is – come in, Father Murphy. Come in, Father. Come in,' said Mary, rushing forward to greet him, her yellow silk dress fitting neatly at her waist, her thin frame toppling forward slightly probably because her silver strappy sandals were just a fraction too high.

Roisin watched her fussing and bouncing around Father Murphy, leading him across the lawn to where their mother and father were sitting alongside each other, sipping champagne. She looks just like a buttercup, Roisin thought.

'Well, a grand day it is for a celebration it is, to be sure. Congratulations, Kathleen and Frank, and God bless you on this day,' said Father Murphy, shaking Frank's hand.

There was only just a faint trace of Irish in Father Murphy's accent.

Perhaps the most Irish thing about him was his name. He loved football and barracked for Collingwood. It was surprising he hadn't worn his black and white scarf, but there again it was probably too warm to be wearing a knitted scarf no matter how ardent a supporter he might be.

'Now, will you be having a small whiskey with me, Father?' said Frank, standing and knocking back the dregs of his champagne.

'Yes, Father, come on now, let's take our drinks into the shade,' said Kathleen.

The humble little inner-city garden had been transformed for the day. Bridget and Mary had hired some flowering plants in terracotta pots. Chairs dressed with calico skirts and yellow organza bows were set around the brick fence. They must have been expecting a multitude. Chinese lanterns hung from the magnolia tree, the old Hills hoist had been transformed into a gazebo and the two Irish musicians were under it, setting up their act. A white cloth covered the trestle table and a huge bunch of pink roses sat in the centre. An upturned fridge was full of the best champagne.

'It all looks wonderful,' Roisin said to Bridget and Mary. 'You should have let me help. And you both look so lovely today.' She wondered if they knew how beautiful they were, her sisters, with their fine skin, slow elegant movements and sleek hair; if they knew the power of their currency. Roisin knew plain women had to try much harder to get what they wanted from life.

Her sisters both smiled at her, the way shop assistants smile at customers.

'Absolutely no need, no need for your help, Roisin. It's all done. Relax. It's all done,' said Bridget, turning away to talk to the musicians.

'So glad you could come, Roisin. Have a wonderful day. Don't look so glum. It's a party, you know.' Mary turned and joined Bridget and they both stood with their backs to her: her sisters.

24 December 2001

Dear Rose,

I am pleased to tell you I have made a new friend – Imelda. Not a writer, but sometimes that can be better. Writers don't always make the best friends. Imelda is in her early forties, maybe. It's hard to tell. Met her about a month ago when I was out walking. I sometimes wonder if she knows how old I am. I must be at least twenty years older than her, probably more. Perhaps that is why she feels she can tell me so many things. We have had coffee a few times now and I sense I will be her keeper of secrets.

And she has invited me to dinner on Boxing Day. 'Don't bring anything, Iris,' she said. 'Just bring your beautiful self.'

How lovely it was to hear that. She didn't mention Arnold, but he wouldn't want to go anyway. He will be happy just to sit on the front veranda and stare at the roses.

I have bought a new dress, although I was tempted to wear one of Mother's Grace Kelly-style dresses, but there is an age where retro dressing becomes just plain silly. And try as I might, I cannot get the mothball smell out of her dresses. I couldn't possibly sit at Imelda's table smelling of mothballs.

This morning, when I was looking through Mother's old dresses, I started thinking about the outback and how it used to attract so many eccentrics. Perhaps I was one of them. Why I began thinking about him, I don't know, but there was an elderly gentleman who I would see every time I went into town for supplies. He would wander up and down the main street in the heat of the day, talking loudly to himself and quoting Keats in the most cultured English accent.

I remember Mr Harris from the stock and station agent told me

Jack, I think his name was Jack, had been 'a remittance man'. How awful to be someone who was exiled to the colonies and paid by their family to stay away. I recall vividly he would wear a thick green hand-knitted jumper no matter what the temperature. You couldn't help but wonder what sins might have been pinned to that tatty old jumper. It was as if he, like some poor goat, had been sent off into the wilderness carrying with him all the problems, failings and perceived evils affecting his family. Was he held responsible for the death of his mother in childbirth, the loss of the family fortune, the disgrace of his sister, or did his schizophrenia remind the family of a certain amount of inbreeding which occurred in generations past and which needed to be denied at all costs? Or none of these things? Was it just that someone had handed him the poison package as sometimes happens in families and he had no choice but to accept?

Tonight, I will go St Margaret's for midnight Mass. I have never been to midnight Mass before but it's not far away. I could even walk there. I can't help but wish that someone in my family – just one of them – would contact me and wish me Merry Christmas.

Arnold hates me talking about my family. He gets angry and frustrated and doesn't understand. It probably has to do with his brain injury. He just sees everything in practical terms, black and white, right or wrong, nothing in between. Most nights, he sits at the kitchen table with his knife and fork in his fists, his lame leg stretched under the table, waiting for me to put his tea in front of him, for him to cover it with tomato sauce. He eats whatever I put in front of him and never complains. When I think about it, Arnold has accepted his situation quite well, all things considered.

Christmas is a strange time of year, the thoughts it sets off in a person. Lately, I find I'm thinking a lot about the notion of fate and the eternal question – is our fate determined by the decisions we make, or are our decisions determined by our fate? Or is there even such a thing as fate?

Iris

Passing Round the Platter

The Irish musicians started up with a reel. Dancers took to the floor. Roisin stood watching, smiling, pretending to listen to the music. Where did it go, the coolness she had in her youth, when she had made a point of standing alone? Never then did she have the feeling of being compelled to find someone to talk to, someone to hide behind, so her aloneness wouldn't be noticed.

'Hello, my darlin', and how would you be keeping on this very fine day?' Sean, her father's oldest friend, had noticed. Perhaps he was feeling a bit the same.

Immediately, she was grateful for his presence; she remembered he was a great talker and his stories and chatter would shelter her, for a while at least.

'Oh, Sean, it's so nice to see you again. I haven't seen you in years. Not in such a long time.'

'You're right, my darlin'. Such a long time. I can't even remember when. Now, who was it who said, "Time is a traitor"? Shakespeare, was it?'

'Might have been Shakespeare's sister,' she smiled.

'Ah, yes, you can't turn back time or fate. But isn't it a wonderful thing that your Mum and Dad can celebrate their life together like this?'

She nodded. It was just easier to agree.

'I only wish my own lovely wife were here with me, today. You heard about it, did you, Roisin? Alannah – when we were on holidays on the west coast. A tree fell. Taken from me in an instant, she was. Ah, yes, my own dearest love, Alannah, taken in from me in the blink of an eye.'

'I'm so sorry, Sean. You must miss her terribly,' said Roisin, thinking how much older he looked. He'd been quite dapper once, when his wife had been at his side.

'Oh yes, that I do, Roisin. That I do, but I like to think that she's never far away.'

She looked into his watery blue eyes. 'Well, perhaps you're right.'

Roisin remembered his two daughters from school. Twins – one equally unpleasant as the other. When she thought about it, Bridget and Mary were a bit like twins. But Sean's girls weren't like Bridget and Mary. They'd had that kind of wiry red hair that always needed to be tied back. Unless they'd changed a great deal, she imagined he wouldn't see much of them any more. They would be caught up in their own lives and each other's. He probably had his meals alone. At teatime, he most likely sat alone at the red laminex kitchen table with the empty chairs. Alannah would have always made sure the table was spread with a clean gingham tablecloth and the salt and pepper shakers and sugar bowl were neatly placed. If she had been out in the garden, there would be a little vase of flowers, nothing too fussy, though, and woe betide any soul who would be coarse enough to put a carton of milk or a bottle of sauce on the table. Alannah had always used a little white jug. Once, teatime had been a noisy, chatty affair with his daughters full of themselves, their schooldays and who said what to whom, and Alannah loving them all in her fussy way. Now, Sean had his tea with the game show host and the newsreader.

'It must have been such a shock for you and your girls, Sean.'

'Oh, a terrible day it was. Terrible! Gone in an instant, she was, when the branch fell. I was but a few steps ahead of her. It could have been me if it had fallen but a second earlier but it was her, her who was taken, her…my one and only love…taken from me… Do you believe in fate, Roisin?'

'You asked me that when we last met.'

'And what did you say?'

'You know, Sean, I just can't remember.'

Sean's eyes were misty now, misty blue. He put his arm round her waist, 'Well, it's all fate, darlin', the whole bloody lot of it. Come, take a turn on the floor with me.'

His hands, soft and fleshy, reminded her of Dave's. They waltzed on the wooden, makeshift dance floor under the canopy of the Hills hoist. She looked at Sean's face; he was somewhere far away. It wasn't her he was dancing with.

They danced until the end of the song. Frank and Kathleen had taken the floor. The band began playing 'When You Were Sweet Sixteen' in the melancholic chords of the Celtic mandolin.

'Sean, shall we let them have the floor?'

'Thank you for taking a turn with an old man, my love. Now, you make sure that you have a nice time today,' he said and he kissed her hand, his wet cheeks brushing her skin.

Together they watched her parents dance a slow waltz. Some of the older guests started to sing and when the song finished, everyone clapped.

The yard had filled up now. Apart from her family, she hardly knew anyone.

'Ah yes, a lovely couple your mum and dad are, Roisin,' said Sean, walking away.

'Yes, they are. My mother looks a picture of happiness,' she said, hoping that someone else would hear her, would come and talk to her. But no one did, so she stood sipping the champagne, trying to look like she didn't care, trying to enjoy the sunshine on her face.

It felt like she had been standing like that for hours, but it was probably only minutes. She picked up a silver tray of sandwiches and began to offer them around. Tiny little triangles, no crusts and fresh brown bread. This would have to be the first time that either of her parents ever had cucumber sandwiches. She popped one into her mouth. It was the first time *she'd* ever had cucumber sandwiches.

'Sandwich, Pat?' she said, approaching him. What an opener, after all these years. She almost said, 'Pat, how you've grown.'

He seemed taller and broader than she remembered. Standing in front of her, he blocked the sun. 'Hello, Roisin. Been a while. Years, I think. How's life?'

She couldn't quite remember how long it had been. Standing there in front of him, holding the tray, she felt a little like the maid of hearts.

'I hear you and Dave split,' Pat said, looking down at his shoes.

Yes, well, Roisin thought, it doesn't seem to matter how ostracised from your family you are, they always seem to manage to gossip about you.

'Yes, we did. What about you? Are you still married?'

'Married to the job, darl. Married to the job. I hear you are a writer now. But I guess you've always been one for making up stories.' He smiled a smile that wasn't a smile.

Sometimes her thoughts overpowered her and it was becoming more and more difficult to stop herself from speaking them out loud. She wanted to say, 'I can hardly believe that you are my brother, that I am related to you. You seem like a complete stranger to me.' But instead she said, 'The sandwiches would have been Bridget's idea, I'm sure. She has such wonderful taste.'

Pat looked at her, raising his eyebrows with disdain or confusion. Roisin wasn't sure.

'The cucumber sandwiches, I mean,' Roisin said wishing she could put the tray down.

'I know what you mean. You know, Roisin, there's something about you. We all feel it, even Mam. You always seem to be watching us, like you're taking notes for your book. Just keep yourself tidy, today. They'll be no note-taking today. You got that?' He looked her square in the eye.

Pat stood for a moment and looked over the top of her head then he turned his back and walked into the crowd and began refilling glasses, smiling, the ever-dutiful son. Standing next to Bridget, he filled her glass and it overflowed down her gold-bangled arm. They laughed loudly and looked in Roisin's direction. The sound of the Celtic mandolin drowned the noise of their laugher.

A whiff of cigar smoke made her stiffen.

Her father approached her, glass and cigar in hand. 'I'm just getting your mother a glass of lemonade, Roisin. Haven't your sisters done us proud today! Have you thanked them for the magnificent job they've done?'

'No, not yet, Dad.'

'And it's Pat who has paid for all this. You know that, don't you? You know that your brother Pat has paid for everything?'

Roisin took a step away from him. She had always hated the smell of his cigar; she had always hated the smell of him. 'They're all wonderful, all your children, aren't they, Dad, especially Pat?'

'You've still got a bit of an old chip on your shoulder, haven't you, Roisin…a real old chip I'd say you have there. There's a barb in you.' He took a slow puff on his cigar. 'Just you mind your manners today, girl.'

'Mum looks dazzling today, Dad.'

Kathleen was a rose on any day but today, floating in deep crimson chiffon, with her dancer's feet encased in diamante-studded sandals, her soft grey hair braided with ribbons, she was like a little girl in her new party dress. Swaying to the music, Kathleen was young again, her cheeks flushed with excitement and champagne.

'I wasn't talking about your mother, Roisin.'

'I'll just be passing some of the trays around.' Roisin's arms were beginning to ache.

'Don't you go causing any trouble today, Roisin, do you hear me?' he said softly as he moved away, his cigar smoke trailing behind him. 'You've always been a trouble-maker, a teller of tales.'

'Yes, well, it's a tragic thing when you feel you have to hide behind a pile of sandwiches for fear of what you might say,' Roisin said, laughing.

The sound of her own shrill laughter shocked her. She would have to keep a check on herself. Her thoughts were beginning to get the better of her. Settle yourself down, she said under her breath and picked up the silver platter again and walked between the chattering groups.

The little backyard was filling up now. She stood behind the rosebush, pretending to inspect the leaves for aphids, and surveyed the guests. People she hadn't seen for years stood around in little chatty groups: grey heads, flower-spotted dresses, white shirts and ties – her parents' friends from church; Bridget and Mary's joint friends, trendy, with fashionable clothes, brand-name types. Her sisters had always shared their friends. Children who she had never seen before were running about playing hide and seek. And Father Murphy, sitting a little apart from the crowd on the brick fence, legs slightly apart and holding a small radio to his ear, his eyes closed, was either drifting into sleep or deep in thought, or maybe listening to the football. It was difficult to tell.

22 January 2002

Dear Rose,

Last night. The writing group. Well, I should have known better.

I was trying to explain how I am struggling to create the bleak internal world of one of my characters. I told the group I often wonder if my character would have ever have written anything at all had it not been for her experience of exile from the family. I tried to explain when I think about this character, I sometimes think maybe if she stopped writing her life would improve, she should stop dredging old hurts, playing with them, reliving the emotion, teasing them out into scenes for the sake of art.

Then Sally piped up, 'I know the type, the eternal victim. There are so many of them about.' When she said that, she looked me straight in the eye.

I find Sally infuriating. A real know-it-all. So I said to her that such characters are actually quite complex and I have read that if you are rejected by your family of birth it may take you years, if not a lifetime, to come to terms with. Then I added, 'But suffering has its uses.'

And Hugh said, 'Most writers know that, Iris. Why are you always stating the obvious?'

Then I read a short, light-hearted piece about scapegoats within families and how a person, especially if they were a writer, might seek revenge by writing her tormentors into her fiction.

Well, Sally's response I can't remember verbatim but it went something like this: 'What both concerns and alarms me somewhat is that you privilege the writer as a seeker of revenge, who writes about life events, involves unwilling parties and hides behind the guise of fiction. I struggle with the ethics of this.'

How pompous. The word 'ethics' puts me on edge. What role do ethics play in artistic expression? None, in my opinion.

And then a man called Ernest who I hadn't met before spoke from the corner. 'There are no ethics in an urge to write,' he said.

Ernest wasn't young, but his skin was brown and stretched tightly across his cheekbones. His hair was still black except for a slight greying at the temples. He had the type of face on which a smile would look out of place. His jacket might have been linen and it was worn over a black T-shirt with the grace of someone who no longer had to try.

'So what is it then, this urge to write? Is it an idea?' I asked him.

He responded in a type of soliloquy, as if he had already rehearsed it. As best I can remember it, this is the gist of what he said. 'The writer takes an emotion, an event and an idea and imposes nuances of meaning or feeling, creates textual light and shade, metaphor and imagery until a story takes shape. Life events are merely prompts. And like most great art, the best writing comes from an unconscious moment. All writers know it. Stories just come to you. They can come from listening to a poem or a song, from a chance meeting in a park with a stranger, from a random memory or a snippet of a conversation. And when they come, they don't hang around too long. They are fleeting, ephemeral, fragile things and must be honoured, taken hold of gently and coaxed on to the page or before long they disappear, fade away.' With that, Ernest walked out of the room.

But that wasn't going to deter Sally. She kept on at me. She said, 'Iris, surely you can't be serious in suggesting writers and artists shouldn't have a standard of ethics?'

And Hugh agreed with her, of course. 'Yes, Iris, you must have some ethical standards.'

I told him he was forgetting the first rule of writing – the character isn't the author. I told him it is my character who is saying this, making this contention, not me. I think I almost yelled at him, 'Do I have to defend the actions of my character?'

Of course, Sally had to intervene. She said with that smugness of hers, 'Far be it from me to challenge your writerly authority. But you might do well to remember the words of another character, Frankenstein's monster.'

Then a tiny voice said, 'Yes, Iris, I think you need to be careful that you don't become so engulfed by your writing that in the end you don't know the difference between reality and fiction. I mean, I think that fiction has the potential to become a monster, and one that can consume its creator.' The voice came from a small shade of a woman who often seemed to attend the group but rarely, if ever, spoke. Nameless, she seemed always in the shadows – the listener, the witness.

An awkward hush fell on us and then Hugh, as he always does when things get a bit strained, topped up glasses and passed around the bowl of nuts. I was glad to go home and get into bed. When I face it, I survived for years out on the cattle station writing without ever discussing my work with anyone. Perhaps I don't need them. Sometimes the best companions are silent ones.

This morning when I woke a voice in my ear said, "There are far more important things in life than cucumber sandwiches.' And last night I had a dream about my mother dancing. I'm not sure that I ever saw her dance, not even with my father.

Iris

Dancing Days

A momentary hush fell over the small crowd when Wesley walked in. Roisin watched him step through the rose arch and stop for a few seconds, waiting for people to look up and notice him. She envied his effortless grace as he smiled and greeted everyone. People just seemed to move towards him one after another, as if he had asked them to dance. He was never alone in a crowd.

Feeling slightly foolish, she walked towards him with the silver tray and she offered him a cucumber sandwich. 'How are you, Wesley? You look so handsome today in your suit and black tie.' Roisin wasn't quite sure why he had chosen to wear a dinner suit on such a warm day, but he could carry it off. Roisin couldn't remember how long she had known him. Had it been Bridget who had introduced him to the family? Would he recognise her now, Roisin wondered.

'Thank you,' he said, smiling widely, clearly expecting her to be impressed.

'Do you know who I am?' Roisin waited for his reply, not quite sure what he might say.

His eyes glazed over and he was silent for a moment. He seemed a little taken back, his smooth charm unsettled. 'You are…Bridget's sister…aren't you?'

Surprised but pleased he remembered, Roisin nodded and smiled back at him. 'Yes, that's right. I am. Now here's a test for you. Do you remember my name?'

Wesley took a cucumber sandwich from the tray. 'You don't look anything like your sisters…'

How many times had she heard this comment? She kept smiling but she wanted to say, 'Sisters hate being compared to one another.

Surely, a man of the world like you would know that?' But she didn't say that; she didn't say anything. She just pressed the thought back down. She would deal with it later.

He smiled again, his teeth white and so straight and even, they could have been false. There was a time, a long time ago, when she had thought that maybe…with his flecked green eyes, his creamy skin, his laugh…but that was before he met Simon and before she met Dave.

'Here's cheers, darling,' he said, raising his glass. 'I'm just going to give my best to your mother.'

Roisin watched him walk away with his elegant swagger that some might have called mincing. Her thoughts were beginning to race. He probably has a new partner now. Simon must be old. Probably a man who worked out at the gym every day, who cooked for him every night, a man who understood his story and who loved him in spite or even because of it. Don't we all have a story? she asked herself, remembering a discussion she had with her counsellor.

'Sometimes I think I live my entire life as if it is a work of fiction, as if I am constructing my own life's plot, as if I am a character in a story…'

'And why does that trouble you so, Roisin?'

'Because we never really know exactly at what point we are at in our lives because we have no way of knowing when the story of our lives will end. We might think we are somewhere in the middle of the plot, but in fact we might be close to the end.'

'I think you have a way to go yet, Roisin.'

Picking up another tray of sandwiches, Roisin made her way through the crowd of guests. How the crowd had grown in such a short space of time. A heavy cloud of perfume had settled over the throng – a blessing because it softened the pungent smell of her father's cigar smoke. She watched him offer Father Murphy another tot of whiskey and then wander off, talking to this one and that one, smoke wafting with him. Kathleen was sitting in the shade, fanning herself. Roisin stood alone, staring down at the stale, shrivelled sandwiches. How much longer could she keep up the pantomime?

Father Murphy was always good for a chat, so she made her way toward him. 'Would you like a sandwich, Father Murphy?'

He looked up, his fair skin flushed and the veins on his nose prominent. His fine grey hair was thinner than she remembered. He put his little radio aside and said, 'Well now, child, you should know better than to offer an Irishman something as English as a cucumber sandwich. Sit down a while, my girl. There are far more important things in life than cucumber sandwiches.'

He moved to make a space for her on the brick fence. He had that stale priest's smell about him still, but the reek of whiskey was stronger. He took a sip and turned his florid face to hers. 'And what have you been doing with yourself, Roisin? It is a grand day for your mother and father's anniversary, is it not? Your wonderful parents, Kathleen and Frank.'

'I've been keeping busy, thanks, Father. Have you been keeping well?'

'I'm an old priest now, Roisin. Can't really complain about much. The good Lord himself watches over us all, you know. I did have a bit of sadness a few months ago, though,' he said, his voice dropping. 'My dear old mother passed away back home in Ireland.'

His deep blue eyes misted over and he seemed not to be looking at her particularly, but through her to who knows where.

'Ninety-three, she was, and I hadn't seen her for nigh on thirty years. She wrote to me every month until the end of her life. I was her pride and joy, you know? Her precious son, the priest. She never missed my birthday once, and every Christmas she sent me a little plum pudding she had made on her wood stove in the kitchen where I grew up.' He took a slow swig of whiskey and water. 'You know the only perfume I ever liked on a woman was the perfume that she wore. Some type of French cologne, it was.' He smiled and patted Roisin's hand, 'Enough of my maudlin self, now. Tell me how you are, Roisin.'

'Oh yes, Father, I am well. I have a little cottage out of town, and

I am studying history and art.' Her voice had taken on the tone of a young schoolgirl wanting to impress.

'A nice place, is it? History and art, eh? And what of your husband – is he here today?'

'No, Father, we are divorced now, but we keep in touch.'

'And no children? Well, perhaps it was just as well.'

'No, Father. I never had a child.'

'It was all for the best, Roisin. Don't you be fretting about it, now. It's all a long, long time ago.'

Frank walked toward them with the whiskey bottle. 'I see I am just in time, Father. It's warming up, is it not? Roisin, go see if your mother needs any help in the kitchen, will you.'

Sometimes it was easier to be obedient. Grateful to get out of the sun for a while anyway, Roisin wandered through the dark house to the kitchen. The old louvres had long since been upgraded with aluminium sliding windows, a modern dining setting replaced the old pine kitchen table, but the picture of the Sacred Heart still hung in the same spot as it had in the little inner-city kitchen of her childhood.

Kathleen and Wesley were deep in conversation bent over the kitchen bench, unaware of her presence.

Wesley was holding a framed photo. 'Kathleen, you were a beauty,' he said, smiling at her, 'a real beauty.'

'My mother was so ambitious for me – she wanted me to go to New York after the war, but I married Frank – she hated Frank, my mother. She thought I had ruined my life by marrying him.'

'Do you regret not going on the stage, Kathleen?'

'Well now, Wesley, there's a question if ever there was one. Do I regret never going on the stage? How is your life in the theatre going?'

'Oh, Kathleen, I love the charade, you must know that. I love the masks I create, experimenting with other selves. You know, darling, I sometimes wonder if I know who I am at all.'

Roisin coughed that deliberate little cough that people make when they want to be noticed.

Still unaware of her presence or not caring, Roisin couldn't tell which, Kathleen said, 'I have four children living, and other precious little ones – three of them there were – that died at birth and you ask me do I regret not becoming an actress. I think I did become one,' she said, bowing her head.

'I'm sorry, Kathleen. I can only imagine how hard it must be to lose babies,' Wesley replied, touching her hand, but only for a second or two.

Roisin watched him and thought probably that would be how he would have delivered the line if it had been part of a script he was reading.

'Yes, maybe to lose one is to be expected…but three… Mary came at just the right time. I thought I was never going to have another… it was the most wondrous moment when she was placed in my arms.'

Roisin stood still for a moment and looked out the window. She had been thirteen when Mary was born. Thirteen.

'Oh yes, Wesley, I was a wonderful dancer in my time.' Kathleen stood up and began slowly twirling around the room.

Wesley took her in his arms and they waltzed.

Roisin coughed again.

'Roisin, what are you doing there? Have you been in here for long?'

'No, Mam, I just walked in. Dad sent me in to see if you needed any help. Now, don't let me stop you dancing.' Roisin felt as if she had walked in on private moment and wished that she hadn't.

'No, my dancing days are over, long over,' Kathleen said.

'No, dancing days are never over, darling. Come, let's take the floor outside,' Wesley said, dancing Kathleen out of the door back into the sunshine, on to the makeshift wooden dance floor under the Hills hoist.

Roisin sat down at the kitchen table, her eyes still adjusting to the darkness after coming from the bright sunshine. You could barely swing a cat in her mother's kitchen, yet she had worked many a minor miracle on that old, black gas stove. Roisin could smell the faint shadow of Kathleen's Chanel, another present from dear Pat, no doubt.

She stood for a moment and watched through the window, her mother and Wesley gliding like swans across the makeshift dance floor.

Roisin walked down the narrow passage into the lounge room. Someone had drawn the red velvet drapes against the high afternoon sun and the room had a rosy glow. The votive candles next to her parents' wedding photograph had gone out. She picked up the photograph in its silver frame.

What a handsome couple they had been – Kathleen with her perfect hourglass shape sheathed in white satin, golden blonde hair framing her face; Frank sleek and dapper in his navy blue pinstripe suit. The hand-tinted photo was faded now but the red pigment on her mother's lips was still strong. They were smiling at each other: innocents.

Roisin put the photo back in its place on the dresser and wandered over to the antique travelling trunk. It had belonged to Kathleen's mother. But Roisin had never known her grandmother. Roisin imagined she could smell the faint familiar lavender fragrance she used to smell as child when she lifted the lid and gazed in awe at her mother's 'precious things' – evening dresses, hair bows, dancing shoes and even a fur stole. But what use did Kathleen ever have for evening dresses or dancing shoes in her life with Frank?

How she would plead with Kathleen. 'Please, Mam, can I play the dress-up game?'

Sometimes, on a very good day, Kathleen would say yes and Roisin would parade up and down the hall in her mother's red taffeta evening dress and her black, high-heeled dancing shoes, swaying and delighting in the swish of the gown and the clatter of the heels on the wooden boards.

'I'm going to be a princess when I grow up, Mam. A real princess.'

'Well, you better get those things off before your father comes home. You know it upsets him to see you dressed up like that – looking older than you are. And I don't think he would be too keen on you being a princess, either.'

No. It wasn't the princess role that had been assigned to Roisin.

Underneath the evening dresses was Kathleen's linen: white linen tablecloths with crocheted edges, table napkins the same, circular doilies with embroidered roses and daisies, ribbon-edged towels and crocheted beaded milk jug covers – perfectly folded and scented with lavender and moth balls but never used, not any of it. Would the christening gown still be at the bottom, where it had always been kept? They had all been christened in it. Mary was the last to wear it. Roisin hadn't been allowed to hold Mary for the photographs. No. Frank had said very firmly that it wasn't fitting for a girl her age to be holding a baby. Not fitting at all.

25 February 2002

Dear Rose,

Lately, I have started to reread *Jane Eyre*. I hope you have read it. I have always thought Jane and Bertha were doubles in a way. I suppose every family has a mad woman in the attic. But I don't think Bertha was always a crazed woman. I mean, she must have been sane once, surely, for Rochester to have married her, before he betrayed her by locking her away. I think she just became that way because Rochester locked her in the attic. Jane married Rochester to escape a worse situation and probably Bertha did too. But it wasn't much of an escape, was it, for either woman, especially for Bertha? Straight back into captivity.

I sometimes wonder if I married Arnold to escape. Perhaps I did, but Arnold surely isn't any Rochester character. Perhaps I am the mad women in the attic in my family. But at least Arnold never betrayed me. But there again, maybe betrayal takes many forms.

The other day in the garden he said to me, 'You know, Iris, I've been thinking, you ought to stop writing about all that dark stuff. You're just using your writing to make sense of that rubbish about your family, but it's just taking you further and further back into it. Nobody's interested, Iris. Why don't you use your talents to write about something people really want to read?'

I was getting a bit annoyed. 'Like what?' I asked him.

You know what he said? He said, 'Why don't you write about wizards like the woman who made all that money from the films they made out of her books?'

Wizards? I had to do my best not to burst out laughing.

He went on pulling up the weeds and then he turned to me and said, 'You've got good writing talent and you should use it for something like that. Put all this misery behind you.'

'Remain silent, you mean?' I said to him, but he didn't hear me, or if he did, he pretended not to.

Arnold would never understand. Even before his accident, he never understood. He has never been a great talker but since his accident he speaks more slowly and deliberately. It was a waste of time talking to him about my writing. But I can't blame his brain damage for everything. On another day, I wouldn't have bothered. But the words welled up in me and I had to speak. I told him if he understood anything about writing and art, he would know that stories are like seeds in the wind and it all depends where they fall as to how they will grow. Sometimes they just die, but you have to give them a chance.

Anyway, this was his reply. 'Yes, well, Iris…the prime aim of any flower is to produce seed. If you remove the spent blooms from roses, it stops the hips from forming and forces the plant to try again. Got to deadhead a rose bush, Iris. Stops it from going to seed.'

Sometimes, I think he deliberately misunderstands me and it makes me so angry. So I said to him as calmly as I could, 'I know that you know a lot about gardening, Arnold. But that wasn't what I was talking about.'

Anyway, I'm pretty sure I read that roses that grow from seed are hardier than the grafted ones. They have to be – they have more to struggle against.

'I know you weren't talking about gardening, Iris. I'm not stupid,' he said to me. And he went on lecturing me. 'No, I just meant for you to do something more worthwhile. Try and make some money.'

So I told him I didn't think he understood anything about art. Sometimes, I feel as if I'm talking down to him. I don't mean to. He just infuriates me so much.

'I was only trying to give you some advice,' he said, and I thought these were his final words on the subject. And then he asked me what the name of my novel was.

'I'm not sure yet,' I had to say.

'Am I in it?' he asked me.

'I'm not sure yet,' I told him.

Iris

That Old, Old Story

Frank was enjoying himself – he had taken centre stage, laughing raucously, telling stories to anyone who would listen. The band struck up another tune, drowning Frank's laughter. People had begun dancing again and Roisin found herself staring at a woman in the crowd. She had long brown hair that fell in waves about her bare shoulders and she was wearing a straw hat with a black bow, no doubt to protect her fair skin. There was something very delicate-looking about her, and familiar. Yes, that was it. She remembered now.

Roisin made her way over to her. Offering her the silver platter, she said, 'Care for a cucumber sandwich, Eliza-May?'

'Thank you,' the woman said, looking bemused. 'Are you related to the family?'

'I'm one of the sisters. Do you remember me? I'm Roisin. I did meet you when you were a lot younger. You used to visit our house a lot.'

'Oh, sorry. I don't think I do remember you. You look so different from the others.'

'Don't worry, I'm used to hearing that.' Swallowing the words she wanted to say at hearing this comment again, Roisin smiled and said, 'I left home when I was very young. But when I lived at home, you used to come over and visit Bridget and Mary quite a bit. You probably didn't see too much of me. I used to hide away in my room studying or sketching in those days. Lurking in corners, making myself dim.'

Eliza-May began to look around the crowd the way that people do, when they want to get away to talk to someone more interesting.

'Yes, I know Bridget and Mary really well, but they've never mentioned there was another sister. They've never mentioned you, not once. How strange. But I do remember another girl who was often in the house. I thought she was someone Kathleen and Frank hired to help out around the home. Maybe that was you… Oh, I'm sorry. That sounds so awful, doesn't it?'

'Well, I am part of the family. Perhaps that is what is so strange. Didn't you work for our father for a while, as a secretary, was it?' Roisin said.

'Yes, that's right. But not for long. Look, I just need to check on my daughter. I don't want her to get sunburnt. Nice chatting to you, Rochelle.'

'It's Roisin.'

'Oh…sorry.' She stepped away and walked towards a man and a little girl standing under the magnolia tree.

Eliza-May stood on her toes and appeared to whisper something in the man's ear and he turned and stared at Roisin. Eliza-May didn't look much older than she did when she had just become Bridget's 'new best friend' all those years ago. How her name echoed. Roisin could hear mother saying, 'She's not coming around again tonight, is she, that Eliza-May? She's never away from the place! Hasn't she got a home of her own?'

Frank was never better than when he was in a crowd, telling stories and drinking whiskey – it was only when the crowd left that the shadow came. Frank had finally spotted her. 'Eliza,' he called through the crowd, walking toward her. 'Eliza, my darlin' girl, how are you? Is this your husband and your own little girl, now?'

Roisin tried not to make it too obvious but she couldn't help but watch how the scene played out.

Eliza picked up her bag and took her little girl's hand and stood closer to her husband. She looked if she was about to leave but then changed her mind.

'A long time it is since I have seen your gorgeous face. You look glorious today and your little girl is just like you.' He blew his choking cigar smoke high above her head, his cheeks flushed.

Frank had scrubbed up well for the occasion. Wearing a spotless white shirt with a light blue silk tie, he looked like he could have been getting married or even going to a funeral. His hair was thinner than it used to be, but he was only grey at the temples and his blue eyes were bright. Teeth stained from years of smoking, they still did the job, and when the spotlight was on him, he smiled like a fifties movie star. Ever the charmer, ever the two-sided coin.

Even now, Roisin could see Eliza-May falling for him. Her head was tilted to the side as she listened to his stories.

He stood close to her, pressing his shoulder to hers. 'You know, Eliza, your sweet, loving hat reminds me of the day my mother took me to the city when I was a boy to see Father Christmas. She had a hat just like it and she only ever wore it on special occasions and you know, in the Depression special occasions were precious few. We were a rum lot, me and my brothers, and I can see my mother's face now, glowering at me under that hat,' he laughed.

Pat joined them. He was laughing loudly too. Bridget joined the group and Mary too.

'Eliza-May, so glad you could come,' Bridget said as she reached over to kiss her.

Eliza-May smiled broadly and hugged Bridget. They were all laughing now.

'Pat, do you remember that old codger who lived on the corner – you know, the one who always plastered shaving cream on his head when he took the funny turns. Heard voices or something, didn't he?'

'No, I don't remember, Da. Must have been after I left for the navy,' said Pat.

'Oh, do you not, Pat? He knocked on the door one Friday night, the shaving cream piled high on his head like an Easter bonnet. Little Mary and Bridget couldn't stop laughing. It keeps the spirits in, you see,' he told us. He needed to lay off the spirits, he did. He smelled like a painter's cupboard – full of the methylated spirits, he was.' His cigar smoke drifted over the group that had gathered around him.

Roisin noticed her mother watching from a distance and, as if by some telepathy, her father turned and called to her, 'Shouldn't you go and see if your mother needs anything, Roisin? She needs looking after now that she's getting older. It's loving care and attention your mother needs now.'

'I'll go over in a minute, Dad.' Roisin put the tray she was holding down on a table next to her. She was done with passing round the platter.

'You know what your trouble is, Roisin? You are a moper and a mooner. You need to spruce up and get out more. You spend too much time in your books. Now, young Liza here, she knows how to live and enjoy herself, don't you, Liza?'

Eliza-May took off her hat, shook her long hair and smiled up at her husband.

'And Pat here, he knows how to have a good time, don't you, lad?' Frank said, putting his arm around his son's stiff shoulders. 'You were a terror when you were a lad, Pat!' They both laughed so loudly it was as if they were in competition to see who could laugh the loudest.

Yes, Roisin had written a scene about a boy just like Pat, with terrible ways just like Pat's.

*

I heard the yelling coming from the kitchen. It was my father screaming at Mick.

The police officer was standing there, notebook in hand.

'Yes, it was definitely him, Ken, no mistake. There were a few others with him, but they ran off. The workshop is burnt to the ground. Nothing left of it. It's going to cost a fortune to fix it.'

'Ye fecking little idiot. You know where you're going, don't you?'

'Please, Dad, it was an accident. We didn't mean to do it.'

'Don't be too hard on him, Ken. He's only a lad – thirteen,' said the police officer.

'Hard on him, be damned. Me, I'm working double shifts every day to put food in his mouth and he's out there burning down fecking workshops. No, he's going to the boys' home. That'll put a stop to his shenanigans.'

My mother was standing by the kitchen sink, saying nothing. Saying nothing. Crying and saying nothing. The next day I came home from school hoping, hoping he would still be there, that our father had changed his mind. I walked into the house. It seemed quieter than usual. There was no sound of playing from the back yard, no smell of scones cooking in the kitchen.

'Mum, where's Mickey?' I asked my mother.

Her back to me, standing by the kitchen sink, her head was bowed and I could hear the sound of her sobs.

I walked down the hallway and looked into his room. His bed was still unmade and the old worn flannelette sheets with the fire engines that he'd had since he was three were crumpled and worn. I sat on his bed, the old mattress, the springs creaked and I picked up his pillow and buried my face in it. I could smell him, his boy's smell, his boy's life.

My throat was so tight I thought I was going to choke.

I couldn't cry, not yet – it would overwhelm me. Little Frannie walked in and sat next to me on the bed. She put her head in my lap and cried. I stroked her golden curls.

'Don't cry, don't cry,' I said. 'Mickey will be back soon.'

'But his billycart is all smashed on the back lawn, all smashed and broken.'

It was twelve months before we saw him again. He was paler, quieter, changed. Somehow the Mick I had known was gone and a stranger came back in his place.

*

Father Murphy was sitting in the shade of the leafy tree. How distant and peaceful he looked. No radio at his ear now. Perhaps the last race has been run. Frank took him another shot of whiskey. Mary offered him some cake. It must be nice for him to have the attention of people, a break from his solitary world. Even Pat was talking to him now.

Roisin wondered about Pat and his life. Success in the navy, and now a thriving business, so why did he seem to resent her writing so much? Perhaps it's a question of authority. Maybe he wanted to be a writer himself, to give his version of events which he might consider had more validity than hers. Sometimes Roisin imagined him cross-examining her and her intentions in a kind of gypsy court, as if it were scene from a novel or a play. Just about everything in life she could imagine as a scene in a novel.

*

'I hear you're a writer now.'

'Yes, that is so.'

'So what's the book about?'

'Well, a family drama, I guess. A bit of a mystery about what might have happened and what might have been hidden in a family. And why.'

'Sounds like you might be writing about us. Your family. Our family. Are you?'

'No, of course not. It's just a story.'

'Yes, but a family story.'

'Every writer brings their emotional experience to their work. We're like actors. You can change facts but you can't change your own emotional landscape. A writer has to be able to use that. Just like an artist with a painting – they can't turn the tap off on their own feelings.'

'Maybe so. You have written yourself as the heroine of the piece, I suppose. Is that how you see yourself? As a heroine wearing a crown of sorrows?'

'Would you rather I wrote you as a hero?'

'I would rather you remained silent.'

*

And the conversation would finish, just falling short of becoming an argument.

'You look miles away,' said Bridget sashaying past in her little tight-waisted dress, so similar to Mary's, and a new model of something their mother Kathleen would have once worn.

'Always romanticising about your writing aren't you, Roisin? I wouldn't be at all surprised if you were taking mental notes at this very minute. Thinking about how you can use us, write about us in your little stories that no one ever reads. What do you think about all of this, Mary?'

Mary looked at Bridget, and spoke as if Roisin wasn't there. 'I don't know much about writing except that sometimes it seems like Roisin is spying on us. Well, not exactly spying. Maybe studying would be a better word.'

'I don't think any of you understand. It doesn't work like that.'

Pat had strolled across the grass and joined his sisters. It was almost as if he were a paid security guard on patrol.

'Well, be careful what you write about, Roisin. Writing can be a bit like wishing you know. It just might happen,' said Bridget.

'Yes, be careful what you write about, Roisin. Writing can be a bit like dreaming, you know. It can be frightening,' said Mary.

'Be careful what you write about, Roisin. Writing that stirs up the past is dangerous. It sets everyone's teeth on edge,' said Pat.

They turned their backs on her in unison.

Roisin felt herself wilting with the effort of trying not to care. She went behind the magnolia tree and pulled out her powder compact. Her nose was shiny, her mascara smudged, her lips pale. Her mask was completely gone. She powdered her nose, slid some lipstick over her mouth and snapped the compact shut. She smiled at herself in the compact mirror. Her mask intact again, Roisin brushed through the unnoticing crowd towards Kathleen, who was sitting in the shade, fanning her face with a folded serviette. She seemed unaware of her daughter's presence. Kathleen's gaze was glassy as if she might be looking out over the ocean; she had an air of waiting, of wishing about her.

Roisin was tempted to say, 'What do you think Virginia Woolf would think of our garden party, Mam?' but her mother would never have heard of Virginia Woolf, and would not know what she was talking about. Such a comment would have been pretentious, and a rude intrusion into her mother's private thoughts.

Perhaps Kathleen was sitting with thoughts of regret, thoughts about who she could have been, what she could have achieved. Roisin remembered her singing lessons, Bridget's tap-dancing lessons and Mary's piano lessons. They were all equally hopeless. Those lessons should have been Kathleen's lessons.

'You can sing quite well, Roisin. You just need to practise more,' Kathleen used to say.

Roisin knew she couldn't sing a note.

'Bridget, you need to try harder with your dancing.'

She had no coordination whatsoever.

'Frank, we need to get a piano for Mary. How else will she learn?'

They never did get a piano, but poor Mary suffered Sister Martha's lessons every Monday after school.

But if Kathleen had gone to New York, taken the stage part she had been offered all those years ago, there would have been no Frank, no children, or at least, not these children. Her life had become a tragedy of unfulfilment that only the gifted know, those who have had to bury their talents to keep others happy. And how hard she had tried to be happy with what she had; Roisin had always been able to see that. But then there had been those little times of 'being away', of being 'poorly', when the family didn't see her very much. Those weeping times, crying times. Frank would send her away to convalesce. For her own good, he would say. She, Roisin, the eldest girl, did the cooking and cleaning, took her mother's part…for a while at least.

And as for Frank's little indiscretions, Roisin could remember Kathleen saying, 'A man cannot go without for too long.'

Roisin wasn't sure what that had meant, but she knew now. Her mother never seemed to mind about Eliza-May.

'You've enough girlfriends here at home to keep you busy, Frank,' Kathleen might have said once.

Roisin wondered if Kathleen knew the truth.

And Frank was big on loyalty. Roisin remembered his private little lectures on the subject. She'd been about seven the first time. Her memory of it was so clear.

He'd call her into the bedroom. 'Stand up straight when I'm talking to you,' he'd say, punching her between the shoulder blades.

She could see him standing in front of her, seeming so strong and tall, towering above her.

'Do you know what "family loyalty" means?'

'No… Yes, I think so…'

'It means not talking to other people about things that happen in our family, private things. There are things that happen in this house that are not to be talked about outside. Is that clear?'

'Yes, Dad.'

'Well, let that be a warning to you…'

Her young cheeks had blazed with shame. The term 'family loyalty' became fixed in her mind, a commandment, an instruction that could have dire and as yet unspoken consequences if it wasn't adhered to. But what was the thing she must keep secret? Her childish innocence had no idea. Her father knew, though. Frank knew the terrible thing she might disclose.

On the day Roisin left home for good, Kathleen hugged her tighter than she had ever hugged her. 'Roisin, I'm so sorry. I wish it could have been different. I wish…'

Sitting across from Kathleen, in the late afternoon of her fiftieth wedding anniversary, it occurred to Roisin that maybe she didn't know her mother very well at all. But the very last thing Kathleen needed at this moment was a daughter trying to read and record her thoughts. What an act of betrayal that would be.

'Do you fancy a glass of lemonade, Mam?'

'Oh, Roisin… I didn't realise you were there. Go offer your father one, dear,' she said, still gazing ahead at the unpainted view.

2 March 2002

Dear Rose,

Today, I met Imelda for coffee down at the pier. I waited in the soft morning sunshine. The breeze off the water was chilly and the sun slipped behind the clouds and I began to feel oppressed by a kind of ambivalence – or was it melancholy? It's not always easy to pinpoint an emotion. All I know is what I was feeling was like the sadness I used to feel in particular places, at certain times, when I lived here all those years ago. I thought maybe I had grown out of it, but obviously not.

Finally, she arrived. Nearly twenty-five minutes late, she was! I was about to go, when she slumped down at the table and sank her head in her hands. I haven't seen her since the Boxing Day lunch. I don't think she once asked me how I had been, because she was too busy telling me her tale of woe. She must have forgotten I had been in hospital for a few days last month. I don't think she has ever once asked me about my life in the outback, or why I left to live in the outback so many years ago and why I eventually returned here to this island. I would have liked to tell her, but then maybe I should be satisfied with the stories I write even though none of them are true.

Sometimes, I think she just uses me as a free counsellor, that she doesn't see me as a friend in the way she sees the other women in her life. I guess I am not a 'girlfriend' in her circle of 'girlfriends'. She probably describes me as an 'older lady' she knows who she takes out for coffee sometimes.

At her Boxing Day lunch, I felt as stiff as cardboard. I don't think I tasted a single thing I ate. I played my part, the part she had given me: the poor woman who has no children and no family except a husband who is, well…and whom she, Imelda, was kind enough to have at her table. I can imagine what she said when I left. 'Iris is a bit of a sad case, really. But the children like her and, well, if I can do something to help.'

I remember when I arrived home that day, Arnold was sitting on the veranda, smoking and drinking beer. He probably had a better time than I did.

Anyway, today Imelda was tearful. Not herself at all. Her eye make-up was smudged under her eyes and she had a stain on the front of her cream-coloured jumper. She confided how she had fallen out with one of her girlfriends because she suspected the friend may have been having an affair with her husband. There had been an incident at a party. I think men sometimes sabotage female friendships, knowingly and unknowingly. Female friendships threaten them.

Perhaps I should have paid more attention when Imelda was telling me her story because I can't remember how it ended. 'Everyone betrays you in the end,' I said, but I can't remember why I said it.

Iris

A Glass of Whiskey and a Good Book

Roisin looked across the yard. Groups had formed and bonded, the guests had eaten and drunk plenty and the tenor of conversations had been set. Everyone seemed to be talking to someone. The party had reached the buzz stage. To try and join a group now might appear forlorn or even desperate.

Frank and Kathleen were dancing the gypsy tap with Sean and the woman who used to live next door to them. Roisin remembered she had an extraordinary collection of aprons.

Wesley was holding forth with Eliza-May and her husband, no doubt entertaining them with one of his many personas.

Bridget, Mary and Pat were standing together all laughing loudly about something or other.

A mass of faces Roisin didn't recognise began to whirl in front of her. The only solitary figure was Father Murphy still at his lone post under the walnut tree.

Bridget and Mary still looked fresh and bright – not even slightly tipsy. Roisin looked down at her feet and the flaking purple remains of an old pedicure. She should have thought to do something about it before she left home. But then she didn't have much warning, did she?

Roisin scanned the crowd in search of someone to talk to, to still her thoughts that had begun to race again.

You complain you didn't have any warning, that you only got a day's notice, but that's not entirely true. You could have been in touch with your brother and sisters. You knew this party was coming up. You only had to ask and they would have told you of their plans. But, no. You would rather be the victim, wouldn't you? Have something to whine about, something to write about. You are always causing trouble.

A fixed smile had settled on her face like a death mask. She watched Bridget, Mary and Pat laughing together, talking together: remember this, remember that. The warmth of it, the comfort of it, the banter, the jokes: the love. But if she succumbed to it, to the seductive dishonesty of it, the family circle, it would stifle her, confine her, silence her. No, she must resist it at all costs. A familiar voice stirred her from her thoughts.

'Come over here and have a bit of a chat now, Roisin,' Father Murphy beckoned to her.

She sat next to him on the old brick fence. *Try and settle those thoughts now. Become aware of your surroundings like the counsellor taught you.* The bricks were warm from the afternoon sun. There is something oddly soothing about old bricks when they are warm, Roisin thought, smoothing her skirt. She took off her stilettos and tried to ease out the sharp piece of shell that had embedded itself into her flesh during her morning walk along the beach. She couldn't shift it. Her feet were aching now from standing with the silver platter for so long. She stretched her legs out in front of her and wriggled her toes. Sitting next to Father Murphy, she began to feel a little calmer.

'I've always been partial to walnuts, you know, Roisin,' he said as he split the thick hard shell open with his thumbnail. 'I think there's something noble about the humble walnut. Bit like the potato. Doesn't pretend to be anything it isn't. Bit like Collingwood, if it comes to it.'

She laughed. It felt good to laugh. To feel it in your belly, a release of a kind. But Roisin needed to be careful. She felt if she kept on laughing she might start crying.

'You'll never give up on them will you, Father?'

'Who, child?'

'Collingwood.'

'No, that I will not,' he said with the conviction of a man who believed. 'Now, Pat's been telling me you've been doing a bit of writing. What's your book about, young Roisin?'

'Well now, there's a question, Father. "What's your book about?"

What did Pat say it was about, Father?' Roisin felt her face; her cheeks were wet.

'What did Pat say it was about? He said it was about a family. In fact, I think he might be worried you might be writing about your own family, Roisin.'

'If that were the case, Father, and it isn't, why do you think that would worry him?'

'People are funny about such things, Roisin. Perhaps he thinks, as the only male child, he should be the one to tell the story, if it is it to be told at all, that is.'

'And what do you think, Father?'

'I know nothing about such things, my love. I put my faith in another book, the only book. Families make for fascinating stuff, Roisin. And hard stuff. Families are never easy for any of us. I know that as a priest and as a person.'

Roisin thought it odd how he made that distinction. 'Maybe you're right, Father. People must tell you all sorts of things about themselves, tell you their secrets.'

'Yes, my child. I hear a lot of secrets.'

Roisin looked across the lawn and there they were – her family. Pat had his arms around Mary and Bridget, and their mother and father had joined them. It was as if there was some kind of an aura around them all, holding them together, protecting them from the world.

'Would you like to have a look at my manuscript, Father? I have it here with me.' She pulled a slim file from her bag hanging over her shoulder. 'I take a copy of my manuscript with me everywhere, I'm not sure why. It's not a massive volume, a tome. Only a slim humble little thing, really. I know it does seem rather contrived, that I should just happen to have it with me and I just slip it to you out of my bag just like a plot device in a novel, but it's true, I carry it with me every day – somewhere between a burden and a treasure.'

'Well now, that I would, child. I'll just sit here and have a glance through it in a while.'

In a stop-start gesture that suggested she might have been having second thoughts, Roisin handed him the slim manila folder

'You handed that to me as if you were passing me a baby to hold, Roisin.'

'Maybe I am, Father.'

He read the title. 'Handwritten in pencil, Roisin, so you can make changes? Is it about you and your life?'

'Do you know, Father, I never know how to answer that question. My own life, the life I lead inside me, changes so quickly my fiction could never keep up with it. Maybe that's why I choose to write in pencil.'

'What about the past – your past, Roisin?'

'That changes too, Father. Nothing ever stays the same.'

A soft breeze stirred his fine grey hair. He stared down at the manuscript and without looking up said, 'Roisin, this writing, this art, this book, it might be precious to you, but you seem troubled by it, somehow. As if it holds some kind of secret, carries with it some kind of danger or blame, something that could harm you. Am I right?'

'Well, Father, fiction can be dangerous because it can become the coincidence of the future, so to speak. Almost like a prophecy.' Roisin looked down at her half-empty champagne glass and took a sip. It had become warm and tasted sickly sweet.

'You mean like a type of manifestation of thoughts, Roisin?' he said.

'In a way, yes, and in a way, no. And there are some things that we have no language for, not even in fiction. Sometimes the more we try to reveal, the more we conceal.'

Roisin was unaware Pat had been standing next to her, until he spoke.

'Don't be flaunting that thing everywhere, Roisin. It's a party not a reading group. Leave Father to enjoy himself.' Pat stood over them both for a moment casting a shadow and then, seemingly distracted by someone in the crowd, walked away.

'I will keep it close to my chest, my child.' He looked at her, his blue eyes smiling.

'I remember reading somewhere that silence is the only companion that never betrays. Might have been Confucius.'

'Well, you would never want that would you: silence?' he said.

'Only in a confessor, Father. In fact, all I would want from a confessor is silence.'

'Well…you have it, child…silence is yours…'

10 August 2002

Dear Rose,

Arnold pruned the roses today. But he didn't prune the red climbing bush. I didn't ask him why. There was sadness about him, a bit hard to describe. He seemed quieter, slower, a little more stooped. He didn't even seem to enjoy the chicken casserole – his favourite. I think, if he could, there is much Arnold needs to talk about. But there again, he's never been a great talker. Most men would say women talk too much.

The other night at the writing group a man called Oscar was deliberating on the form of the Greek chorus and his attempts to include it in his novel as a way of underlining themes or issues in his fiction. I couldn't help sensing his fragility, as if he could be blown away in a gust of wind. I noticed his skin was the colour of aged parchment and his fine hair grey and wispy. Everything about him seemed delicate. He had the air of someone who could be wasting away on a chaise longue, and who should have been wearing a smoking jacket and a silk cravat. I said to him I'd be a bit wary of' 'underlining' themes and issues because it might come across as hitting the reader over the head.

Anyway, I'm going to have a go at Greek chorus myself. I thought about it today when I was in the garden helping Arnold with the roses. I'd like to share it with you, Rose.

Notes for a chorus scene

VOICE ONE: Why do you think a person feels the need to write?
VOICE TWO: That's a hard question, but an obvious one to ask a writer and one that seems to fascinate people. Why does a painter need to paint? For the same reason a writer needs to write, surely?

VOICE ONE: Yes, but that doesn't really answer the question, does it? Where do you get your inspiration from? Where do your characters come from?

VOICE TWO: Well, people who read stories often assume the narrator in the tale is the author and the characters are real figures from the author's life. And that is exactly what fiction is not.

VOICE ONE: So what is fiction, then?

VOICE TWO: Fiction is an art form, a fabrication, an imaginative creation, a fanciful construction – in short, a lie.

VOICE ONE: Yes, maybe, but it must come from somewhere.

VOICE TWO: Yes, it does. It starts with a word, a nod, a wink, a smile, a tear, a colour, a voice, a laugh, a fear, a dream. Sometimes the writer must journey far and wide, go to fearful and strange places, before the idea becomes a story.

VOICE ONE: You haven't convinced me. I bet that's not how Dickens did it.

VOICE TWO: I've never asked Dickens.

Life seems to be full of choruses.

    Iris

The Party's Over

Roisin left Father Murphy to his silence. The lawn was cool and soft against her bare feet. Kathleen and Frank had taken to the floor again, Kathleen floating in a cloud of pink chiffon, Frank a little unsteady. Or was it Roisin who was unsteady? She found herself a chair next to someone she thought she should know, but she couldn't quite remember who they were. One of Bridget or Mary's friends, perhaps. It didn't matter, because they didn't recognise her either. Roisin was grateful not to have to speak any more, to make stilted conversation with people who were only being polite. All she wanted was to be alone and to have peace from her thoughts that would not be still. Her parents continued their dance.

The party seemed to be thinning out a little. Roisin thought of the night before. Nick was probably back at home with his wife now. Funny that he sold beds. Last night at the hotel there had been a possibility of human contact, of some kind of tawdry intimacy. But she'd seen the look on Nick's face when he left her at the lift. He must have considered it momentarily like you would consider the last stale biscuit in the barrel when you were hungry. He decided against it, backed out in the end. She wasn't his type. He had a wife anyway. He had told her so. She was most likely a blonde, suntanned (the fake kind), with long painted fingernails, a snappy dresser who watched TV reality shows, gave him two kids, a boy and girl, and blow jobs. Some women like sex. It's important to them. Not just a chore at the end of the day, keeping them from sleep. Dave had missed out in that department. For Roisin, sex was never important.

She could never feel any real bitterness towards Dave. Perhaps she never loved him the way she should have loved him. He served a purpose in her life. He provided her with a home but she failed to provide him with children, failed at her part of the bargain. You couldn't blame him for being disappointed. Most men want children and when she discovered she would never be having any, who could reproach him for leaving? It had been okay between them for a while but, towards the end, they had very little to say to each other. No, that wasn't altogether true. As Roisin remembered it, she had plenty to say, plenty, but nothing Dave seemed to be interested in hearing.

'All those words, Roisin – don't you get tired of them, those endless fucking spruiking words?' Dave said, one day, just before their second anniversary.

So silence became an easy option for her. She pretended to listen when he spoke, and in the end she spoke less and less. That seemed to suit him better. He thought they weren't trying hard enough to have a baby but how hard do you have to try? It became obvious in the end.

'It's never going to happen, Dave. The doctor told me – I can't have babies. Something went wrong when I was young and they can't fix it,' she'd told him.

Roisin had never written about that conversation with Dave like her counsellor had advised her to. If she had to write about it, perhaps it would have gone something like this:

He looked away from me, and then when he turned to look at me again he had become someone I had never met before, like someone I had never known…

One day, she would use that memory in her fiction.

'Roisin…Rose…' Her mother was calling her. 'Don't sit over there moping all by yourself, you silly girl. Come over here and be part of the family.'

Well, she would give it a try. Roisin felt herself get up from her chair and heard herself apologise to the woman sitting next to her for bumping her arm and her spilling her drink. She watched herself move with smile fixed on her face through the crowd, trying not to bump anyone else.

The second she approached them, her family – Frank, Kathleen, Pat, Bridget and Mary – the conversation ended. Her brother and sisters moved away.

Her mother whispered, 'Roisin, your shoes…go find your shoes, dear. And you've spilled your drink down your dress. Please don't embarrass us, today of all days.'

The old neighbour with the apron collection called Kathleen to join her, leaving her father and Roisin facing each other. There was nothing to say. Nothing. He inhaled deeply on his cigar and blew the smoke in her face, turned his back and walked away. Only a few nights ago when she had been sitting on the back veranda in her little cottage, she was sure she could smell that same cigar smoke. That familiar yet dreaded smell.

Roisin was unable to smile with that fixed smile any longer. She leant against the magnolia tree. Her father was talking to Eliza-May, again. Did he really say, 'Yes, Roisin is the plain one and I'm disappointed she hasn't helped her mother more'? Roisin was sure that was what he said, but she couldn't swear to it. The moment was blurred.

The counsellor had warned her about drinking too much. 'It's not good for your depression, Roisin. Try not to drink too much. Sometimes alcohol reacts with certain medications and I generally advise against it.'

Roisin began swaying to the sounds of the Irish band.

'Roisin, I'd be watching what I was drinking if I were you,' Frank said. He brushed against her shoulder as he escorted Kathleen back to the dance floor. 'We don't want you making an exhibition of yourself, now.'

'No, Daddy, we don't want me making an exhibition of myself, do we?' She sat down on the old stool behind the garden shed with the champagne bottle beside her. No one could see her. She took a swig from the bottle. No, the counsellor wouldn't be pleased with her at all.

Her last appointment was about a month ago. She looked forward to visits, to the unloading of emotion, the sense of being heard by another human being. Lemon verbena and lavender, the smell of furniture polish, soft strains of classical music; a glass bowl of peppermints; the rosewood bookcase; dark leather chair; framed seascape: these things had become so familiar the past year. At first, her outpourings had been fraught and fragmentary. But lately what had, in the past, been shaded by fear and doubt, had begun to surface.

*

'How have you been feeling since last we talked?'

'I have been feeling perplexed about the nature of truth.'

'How so?' The counsellor offered her a peppermint from the glass bowl, as she always did at the beginning of their sessions.

'I guess when you are a creator of fiction, an architect of imaginings and memory, a sculptor of thoughts and dreams, you can't help but wonder about truth.'

'How would you define truth?'

'I couldn't really say, except maybe it is that which is not false.'

'Do you think that maybe we create the truth?'

'Yes, maybe we do create truth but if we create the truth, what is fiction? Maybe fiction is truth.'

'I see you have brought your notebook with you. Maybe you have a lot of truth in your journal. When we last met, I asked you to go back in your mind, to think of a room from your past that was significant to you. How did you describe that room? Take your time.'

...thin, torn curtains blow in the wind that whistles through the open window and stirs the ash in the black grate. Walls hospital green. Grey shadows fall across the bed. But it's hard to recall the carpet... I think there was carpet...

'Have you ever used these images in your fiction writing practice, Roisin?'

'Do you think I should?'

'Only if it fits, Roisin. There would be no use if it didn't fit. When these memories come, Roisin, how do you feel?'

'Are they memories?'

'Do you think they are memories, Roisin?'

'I'm not sure. All I know is when I feel tormented, writing fiction helps.'

'Whatever happened to cause you such distress is wedged deeply in your psyche like a vicious tumour…so writing about it, even if you feel unsure about what happened, is good. Do you agree, Roisin?'

'I couldn't have put it better myself.'

'Roisin, next week, what do you want to write about?'

'Well, maybe the carpet. Maybe I will go away and write more about the carpet.'

*

For Roisin, words spoken into the air were ephemeral and transitory. So often she couldn't even remember what she had said, but words on the page for her were tangible, corporeal, material, even if meaning was incomplete. The idea of someone filling in the blanks was as cleansing as a prayer of penance, as if the burden was taken from her and someone else would carry the weight from here on. Someone else would be left to sift through the words, to look for meaning, to look for reasons.

No, the counsellor would not be pleased with her for drinking so much today, but she would never know. The band was playing the last strains of 'The Anniversary Song' and the guests were starting to take their leave. Women kissed her mother, men shook her father's hand and echoes of 'A wonderful afternoon', 'Congratulations', and 'A beautiful family day' followed the guests as they left by the garden gate, adorned with a huge white ribbon.

Roisin drank the last of the bottle. She drifted into the blur of the plot lines of her novel, as she often did. The world she created in her fiction was never far from her thoughts. Sometimes she wondered where she lived most, in her fiction or in the world?

A wasp buzzing close to her ear stirred her from her reverie. She looked across at Father Murphy; his head was down. At first she thought he must be absorbed in her story, but as she wandered across the lawn towards him, she noticed he had nodded off. A warm afternoon and too much whiskey, perhaps? He looked up at her with a start. It probably was too much to expect him to read much of her work in such a short time. But it might have given him a bit of an idea of what she was writing about. He might have some thoughts to add.

'Sorry, Father. I have come to relieve you of your burden. Did you have a bit of a read of my scribblings?'

'Well yes, of course I did. I think I sailed away for a while. You've brought me back just now, my child.'

Father Murphy patted his chest, looking for the manuscript as if it was stuffed inside his priest's garb. 'Oh, now did I put it down next to me while I had a little nap? Child…don't worry…it can't be far way.' He stood up and began to look under the tree, brushing away the leaves from the roots. He patted his chest again. 'Don't worry, child. I'll help you find it. Roisin, you look like you've seen a ghost. Oh, Roisin, I'm sorry. I'm a silly old fool to have let it out of my hands. Perhaps Bridget may know.'

Her mouth went dry. Roisin's thoughts tumbled over each other. Perhaps, if she found Bridget before she had a chance to read it… She could see she was talking to Mary. She didn't want them to read it yet. She didn't want them to read it ever. She had an odd feeling in her feet as she walked over to them, as if she was in shackles, in chains, like a prisoner stumbling to the dock.

'Bridget, did you by any chance find…pick up a…?'

'Not now, Roisin,' snapped Bridget.

'Not now, Roisin,' whispered Mary.

'Just a little folder. No value to anyone but me. Are you sure you haven't seen it? Father Murphy was just reading it.'

'Well, ask him what he has done with it then,' said Bridget. She frowned as is she had just been accused of a theft.

Mary and Bridget turned their backs and walked into the house.

'I'm so sorry, Roisin. I can't think what might have happened to your precious writing. I mean it wasn't as if I went anywhere. Perhaps

I dropped it when I nodded off and one of the guests has put it somewhere. And anyway, my love, you'd have another copy somewhere at home, surely?' said Father Murphy, mopping his forehead with a white handkerchief.

'It's not that, Father. Yes, of course I have a copy at home. I just didn't want anyone else here to read it. Did you read any of it? If you did, you'd know why I don't want my family to lay their dirty hands on it. It's my story, not theirs,' said Roisin.

'Now then, Roisin. Don't be getting angry with me. I'm an old man and I'm sure your writing folder will turn up.' Father Murphy picked up his empty glass and walked towards Frank.

She shouldn't have been so careless as to have handed it to him in the first place. Roisin knew that. But he was a priest after all, a confessor. She thought he, above all, would have guarded her confessions; her secrets should have been safe with him. Now they would just rub her out, erase her and her story would be taken from her.

A strange quietness came over the scene, the remains of the garden party – discarded chairs scattered carelessly in disarray, overturned crystal champagne flutes stained with lipstick, and plates of half-eaten pieces of cream sponge now spotted with flies. The cucumber sandwiches had hardened, the edges curled and the once elegant little triangles were spread about untidily on the silver platter. A solitary white linen handkerchief embroidered with pink roses and probably smelling of perfume lay on the makeshift dance floor.

Father Murphy filled his glass again from the whiskey bottle. He and Wesley were the only guests left who were not family. The air was dense and heavy, the sun had clouded over, but there was no smell of rain in the air yet. A blanket of humidity enveloped them all. Even Wesley was looking wilted. He had discarded his black jacket and tie and his shirt was half untucked and stained with red wine. Somehow he had lost his sparkly aura. He looked more like a tired waiter than a movie star.

The hot wind blew the white handkerchief across the lawn. A storm was building.

5 October 2002

Dear Rose,

Arnold made a boiled fruit cake today but he forgot to stir in the flour. When I came home, the whole house smelled of burnt sugar. I had to open all the windows. He became so angry when I told him he'd forgotten the flour. He threw the whole thing, cake tin included, in the rubbish bin. Then he went out and chopped wood for over an hour. It's my birthday soon. Maybe he was thinking it would be my birthday cake.

I was thinking today about my work, my writing. I think, when I am working on a book, I love my manuscript more than anything or anyone in this world. It's like a baby to me. When I am done, I am done and I can let it go, but not until that moment, and all writers know it. That moment when there is nothing more to say, nothing more to write, when the characters have fulfilled their roles, when the script is finished, when the job is done. I know if someone read my unpublished work without my permission, it would seem like a violation, a kind of rape. I hope you don't mind me sharing this with you, Rose.

It's just sometimes I feel fiction is a little like Cinderella's slipper. People will try and make it fit them if they can. Especially the author's family. That's the very problem Roisin now has. Her family will try and find themselves in the work. But try as they might, they will never make it fit. Never. It's Roisin's glass slipper. It's her story.

Iris

Banished From the Garden

'You'll stay for a bit of supper with us won't you, Father? And you too, Wesley,' said Kathleen.

'Well, of course, Kathleen – I'd be delighted,' said Father Murphy.

'Yes, nothing would be nicer,' said Wesley. He'd managed to clean the red-wine stain off his shirt but one of the sleeves was undone now. 'I appear to have lost a cufflink. It's silver – probably out there on the grass somewhere.'

'Well, we'll keep an eye out for it,' said Frank. 'Come on inside now.'

They filed slowly inside, taking their positions, like characters on a stage set, each with a part to play. Bridget had a type of power that had been bestowed upon her by some unknown force within the family. Or perhaps it wasn't unknown. Maybe it was Frank and Kathleen who had anointed her as their second in command, with Pat as her deputy. Mary just went along for the ride, protected by all. And Roisin…well…

The lounge room was hot and airless and seemed smaller than ever. Bridget tapped her glass with an Apostle spoon.

'Open the curtains and windows,' suggested Wesley.

'Not yet,' said Bridget. 'I have a slide show for you all.'

Kathleen moved towards Bridget and hugged her. 'Thank you, my darling girl,' she gushed. 'And I wouldn't be surprised if you had a hand in it too, Mary. Am I right?'

'Yes, I helped her, Mam,' Mary said, her cheeks flushed.

Kathleen stood next to Mary and hugged her too. 'Two beautiful girls,' she said.

'Yes, indeed. Two beautiful girls,' echoed Frank.

'I'm in on it, too,' said Pat. 'I have a grand story to tell.'

'I knew I could rely on you, Pat,' said Frank. 'You are the keeper of the faith, to be sure, my son.'

Frank switched on the old green fan and it cranked noisily and blew the hot air. Roisin decided to stay standing and leant up against the faded wallpaper. Honeysuckle, the pattern was, before it paled to faint patches of brown. Strange they never replaced it even though it was peeling and mouldy in parts. She put her glass in a space on Frank's bookshelf, next to his poetry books. She tried to steady herself, to stand up straight, remembering her lesson in 'family loyalty'.

Bridget looked unnaturally bright, over-excited maybe. She reached over and blew out the votive candle and shone the slide projector on the wall opposite. The heavy red velvet drapes remained closed for the show. Well, if Bridget has had anything to do with it, the slide show will be a good one. It would have all the bells and whistles. She never does anything by half, Roisin thought. She began to say, 'If you have had anything to do with it, Bridget…' but stopped midstream. No one seemed to hear her.

Kathleen was sitting in her special chair she'd had re-covered last year in an old-world floral. Frank sat expectantly on the arm of her chair with his hand over Kathleen's. Pat stood behind them, tall and straight-backed as always. Father Murphy, on the stool by the fireplace, rested his chin on his fist like Rodin's *The Thinker*. His face had taken on a warm glow and his blue eyes were red and glazed. He was humming a tune softly to himself. Roisin felt herself sway. If only she hadn't drunk so much champagne, she wouldn't have felt so unsteady, so uncontained, as if something within her was about to shatter.

Mary was hovering about nervously.

Bridget tapped her glass again. She began. 'My dear and wonderful family, Wesley and Father Murphy, it has turned out to be a great day for us all. Mary and I have prepared a slide show in honour of Mam and Dad and their life together. But before we start, I have asked Father to say a few words. Thank you, Father.' Bridget sat down next to Mary, smoothing her hair and adjusting her gold fob chain.

Father Murphy stood up from his stool by the fireplace. He looked around the room at them all as if they were his congregation and he was about to deliver a sermon. 'Well, it is my pleasure and privilege to be here and talking to you today. A finer, more gracious couple you could not wish to meet. I have known Frank and Kathleen for most of their marriage and I have seen them grow together. I still have not yet been able to convince them to barrack for Collingwood but, ah well, I will not hold that against them.'

Bridget and Mary giggled.

'And it's not that they've been without their challenges. Oh no, we all have those. But they have battled bravely and they have succeeded. They have raised a fine and wonderful brood and I am proud to know you all. It has been a joy to know you, Frank and Kathleen. In your honour, I will just read a few words from our precious Lord. If you'll all be upstanding, please.'

He took a small Bible from his pocket, put on his glasses and slowly turned the pages. He cleared his throat and took a sip of whiskey. 'It has been wonderful to know you and your children all these years, Kathleen and Frank. I wish you and your family many, many more happy years together. Now, if you'll all raise your glasses. To Kathleen and Frank, God bless you both!' Father Murphy's nose was bright red.

'Please all raise your glasses, to Mum and Dad!' Bridget said, beaming her smile at them all.

'Thank you, Father, that was a truly beautiful reading,' said Kathleen.

Frank stood now. 'Thank you one and all, and thank you, Father, for the beautiful reading. It is a proud man that I am today, to be sure, to have my lovely Kathleen by my side. Thank you, my darling, for the precious years that we have had together.' He turned and kissed her cheek.

She wiped her eyes with a tissue Mary offered her. 'Oh, I must have lost my linen handkerchief in the garden, Frank. It was my own mother's,' she said.

'No more tears, my darlin' one. This is a happy day for us all,' Frank said and he sat on the arm of Kathleen's chair.

'Okay, everyone,' said Bridget as she began the slide show, 'Pat has his own story to tell you now.'

Pat, confident and smiling, took the floor, pressed the button and the show began. Pavarotti's voice – 'Nessun Dorma' – resounded in the background.

'Nice touch, Bridget – classy. Oh yes, so tasteful,' said Wesley.

Roisin's head was spinning now. 'Oh, so tasteful,' she muttered.

'Now,' began Pat, 'this is a little history of our family. The true history, if you like.'

Roisin heard herself laugh, loudly.

Bridget glared at her. 'Roisin better not spoil this,' she whispered to Mary.

'This is Mum and Dad on their wedding day in Dublin, all those years ago,' said Pat.

He had his story all under control. Today, his story was one that was going to be heard; his story was the one that would be believed. Their parents' struggles, their mother's uncomplaining sacrifice, stoicism and faith, their father's heroism and devotion, his respect for his mother and father, the happiness of his childhood, of all their childhoods, the laughter, the joy, the memories: the love. He flicked through the slides, pausing just long enough at each one. Bridget had included one of Pat in his billycart.

He hesitated for just a second, no longer. 'You did a beautiful job on that, Dad,' he said smiling.

'That I did, son, that I did,' said Frank.

'It's a fine father who crafts a billycart for his son with his own hands,' said Father Murphy.

Absently, Roisin picked up a poetry book from the bookshelf she was leaning against and turned the first page.

'Roisin, are we keeping you from your books?' said Bridget.

'Sorry…sorry, Bridget,' Roisin said. She snapped the book shut. 'I need some air.'

'Why don't you just sit down and be quiet. Go on, Pat,' said Bridget.

'Now, this is Mary and Bridget playing on Christmas Day, all those years ago,' Pat went on.

'That was the year we got yo-yos,' said Roisin.

Where was Pat's? Was that the Christmas she found him hiding behind the garden shed, his jaw bruised and crying holding his cracked and broken yo-yo stomped on by some deliberate and angry boot?

Bridget laughed, 'Yo-yos? What are you on about, Roisin?'

'I think I just need to get some air,' she said, turning towards the door.

'Roisin, just shut up,' hissed Bridget.

Pat moved on to the next slide. 'What are you babbling about, Roisin? Concentrate if you can – Bridget and Mary have put a lot of effort into this,' said Pat.

'Goodness, these girls have covered just about everything, not a stone left unturned, things I had almost forgotten,' said Kathleen.

'Bridget is the researcher, the detective,' laughed Mary. 'I can't take much of the credit.'

'I can take no credit at all,' said Roisin.

Bridget stabbed her with her eyes.

Carefully selected pictures of happiness flickered one after the other on the wall. Birthday parties, graduations, holidays, anniversaries.

Wesley had moved next to Roisin. His musky perfume had settled throughout the room. 'It's an amazing story, Roisin,' he whispered.

'Yes, Wesley. It's an amazing story,' said Roisin for all to hear.

'Hush…please, Roisin,' Mary mouthed at Roisin, catching her eye.

Roisin looked away and took another sip of champagne.

And finally the last slide: the christening scene – Frank and Kathleen outside the church, in front of the stained glass window at the top of the steps. Kathleen, smiling, holding little Mary in the lace christening robe.

'The last child,' said Pat.

'Why wasn't I allowed to hold her?' Roisin's voice was becoming shrill and loud.

'Roisin, what are you babbling about?' said Bridget. 'I think you've had too much to drink.'

'Don't go spoiling things for Mum and Dad like you always do,' said Mary.

'Shut up, Roisin. Shut up!' Pat yelled at her.

'Why wasn't I allowed to hold her?'

'Calm yourself, my child – don't distress your family in this way. You know it was all for the best,' said Father Murphy.

'She's hysterical. She's always been nuts. She's drunk. What is she going on about?' said Bridget.

'Pat…' hissed Frank, motioning to his son.

Pat didn't hesitate. He moved forward and took Roisin's arm and forced it high up her back. She held her breath. If she didn't move with him, her arm would break.

'Get out, cunt,' he said under his breath.

Pat flung the front door open and just before he pushed her out of the door, she looked back at the frozen image on the wall. Her parents staring back at her from the slide. The christening gown falling in soft folds around Mary's little body, Kathleen holds her close, smiling, her lips a streak of scarlet. Her father stands straight-backed with his medals shining bright through the sepia.

20 November 2002

Dear Rose,

I was thinking this morning about when I lived in this house as a child. I'm sure the wallpaper in the hallway is still the same. It's so old and faded it must have been there for years. More has peeled away and there seems to be another layer underneath and maybe another under that like a palimpsest. In my old battered dictionary (which Arnold keeps taking for his crosswords), the definition is 'Writing material or manuscript which has been rubbed away to make room for a second'.

I hope this novel will be a bit like that in the end, that what is changed might still bear traces of its earlier form. And carpet has that same layered quality. A type of covering up, only revealing what is underneath after being worn down by time. The fascination of surfaces.

Last night at the writing group, we did an intense exercise. The woman who sits quietly in the shadows suggested it. Insisted on it. She handed out blank envelopes and asked us to write a memory on the back. This is what I wrote:

I was sick that day. I had thrown up in my soup bowl. The lady in charge of the crèche called my father to collect me, which meant he had to knock off work early. Strange that I should be aware of that small fact – I was only three years old – but I must have sensed this was the cause of his anger: initially. As soon as we were clear of the crèche he picked me up in his arms, roughly, and held me in a vice-like grip. I began to cry – I was feeling sicker and afraid. The more I cried, the harder and tighter he held me, so that I could barely breathe. It was as if he was trying to crush me. 'Put me down,' I screamed and screamed. I held in the vomit. He carried me this way, walking fast down the unmade road to our house. He threw me on the bed and hit me and yelled he was going to hit me until I stopped crying, until I was silent. I remember I stuffed my fist in my mouth trying to stifle my sobs. At some point, I must have passed out. The next thing I remember I was lying alone in the pitch dark when my mother opened the door and light shone through. She said, 'Do you want some fish?' It must have been Friday.

Maybe none of this ever happened at all. Memory is an unreliable witness, I think. But this memory comes often, so I usually don't doubt it. But it could have been just a dream, I suppose. I have always been a dreamer, Rose.

Iris

It Was All Quite Simple

The rain pelted down through the leaves and branches, shards stinging her flesh. The oak tree had offered little shelter from the storm. Roisin got up slowly, peeling herself off the park bench. She was sober now. Wet and sober, drenched through. Now the rain had stopped, she walked slowly back to the hotel. It was nearly dark.

When she stepped through the sliding doors, the woman at the hotel reception desk looked up.

'Can I help you?' she said.

Roisin looked nothing like the woman who had left the hotel that morning. Not even Nick would have recognised her. She held up her key to show the receptionist that she was a guest and took the lift to the seventeenth floor.

What sort of woman gets thrown out of her parents' fiftieth wedding anniversary party? Roisin caught sight of herself in the lift mirror – a woman in late middle-age, clothes stuck to her body like melted candlewax, her hair plastered to her head. She looked down and realised she didn't even have her shoes on. Now she was sitting on the edge of the bed, knowing she was making it wet, but that it didn't matter because she wouldn't be sleeping in it that night. There would be no redemption.

It was all quite simple, really. Once the bath was full, she tested it with her elbow, as if for a baby, and climbed in. She didn't take her clothes off, a modesty thing. How terrible to be found naked. Roisin felt her muscles relax in the warm water, reached for the hairdryer and began drying her wet hair.

1 January 2003

Dear Rose,

Happy New Year. Such a quiet day, today. Not even the sound of traffic on the road. I'm not sure it is the best day to be thinking about funerals, let alone writing about one. It's difficult to write about a funeral without recalling all the funerals you have ever attended. And when you get to my age, you have attended a few. I have never – touch wood – attended a child's funeral. I hope I never do.

I remember my father's funeral. Bridie and Marie arranged a wake and there was some kind of argument, some kind of scene. I can't even remember what it was about. Jim got horribly drunk and threw me out.

I am not sure if there will be a funeral scene in my novel but if there is, I will write it like this:

Behind the altar, the sun streamed through the leadlight window of green, yellow and rose coloured glass. The tiny white coffin was covered in pale pink rosebuds. She took a sideways glance at him and sensed more than saw his strong broad shoulders stretching the seams of the silk suit jacket. She leant against him and felt his shoulders begin to shake. The smell of honeysuckle from the altar flowers drenched the hot thick air. If she could have looked down on herself from above she would have seen how like a yielding, bending daisy on a long stem she looked.

Perhaps there will be a funeral.

Iris

After the Funeral

Frank seemed composed enough. An objective observer might even say there was an air of relief about him or might think his eyes were too clear and bright for those of a grieving man. He was wearing the same white shirt and blue tie he wore to his anniversary party.

Kathleen was wearing a pink linen suit, the lining hanging a little below the hem, rosary beads entwined in her hands. Her dancer's poise had abandoned her and her shoulders were hunched like those of the old woman she was. The young woman she had pretended to be a few days earlier had disappeared into the past.

'For the rest of my life, I will pray every day to our blessed Virgin that my Roisin will be allowed to enter the kingdom of Heaven,' Kathleen said, tears falling down her soft pink face, so fresh a few days earlier, now crushed like a trampled, spent blossom.

Wesley had come to pay his respects but today, he looked more like an undertaker than a dancer.

'Have faith, Kathleen, my love. Father Murphy said he will pray at mass that Roisin will be forgiven. Try not to worry too much,' Frank said, his arm under her elbow, helping her out into the garden, the same garden where just a few days earlier they had celebrated their golden wedding anniversary.

They sat down together in the shade of the walnut tree.

'But I fear she will go to Hell, Frank. And she doesn't deserve that, no matter what she has done, no matter what sin she has committed,' she said.

'She made her own choices, Mam,' said Bridget, putting her arm around Kathleen's shoulders.

Kathleen held her head in her hands and began to cry. 'We've failed her, Frank, we've all failed her,' her voice choked and muffled.

'Well, let's hope not. All we can do is pray for her soul,' said Frank.

If it had been a scene in a play, the lights would have dimmed for a few seconds and the characters would freeze. But it wasn't a scene in a play. Frank and Kathleen had just lost their daughter and they sat in the shade under a walnut tree on a glorious summer's afternoon.

Frank patted Kathleen's hand. 'We have two lovely girls and a strong son. We must make the best of all we have, my love. Father Murphy gave her a lovely service, now didn't he?'

Mary and Bridget sat down together on garden chairs next to Frank and Kathleen. Bridget had chopped up some fresh fruit and passed it around on a silver platter. Frank and Kathleen both shook their heads but Pat, who had been leaning against the tree trunk, reached across and took a large slice of pineapple.

'You know, I considered wearing red today, but I thought maybe it wouldn't have been appropriate. I thought it might have been better for the photographs, though,' said Bridget.

'But it's a funeral – Roisin's funeral. Why would you wear red? Shouldn't we be sad? I feel I should be sad, crying even,' said Mary.

'I couldn't really say what I feel. It was such a selfish, selfish act,' said Bridget.

Frank said quietly, 'No more in front of your mother, now.'

Pat opened a bottle of champagne. 'Still plenty left from the other day – I didn't have to buy any more.' Roisin's death had bestowed upon him the position of the eldest child, not just the eldest son.

'That's what I call forward planning,' said Mary, laughing a bit too loud.

'Do you want to lie down for a while, Mary? You seem a little upset,' said Bridget.

'My…my…sister…she was my sister, wasn't she?…has just died,' she said, still laughing.

'Pat, take her inside,' Bridget ordered. 'She needs to lie down in a dark room.'

Mary stood up. 'No, I don't need to lie down anywhere. My sister has just died…your sister, Bridget, your sister, Pat,' and looking across at her Grace and Frank, 'and your daughter has just died.'

Kathleen and Frank were sitting, side by side, staring ahead as if they are waiting for a train.

Wesley was standing next to them looking like an extra on a film set. 'Poor Roisin. It was only a few days back she was here with us here in this garden, handing around the cucumber sandwiches,' Wesley said.

Pat had given him a glass of champagne too.

Wesley took a sip. 'I couldn't say that I knew her well but I feel that's she's still around, though. It's almost as if she has something still to tell us.'

Father Murphy joined the little group. His pale Irish skin looking pinker than ever, he mopped his brow with a crumpled white handkerchief, perhaps more out of habit than need. 'Yes, it's hard to believe she's gone when just a few days ago…her parents were a vision of joy,' said Father Murphy. 'They are a vision of tragedy now.'

'We never did get to the bottom of whether there was a note or not, did we? The housemaid said something about a note. Apparently, Roisin didn't want any flowers. But the note has been lost or was so wet that the message disintegrated. Anyway, Mary and I made sure there were no flowers,' said Bridget. She was wearing heavy make-up – bright red lipstick and pale powder. She looked a little like a caricature of a professional mourner.

'Did she leave a will, do you know?' said Pat. He was dressed in a stiff white shirt and black pants. No tie, his collar open. It seemed strange. A mark of disrespect, almost.

Bridget and Mary both said at the same time, 'I don't know.'

Wesley drained the dregs of his champagne, and handed his empty glass to Pat for a refill. 'Did anyone find the story she was so distressed about? The one Father Murphy accidentally misplaced?' he asked.

'It is with her now, in her coffin,' said Bridget

The scene could have been rehearsed. Pat, Bridget and Mary raised their glasses on cue.

MARY: To Roisin, I never really knew you. I wish I had.

BRIDGET: To Roisin, What a foolish act. Such a tragic waste. But she is ashes now.

PAT: To Roisin. At least, she took her story with her. But her story is ashes now.

As if about to begin a prayer, Father Murphy hung his head and said, 'Well, it's a peculiar thing, now. Did you happen to notice Roisin's ex-husband, Dave, at the back of the church? He had a few words to me after the service and asked me to pass on his condolences to you all.' He paused and looked. 'And a wonderful thing…he's found a copy of her manuscript among her effects …the one that went missing because of my careless inattention. He's passed it to her solicitor, apparently.'

Kathleen and Frank blurred into the background, like figures in some ancient fresco; the faint smell of Frank's cigar smoke wafted in the breeze. Bridget, Mary and Pat stood staring in silence at Father Murphy.

'The title,' he said, almost in a whisper, 'is the same as my own dear mother's favourite rose.' He turned and walked under the rose arbour, as if he were a character leaving a stage set.

Rosa

14 February 2003

Dear Rose,

Today, I was telling Arnold I sometimes think my choice to leave my family and head inland like a scorpion seeking the desert set my entire life's course. He was working in the vegetable patch and I don't think he heard a word I said. So I went on talking anyway.

I continued my speech. The short version went something like this: 'I imagine people would think a girl who could leave her family behind like that must be hard-hearted, callous even. I can see how a girl who did such a thing could be judged as a very selfish girl, and you might say one without too many morals, a girl with a dark psychology.'

Arnold's only response was 'This spinach is full of bugs, Iris. It has to go.'

I speak so many words into the air. I feel thankful at least I can sometimes capture them like butterflies in a net and put them down on paper. I've been working hard on my novel, especially these past nights. Arnold goes to bed so early. Sometimes, I think fiction and poetry make all things possible. Everything can be revised, rewritten on the page.

There was a heavy smoke haze around the mountain, today. Arnold is used to the heat but not bushfires. I think the smoke might have given him a bit of asthma. Not too many bushfires in the desert, if any during the many years we were there. This old weatherboard house heats up after a few hot days. I sent Arnold out to the shed to see if he could find a fan.

He came back with an old, dusty, green thing with a cord so frayed you could see the coloured wires. 'A bit past its use-by date, Iris,' he said. And I replied, 'Just like you, Arnold.'

He laughed – the first time I have heard him laugh in ages.

Iris

Not All Legacies Are an Act of Generosity

'Where's Mama?' Rosa closed the back door quietly. 'Where is she?'

No warm familiar smell of her mother's cooking, only the suffocating smell of her father's cigar. He was sitting, smoking, beer can open on the kitchen table. He had that black look about him that made Rosa's twelve-year-old body stiffen.

'Where is she, Dad?' Rosa lowered her voice almost to a whisper.

Her father didn't look up. He blew cigar smoke high into the air. Rosa looked in the little pantry. Her heart was beating hard. Her mother wasn't in there. She crept down the hallway. Perhaps her mother was asleep. She peeped into her parents' bedroom. The bed was unmade. She took a breath, walked in and quickly pulled open the wardrobe. Her mother's soft pink chenille dressing gown was gone. Gone. Rosa's stomach lurched. She knew where her mother was. She'd been there many times before.

'You, Bones, you get down here and start the tea. Your brother and the little girls will be home soon. You have to take your mother's place for a while,' Joseph Kabanosy yelled down the hall.

Rosa felt her throat tighten. How long would it be this time? Last time it was three months and the time before that, two. Please, Mama, please get better soon.

'Did you hear me…get down here and start the tea and get your father a beer from the fridge,' he shouted.

Funny how his accent disappeared when he yelled. Delphine and Camille, her father's little princesses, bounced in the door just as Rosa had begun to peel the potatoes.

'You make a nice tea for these little pets, Bones,' her father laughed.

The little blonde-haired girls laughed with him. They jumped up on his knee.

'You are so funny, Daddy. It's so funny when you call Rosa that name. She's ugly, not pretty like me and Camille. People think we are twins but we're not,' said Delphine.

'That's why I call you my princesses. You are both my beautiful princesses, with your beautiful blonde curls. Your sister's hair is dark like her grandmother's was. She was a filthy old gypsy,' said Joseph Kabanosy.

Rosa smoothed her hair – she wasn't going to wash it until her mother came home.

'Where's Mama?' asked Delphine, looking up at her father.

'Where's Mama?' echoed Camille, pulling at his shirt sleeve.

Rick walked through the back doorway and dropped his school bag on the floor with a thud.

'Not so much noise there,' his father barked. 'I make the noise around here.'

'Where's Mum?' asked Rick, as if he already knew the answer. Just a year younger than Rosa, his hair was dark like hers and his eyes were dark too. Rick and Rosa were the dark ones.

'Just gone away for a little rest… She won't be away too long. Maybe just a few months. Rosa will look after us all, just like she always does.'

'Time to get up and get ready for school,' Rosa called to her sisters.

It was the first call. She would have to go back in five minutes and give them both a shake. Rick was already up; his bed was empty. She could smell her father's cigar smoke. She walked in to kitchen trying to sense his mood.

He was sitting at the kitchen table and he was bending down pulling on his work boots. His feet always smelled. 'Your mother will be home today and she doesn't want to come home to you telling tales and lies. You understand…no tittle tattle…you hear me? You don't want to make her sick again, do you?' said Joseph.

'No, Dad,' said Rosa. 'I don't want to make her sick.'

Rosa felt her heart leap in her chest. To see her mother again, to have her mother home. She would be safe again, for a while at least.

She walked back down the passage to shake Camille and Delphine. 'Wake up sleepy heads. Mama is coming home today.' Rosa almost sang the words.

Rosa ran all the way home from school. She rushed into the kitchen. 'Mama? Mama…oh Mum, you're home at last,' She hugged her mother's motionless form.

Sitting at the kitchen table, she was wearing her pink chenille dressing gown, the one she always wore when she had been away, and she sat with her hands folded across her stomach.

'Are you better, Mama?' Rosa hugged her mother, who didn't move from the chair. Her body felt rigid under the soft fabric of her dressing gown.

'A bit better.'

'I have looked after Delphine and Camille, Mama. They will be home soon and Rick is good, too. He's been playing lots of soccer.'

'And your father, Rosa. How is he?'

The woman from the house next door, Mrs Daly, was in the kitchen making a pot of tea. 'Now, Grace. Let's get you a good strong hot cup of tea,' Mrs Daly said to Rosa's mother. 'You look like you could do with one. Let you mother settle for a bit, Rosa.'

Mrs Daly poured the boiling water into the aluminium teapot and smoothed the stained, orange tea cosy with brown pompoms over it. 'We will all feel better after a good cuppa,' she said, taking the beaded crocheted cover off the milk jug.

She placed a plate of buttered scones with jam on the kitchen table and pushed it towards Rosa. 'Help yourself, dear.'

Whenever she visited, and she only ever visited when Joseph wasn't there, she always wore an apron. On this day, she was wearing a black and white one with red cross-stitching at the hem and roosters embroidered on the pockets. Rosa imagined Mrs Daly must have had quite a collection, because she had never seen her wearing the same one twice. The good and bad times in Rosa's life, so far, had been punctuated by the appearance of Mrs Daly's aprons.

'The baby died, Rosa,' said Grace.

*

'I had that dream again last night – that dream about the room, Mama.'

'You're always dreaming, Rosa. Go on, tell me about it then,' said Grace.

'It's always the same… I open the door, the window is open and something cries…and it seems so…real.'

'Oh, dear. It's only a dream. It's not real. Your father will be calling you a liar again if you don't stop this nonsense,' said Grace.

'But Mama, I don't know if it is a dream,' said Rosa.

'It's a dream.

*

The weeks passed and Grace seemed slowly to return to her mothering role. Rosa wondered how long it would last. It never lasted for too long.

'You can start babysitting again for Mrs Bird, if you like. It brings in a few extra shillings and Lord knows I can use them,' Grace said.

For Rosa, babysitting the little girl, Angela, for Mrs Bird while she was at her oil painting classes was like a holiday, a different world. When she returned, Mrs Bird used to give Rosa a glass of lemonade and a biscuit, show her some of her work, and they would sit and chat.

'Everything all right at home, Rosa?' she would sometimes ask.

Once, when she asked, Rosa started crying and Mrs Bird hugged her so tightly. Rosa could never remember anyone hugging her like that. Even little Angela stroked her hair. Grace only hugged her when she was crying, when she needed comfort. And her father Joseph, well…

Mrs Bird's stories about how she had met Mr Bird when they were both travelling in the outback captivated Rosa and filled her young imagination with hope. Mrs Bird told her stories of a different world, a world of freedom, a world of escape.

'Such an interesting place. Boat races in the dry creek bed. And we used to go to a little outdoor theatre with red and white striped deckchairs and watch films under the stars. And the skies,' said Mrs Bird, picking up a tube of cerulean blue oil paint from her kit on the table, 'are this colour…even in the winter.'

'I might go there, one day,' Rosa said, 'maybe when I turn sixteen.'

'It's a long way from home, dear.'

'Yes, a very long way from home.'

23 March 2003

Dear Rose,

This is what I scribbled on a napkin at the coffee shop this morning. Might be able to use it in something. It just seemed to come from nowhere. I think I may have dreamt it.

He sits on the green couch. The arms are white vinyl and grubby from the Vegemite fingers of my younger brother and sisters. How many of them are there now? Let's see. Me, my brother, my sister, my other sister and all the dead ones, the ones my mother grieves for. She calls them the angels. And always others are waiting in the wings. He sits there in the brown check dressing gown with egg down the front, bitten fingernails, chain smoking non-filter cigarettes, silent, smouldering and staring. I had to stay home from school. Where is our mother? I don't know whether to stay in the room or go outside. His eyes are piercing me. Where have all the others gone. Why am I here alone with him?

I don't suppose I will ever use it in the novel. Someone said to me once that my characters are such strange, repressed figures. So lonely and alone. But heroines always travel alone. And how often does the heroine escape an intolerable situation only to discover that before too long, after a brief glimpse of freedom, she finds herself held captive again?

Arnold was very quiet today. He sat watching television most of the day.

Iris

Heading Inland

The bus pulled into the depot, a corrugated-iron shed alongside a dry creek bed lined with red gums, tall and motionless in the still hot afternoon air.

'This is you, love,' the driver said. He jumped out in front of her and put her suitcase on the dusty curb.

'Thanks.' Rosa was the only one who got out of the bus.

'There's a hostel just down the road, darl'. Look after yourself,' the driver called behind her, pulling out in a veil of dust.

Through the dust cloud, a man in shorts and wearing a stained white cap strode towards her, smiling as if he knew her, as if he were an old friend. A blue heeler sat in the back of his white Holden ute, chained. For a moment, Rosa felt a sense of relief. Someone was there to greet her.

'You need somewhere to stay, love? I've got a room and a bed. My ute's just over there,' he said, reaching down to pick up her case. 'Not much in here. Light as a feather. Did you leave in a hurry?'

Tempting. He was offering a room and a ride, but something about him reminded her of when she was a little girl and a man in a park years ago offered her lollies. She'd wanted to take the lollies but, without knowing why, she didn't and she had run as fast as she could all the way home. Don't talk to strangers, Rosa. She had a feeling she would be meeting a lot of strangers in this strange, remote place.

Rosa looked down the dusty unmade road that stretched in front of her and brushed a fly away from her face. 'Oh, look…thanks…but I'm going to the hostel. I'll be right. Thanks anyway,' she said, snatching back her case.

'Oh, yeah. That's what they all say, love. Good luck.' He turned and walked towards his truck, the back of his shirt plastered with black flies.

Rosa began walking. There was no shade. But what did she expect? It was the outback, wasn't it? She was thankful for her floppy, brimmed felt hat, even though it was black. She always felt a bit like Janis Joplin when she wore it. Months before she had left home, she heard her heroine had died. She had written in her diary – *Today is Sunday, 4 October 1970 and it is the day Janis Joplin died. The world will never be the same. Soon I will be gone too, but just not from the world, but from my life here in a cold and dark place.* Just as well her case was light. She should have worn her summer dress, the pink, paisley one, the dress her mother always said was far too short. But instead she was wearing blue jeans and a thick green velvet jacket, the clothes she had dressed in the rainy morning she left the white weatherboard house with its peeling paintwork, many miles away from where she was now.

'Don't you think sneakers would be better for the outback than those spiky-heeled boots?' her mother had said.

Perhaps her mother had been right. Her feet were sweating and her favourite red vinyl boots were rubbing her toes. I'm going to have a huge blister, Rosa thought. Surely it couldn't be too much further. Sweat ran down her back. Finally, she stopped in front of a grey Besser brick building with a sign: Female Hostel. Permanent and Casual Accommodation. Well, this must be it.

She waited at the front desk. The man behind the glass window would have to look up, eventually. He sat very close to a noisy air-conditioner, smoking, feet up on the desk, reading a paperback with the cover folded back. Music played loudly on the scratchy-sounding radio – 'Hotel California'. Rosa rang the bell twice. She was just about to call out to him when he got up from the desk, slipped his feet into thongs that bore the heavy imprint of his swollen feet, shuffled to the reception window and opened it. His belly wobbled over his belt.

'Hello,' he drawled, through heavy, wet lips.

'Do you have a room?' said Rosa. Her voice came out high and light. She had been rehearsing the question as she walked along. She was trying to appear confident, as if she were an experienced traveller well-used to being far away from home.

'You from down south, I suppose?' Without waiting for an answer, he slid a form across the counter. 'Fill this in. Here's the key. Room 10, women's block. There's only one block, but. It's a women's block. Any blokes and you're out. Here's your sheets and towel. Just through there.' He pointed and closed the glass window and then opened it again. 'Rent's due on Friday and no arrears. And no smoking in the rooms either.' He slammed the window shut.

The building was single-storey and Room 10 wasn't hard to find. She picked up her small suitcase and put it on the bed. The stained blue and white striped mattress was pocked with cigarette burns. Two single beds, two built-in wardrobes and no carpet on the concrete floor – it would have to do for now. This would have to be home for a while.

She thought of the home she had just left, of the lounge room, the ashes in the fireplace, the threadbare couch and dusty green curtains. Only been gone for a few days and yet she couldn't remember what the carpet was like. It most probably would have been grey, yes, grey, with faded pink flowers – roses most likely – and there would have been holes showing the worn, green, felt underlay. Strange, she had lived in the house for all her sixteen years, but she couldn't remember the carpet.

Here there wasn't even a rug on the floor to sweep dust under. What would her room-mate be like? she wondered. On her side of the room there were two large posters: one of a huge whale and the other of white horses galloping through a field. Neither would have been Rosa's choice. The wall above her own bed was blank. Maybe she could find a Bob Marley poster somewhere, or even one of the Rolling Stones. She looked at her room-mate's neatly made bed and the small alarm clock on the bedside table. A clock was something Rosa hadn't thought to bring. Two-thirty. Plenty of time left to look around before nightfall, to go buy cigarettes, have a coffee, to look for others like herself. She left her unpacked suitcase on the bed and walked out again into the afternoon heat.

Walking along the dirt road, Rosa thought about the French woman she had sat next to in the bus. She was travelling on to Darwin to meet her boyfriend. Rosa imagined her in a little flat, small, minimal, but every object in it important, stylish, carefully considered and placed just so. Presumably she'd stayed on in the city while he found work. The woman told her he'd promised he would send for her just as soon as he got a job, just as soon as he found a place. But something had happened and she hadn't heard from him. He was an American, she explained, and they hoped to get married soon but they needed to work things out with immigration. He'd proposed in a sweet but flamboyant way. She had been out shopping for groceries for their tea – just a few things, rye bread, cheese, milk and tarragon. She walked into to the bathroom and he had written in her red lipstick on the bathroom mirror 'Will you marry me?' And she had written in a space underneath 'Yes'. That night they made love three times.

Now she hadn't heard from him in a while, not since he left. He'd promised to wait for her in Darwin. She still had his address and even though she hadn't heard from him in a month she was sure he would still be there. But she couldn't wait any longer, especially with the baby on the way. And she wasn't young, this woman. Rosa noticed she had deep lines under her eyes. She didn't think people that old had babies, except maybe her mother, Grace. Perhaps it was different for French women. Rosa was pleased she was able to practise her schoolgirl French but after a while, the woman, lost in her own thoughts, only answered with *oui* and *non*. Every now and again, the driver had chipped in, offering his opinions on this and that, most likely to keep himself awake on that long dusty highway. There didn't seem to be too much the driver didn't have an opinion on, even though he didn't seem to understand a word of French.

He launched into a monologue on love and marriage. 'I don't think it's natural for a man and woman to stay together all their lives. Things change, people change. Life doesn't stay the same. People who think love is forever are fools,' he said.

Somewhere on the dark highway the chatter must have stopped and Rosa drifted off to sleep. When the bus bumped her awake, the pitch-black sky had become golden on the dark horizon. A day and a night on the rickety bus is long enough to get used to people, to get to know them, to feel at ease with them. Rosa missed her friends, the bus driver and the French woman now, on her first day alone in the outback.

She turned the corner and walked alongside the dry creek bed. Groups of black men and women were sitting in groups around campfires, talking loudly in a language Rosa didn't understand, and drinking from Coke cans that had been cut in half. It was hard to know if they were fighting or just talking, so she kept her head down when she walked past them. Should she be frightened? She wasn't sure. It was as if she was watching herself from a distance, as if she was a character in a play, as if all this was happening to someone else, not her.

Rosa stopped and sat on a seat outside Win's Café. The air conditioner whistled through the blue plastic curtain that hung over the doorway. She realised she was still wearing her green velvet jacket. No wonder she was hot. Why hadn't she changed into her dress? She took off the jacket. It was covered in a mantle of black flies. Just as she began searching for her cigarettes in her bag, she felt a soft, insistent tapping on her shoulder. Someone with what appeared to be a mountain of whipped cream piled high upon his head was standing behind her.

'Smoke?' he said. He offered her the packet, his arm outstretched.

She took a cigarette from the gold pack.

'When only the best will do,' he said, striking a match and cupping his hand to light her cigarette. She smelt the familiar whiff of Old Spice. It must have been shaving cream on his head, and not whipped cream. Somehow that seemed more rational. And maybe it wouldn't melt so fast in the blistering afternoon sun.

'It's to keep the voices still,' he said quietly, leaning closer to her, as if he was speaking confidentially, as if he didn't want anyone else to hear. He sauntered on down the road.

Rosa could hear him talking to himself, or was he reciting poetry?

Rosa remembered the poem from school. What was it now? 'Ode to a Nightingale'? No, not that. It would come to her. He must be so hot in the matted green hand-knitted jumper he was wearing. The jumper looked so tight, like it had been painted on him. And it was short at the back like it had shrunk in a hot wash. Her little brother had a jumper the same. Her mother had boiled it in the copper by mistake.

She got up and walked through the sticky plastic strip curtain and breathed in the familiar smell of vanilla ice cream. Rosa counted her silver. She'd have to be careful, but one ice cream in a cone wouldn't hurt. Still have enough for cigarettes and a bit of food till the end of the week. But she wasn't sure what she was going to do about the rent.

'There ya go, love,' said the woman behind the counter, handing her the ice cream. Her dark hair was tightly permed and sat close to her head. Her mouth was a straight red line and her thin half-moon-shaped eyebrows looked like they were drawn on with a blunt grey lead pencil. 'You from down south?'

Rosa felt the woman's hard gaze looking her up and down. Rosa nodded. She supposed she was from down south, although she'd never thought of it that way until now. Seemed like to outback people 'down south' meant everywhere else; anywhere where it wasn't scorching hot by midday every day; somewhere where there was water and a sea breeze, anywhere else but here.

'Tourist sheila, huh?' The woman turned her back and began stacking cigarettes on a shelf. 'What are you going to do, love? There's dishwashing work here. Come back if you're interested. We work nine till nine. All meals included. No smoking in the kitchen, though.'

'Oh, thanks. I might be interested in that.'

'The name's Win. No one ever calls me Winifred. Last time I was called Winifred was when I got called up for jury duty but I was excused on account of my personal beliefs.'

Rosa took her ice cream back outside, protecting it from the flies with her hand, and sat again at the only outdoor table. The ashtray was overflowing. She licked her ice cream, covering it again with her hand after each lick.

A little girl came out of the shop with an ice cream in her hand. The tip of her nose was black with flies feasting on the yellow snot. Her blonde hair stood up stiffly on her head and her yellow shift dress was soiled and stained. Rosa watched her. The girl was undaunted by the flies; she stuck out her pink tongue and licked the white ice cream from the cone. Just as she was about to take a second lick, the ice cream fell – plop – on to the ground. Holding the empty cone in her hand, the little girl stood staring at the puddle of ice cream on the pavement.

'Tough,' Rosa heard the woman behind the counter yell. 'Go and ask your mother for some more money.' The woman stuck her head through the blue curtain.

Rosa watched as the little girl walked away, still holding the empty cone.

'Filthy little devils. Gawd, they make me feel sick. It's our money they're spending, you know. None of 'em ever worked a day in their lives. Sit-down bloody money. Got plenty of money for grog and cigarettes, though. See you tomorrow, then?'

'Yeah…yes, thanks. I guess so. See you tomorrow.' Never in a million years would she work for that old bag.

She limped back to the hostel, wondering where she might be able to find a Band-Aid for her blister. She was beginning to feel hungry. It was teatime. At home, her mother would probably be cooking a lamb stew for tea or maybe a potato pie. Her sisters would be fighting about something. Would her mother wipe her brow with the back of her work-worn hand and think of her? Soon her father and her brother would be tramping through the kitchen in their work boots and her mother would yell at them the way she did every night. 'Boots! Boots on my clean floor!'

The lump in Rosa's throat hurt. Why did she ever come here, here to this hot dusty place? She would have to go back. She'd made a mistake.

It was nothing like Mrs Bird said it would be. She could go back. She was only on a working holiday after all. She didn't have to stay away for good. It didn't matter what people said. When she got home, she could stay with her friend Lisa for a while and not tell anyone she was back. She would pretend she had been away for weeks, not just a few days. Lisa wouldn't tell. One of her sisters would probably have already moved into her room. But that wouldn't matter. They could keep it. She had just enough money for the bus fare home if she didn't buy any more cigarettes. Or maybe just one more packet.

How her father would gloat. She could hear him saying, 'So you come running back home, do you? Couldn't you find enough to eat?'

She would have to think of something smart to say. 'I was away for a while. It was very interesting.'

'Oh yes, very interesting. So interesting that you come running back.'

'I had a job offer. I just decided not to take it.'

And he would laugh a loud, hoarse laugh that carried no humour with it. 'Well, you can stay home now, Bones. You stay home and help your mother.'

Back at the hostel, hungry now, she went into the kitchen and opened the share cupboard for Room 10. It was neatly stacked with packets of sweet biscuits, pasta, rice, tomato sauce, sugar, tea and even Gravox. And a jar of instant coffee.

Coffee would go down so well with her cigarette. Surely, her room-mate wouldn't miss a spoonful or two and maybe even a couple of biscuits. She plugged the frayed cord into the yellow electric jug that looked like it had been there for years, took a cup from the cupboard and made herself a cup of strong coffee. Rosa reached in and snatched a biscuit.

A stocky-looking woman dressed in jeans, a checked shirt and riding boots was sitting at the table eating a meal of chops, potatoes and peas. Rosa heard the chair scrape on the concrete floor and the woman came and stood next to her.

'Got a tip for you, love. You won't be very popular around here if you steal food,' she said.

'But I wasn't stealing…I just thought…'

'You just thought what? That you would help yourself?' The woman shrugged her broad shoulders, walked away and went back to eating her chops.

Rosa took her coffee and the biscuit out onto the lawn and sat under a tree and watched the sun setting behind the purple-tinged ranges. She counted her cigarettes. Three. She counted her matches. Two. But you could always ask somebody for a light. She looked again at her purse. It was either going to be dinner, or more cigarettes. The rest would have to be for her bus fare home.

The next morning she woke: hungry. Rosa stretched her arm out, pulled a cigarette from the packet and lit up without lifting her head from the pillow. Her room-mate was up and pulling a white uniform over her head. She's too fat to fit in that size uniform, thought Rosa, watching her pull her stockings over her lumpy legs. Not my type. Doesn't even shave under her arms. Don't think we're going to get on. Won't be here long anyway. Bet she hasn't got a boyfriend. She wished the French woman on the bus could have been her room-mate.

'You from down south?'

Rosa nodded, drawing deeply on her cigarette.

'Why'd you leave home?'

Rosa didn't answer. She could have said, 'I am on a working holiday. I heard about this place from a lady I used to babysit for.' But instead she thought of her father, sitting in the lounge room, night after night. Not speaking but spilling hate and anger into the air. Waiting for her to come home. Not one minute after midnight. Not one second. And she thought of her mother. Always pregnant. Always losing babies. And then she would go away to 'the home'. When she came home, she wouldn't speak to Rosa again for days, not until she had regained her authority as mother. And as wife. The wife of Joseph Kabanosy, the man who drank beer, ate pickled onions straight from the fridge every night and smoked cigars. Then she would be Rosa's mother again, until the next pregnancy, the next dead baby.

'I was hoping I wouldn't get a smoker. You're not supposed to smoke anyway. Do you reckon you could ask the manager to give you another room? Actually, I'll ask him for you if you like.'

'Go right ahead. Ask him,' said Rosa, drawing on her cigarette.

Rosa looked at the posters on the wall opposite her bed: the horses and the whale. She thought of the home she had just left. Breakfast time would be noisy. Her brother and father would already have left for the building site, but her mother and sisters would be eating their porridge. Her sisters would begin their usual morning argument about who was going to wear what, until finally, they would leave for the bus. Her mother would take her cup of tea back to the kitchen table and sit for a while before beginning the housework. Would her mother think of her this morning? Would she look at the empty chair and wonder what her daughter had had for breakfast? And her father? Did he glance at her empty bed before he left for work? Most likely he did. He was her father after all. He would be angry.

'So she's gone, has she? Left her mother to do all the work, and for her father, no goodbye.'

And it would be for Grace to pacify him. 'She did say goodbye to you, Joseph. You've forgotten.'

Rosa hadn't said goodbye to him.

'You wait. She'll be back. She's got no money and no brains. Stupid, that one.'

'She might find a job.' Grace would fill his cup again with coffee. Clear his empty bowl from in front of him. Put his lunch box next to him, ready for the day.

'A job? What doing? Sweeping up dust? Plenty of dust where she is. Her sisters, they're still here. They love their father. And even her brother, even he loves his father. She's no good. Big problem for somebody one day, that one. You just wait and see.'

Rosa could picture the blue veins in his red cheeks, she could smell the sour stale beer on his breath from the night before, could hear his breathing, could feel the sharp blunt bristles of his unshaven beard.

Today, Rosa wore her summer dress and Indian sandals. She'd packed her red boots, black felt hat and green, velvet jacket in her case. Southbound buses ran every day and she had exactly enough money for the fare. Her cigarettes would have to last and maybe she could borrow a few from someone on the bus. She'd only just arrived, but here she was after only one day and night, trudging down the dirt road again, going back home. The sign on the door of the bus depot read 'Open at 9.00'. She would wait.

The red earth was hard when she sat down underneath the tall ghost gum, and the great trunk smooth against her back. Smoke from a camp in the dry riverbed a little way off drifted, and the morning air was already warm. Rosa didn't have a watch and she often measured time by the number of cigarettes she had smoked. Her mother had never let her smoke. 'I will tell your father,' she used to threaten. She flipped open the Marlboro packet. No, she would have to save them for later.

Rosa didn't mind smelling of smoke. It was kind of cool. Mrs Watson, the English teacher she'd had at school, always smelled of smoke. The nuns only ever smelled of chalk and a musty kind of soap.

Rosa loved Mrs Watson, her tight slim skirts, her seamed stockings and her English lessons. In her last year at school, they had studied *Frankenstein*.

'This novel,' Mrs Watson said, 'is about fate or destiny. Hands up those of you girls who believe you have a destiny in this world, one that you can't change, no matter what?'

None of them raised their hands but they knew Mrs Watson would find her answer somehow.

'Well now, Rosa Kabanosy, tell us, do you think that our fate is determined by the choices we make, or our fate determines the choices we make? What do you think?'

Rosa felt the colour rising, creeping up her neck, making her cheeks burn.

'Help her, girls. What do you all think?'

They all sat in silence.

'Well, life will teach you all, girls, life will teach you.'

Rosa looked up at the sky. Clear, blue, cloudless. At home it would most probably be raining and her mother would be cleaning up the breakfast things.

Rosa thought of her mother and the morning she had stood at the kitchen doorway and said, 'I'm going now, Mum.'

Her mother had looked at her, walked over and kissed her. 'I am pregnant again, Rosa,' she whispered.

The sound of a bus pulling up snapped her out of her reverie and she jumped up realising she had been sitting on a bull ant's nest. One was crawling over her foot and she brushed it off.

The driver got down from the bus and opened the door of the depot. 'Can I help you, love?' he called.

'Oh…maybe…not today. I might come back tomorrow. Thanks anyway.' She dusted off her dress and picked up her suitcase.

'Well, let me know when you make your mind up, love.' The man shook his head.

Rosa began walking slowly towards the main street. When she reached Win's Café, she stopped at the door.

Win pushed her head through the grubby plastic curtain. 'So, you showed up. Good. You can get the sandwich board and put it out. Don't be late again. And stick that suitcase behind the door. We don't want the customers thinking you're not staying.'

Rosa stubbed out her cigarette and went inside. She carried out the board and steadied it on the uneven path.

25 March 2003

Dear Rose,

I have become friendly with Sister Anne at St Margaret's. I met her one day when I visited the church to say a prayer. She said I could come and talk to her anytime I liked. It's such a relief to have someone to talk to. Sister Anne said not to worry too much. She said most creative people struggle with themselves and to just use the voices in my writing. And she would love to hear some of my writing, she said. She seems to understand things, many things, despite the fact she has lived her life pretty well locked away. I don't think she has ever travelled anywhere.

I've been working hard on my novel, especially these cold nights. Arnold goes to bed so early. Sometimes, I think fiction and poetry make all things possible. Everything can be revised, rewritten on the page. Things don't have to stay as they are. Sister Anne didn't object when I told her I thought we have a choice – we can live our lives as fact or fiction, we can choose our reality.

Then she asked me the strangest question. 'Do you think that writers believe their writing makes their experiences immortal?'

I didn't know how to answer her. So I just said I thought whatever we have seen, wherever we have been, whatever we have done is always with us. Even though time passes, the past is always with us. The tracks of our past follow us. I can't remember what she said to that.

Sister Anne usually offers me a cup of ginger tea. It has become part of our ritual. Today when she offered me the gold-rimmed teacup, she said, 'I'm not sure why, but today it occurred to me that many travellers set out with the view their lives will change, that they will change, that they can leave everything behind them, all their sorrows and mistakes, all their secrets. The sad truth is, that just isn't so.'

I think I replied something along the lines that possibly everyone carries an invisible backpack with them, wherever they go, bursting at the seams, full of everything they thought they left behind. I mean, if something has happened to you, you can't leave it behind. It is in you, part of you, forever. Sometimes when Sister Anne and I talk, I feel our words are just seeds in the wind.

Iris

A Friend In Need

Rosa looked at the untidy pile of greasy plates and knives and forks stacked on the side of the sink. She was used to washing dishes for her mother, but not this many.

Win looked the same as she had yesterday, only more so. Her tight, curly hair looked more like a helmet than hair and her thin lips seemed to have faded to a fine red slash on her face. 'You can start on them dishes. We had a mob in last night. Lots of trucks and a bus. The other girl will be along in a minute. She'll show you the ropes. Her name's Gypsy. Nice kid. Behaves just like a white girl. You'd never know,' said Win, wiping her greasy hands on a tea towel. 'And yeah, get the cook to make you a hamburger and chips when he gets here. Looks like you could do with a feed.'

Rosa nodded, 'Sure.' She didn't want to seem too eager to eat.

'Morning, Win.' A slim woman with long black hair and dressed in jeans and a white shirt walked in to the kitchen and beckoned Rosa to the sink and the pile of dirty dishes. 'I'm Gypsy.' She turned on the sink taps.

Rosa noticed her fine-boned hands and her silver rings – one on every one of her long elegant fingers – and the sweet smell of patchouli oil. 'Win likes you to have the water hot. Been in town long? Staying at the hostel, I suppose?'

'Since yesterday,' said Rosa, but it seemed like she had been there for ever. Home seemed a long way away now.

Gypsy pushed her bangles up her glossy, dark-skinned forearms before thrusting them into the water. 'You can dry and stack.'

'Yeah. I really like it at the hostel. I've got a good room-mate.' Rosa looked through the grubby tea towels on the bench and chose the cleanest one.

'That's where they all stay, till they either get married to a local bloke or move on.' Gypsy began scrubbing a large pot with steel wool that looked like it had been used for years. 'Not that easy to become a local here, but.'

'How about getting on with some work in there,' Win called from the front counter.

Gypsy winked at Rosa. 'Make sure you don't use too much hot water. You've got to make one sink-full last till it's thick with grease. Win always says, "That's good hot soapy water – don't waste it," like it's holy water or something.'

Rosa laughed, not too loudly, though, because she didn't want to upset Win, especially not on her first day. She needed the money too much. She began wiping the plates and turned to put one in the rack when a man dressed in baggy white pants and a cook's shirt walked in. He looked as if he had just got out of bed.

'Well, look what the cat dragged in! You look like you had a hard night.'

Gypsy called to him across the kitchen. 'Rosa, this is Charlie – he's the cook. Cook us a hamburger, Charlie. We can't work if we're hungry.'

'You from down south?' he said.

Rosa was getting used to being asked that now.

Charlie threw some onions on the hotplate. The smell took her breath away. Rosa hadn't eaten since yesterday's ice cream and the borrowed biscuits. She was beginning to feel nauseous now. It seemed like the hamburgers were going to take forever to cook. Finally, she followed Gypsy out to a little courtyard where two overflowing plastic rubbish bins took up most of the space. Gypsy pointed to a couple of upturned wooden boxes. They both sat and Rosa sank her teeth into the hamburger. Egg yolk ran down the side of her hand. She licked it.

'You hungry?' Gypsy watched her eat.

'Yeah, just a bit.' Rosa tried not to eat too quickly.

When they had finished eating, Gypsy offered her a cigarette.

'Make it snappy because Win's going to smell the smoke in a minute and call us back inside,' she said as she struck a match.

'You girls gonna to stay there all day? There's work to be done in here,' Win called through the door.

'See, I told you,' laughed Gypsy and they both went back inside.

'You made cappuccinos before, girlie?' said Win.

'Yeah…I have. Lots of times.'

'Well, be careful with the machine. It's the only one in town,' said Win. 'You've got to keep up with the times in business.'

Rosa picked up the silver jug and held it under the steaming nozzle. After a minute, she looked inside the jug. No coffee had come out.

Gypsy came over and laughed. 'Here, let me show you,' she said. 'You put the milk in first and then you froth it.'

Rosa felt her cheeks colouring. 'Don't tell Win.'

Towards lunchtime the café became very busy – a few tourist buses came through and a stream of truckies all wanting steaks. Gypsy helped Charlie with the cooking and Win did front of house.

Win yelled at Rosa, telling her to start chopping more onions and to hurry up about it. Just as she had begun chopping the onions, Win was yelling at her, 'Get out here and clear some tables.'

Before she knew it, it was five o'clock.

'Wanna come to the pub tonight?' said Gypsy. 'I'll introduce you to my brother, Archie.' She hung her apron on the hook and held her hand out to take Rosa's from her.

'Sure,' said Rosa.

She'd made a friend. And before she knocked off, Charlie had made her another hamburger, with two eggs. Not so lonely now, she strolled back to the hostel vaguely wondering what Gypsy's brother would be like.

3 April 2003

Dear Rose,

It is Arnold's birthday today. I'm not sure why, but this morning I asked him if he missed our life in the outback, the days working on the cattle station.

'Iris,' he said, 'are you a jumper short of a stitch? What do you bloody well think?'

I shouldn't have let him get away with being so rude to me, but it was his birthday so I let it go.

I took him a cup of tea out in the garden. He was down on his knees pulling out clover that had been growing thickly in between the daisies.

'Cup of tea for you, birthday boy,' I said to him.

I asked him what he would like for dinner. Would he like me to cook him a good steak? But when he looked up at me, I saw tears rolling down his poor weather-worn cheeks.

It's the first time I have ever seen him cry.

Iris

Archie

Cigarette haze framed the checked-shirt and blue-singlet clad figures that lined the long mirrored bar. The pub was packed. And the barmaid could have been Win's sister – same hair, same eyebrows. Gypsy bought herself and Rosa a Marsala and Coke. They inched their way through the sweaty male bodies and found a table in the corner and sat sipping their drinks. Rosa had never been in a bar where there were so many men before. 'Hotel California' rang out from the sound system.

'That's the second time I've heard that song since I've been here,' said Rosa.

'Do you think someone's trying to tell you something?' Gypsy said, laughing. 'Oh, there's Archie.' Gypsy waved to a slender young man at the door.

Beer in hand, he sauntered towards them, and sat down on the chair next to Rosa. His long legs stretched under the table and his riding boots looked well worn. He was a lot like Gypsy: dark skin, hair the colour of pitch and that same natural elegance. 'Hey, sis. Who's this you got with you?'

'Rosa, this is my big brother… He never did have any manners,' said Gypsy, laughing again. Gypsy was always laughing.

'G'day. How long you been in town?' said Archie.

Rosa looked at him and into his dark eyes a moment too long. She caught her breath before she spoke. 'Only two days, but it seems like longer, much longer.'

'I think I might have passed you in the street yesterday.' Archie took a gulp of his beer. 'Have you got a big floppy hat?'

Rosa didn't remember seeing him. 'Oh yes, I remember now.'

'Yeah, I was sure it was you. I was like a black cat crossing your path, I reckon,' said Archie, draining his glass. Archie had the same smile as Gypsy. Clear and open, a real smile, not just a show of teeth.

Rosa laughed. 'Do you like living here?'

'Got no choice, really. Not yet, anyways. What about you?'

'Got no choice, really. Not yet, anyways,' Rosa said, laughing.

The music became louder and a man walked over and asked Gypsy to dance. Rosa felt Archie edge a little closer to her.

He spread his arm across the back of her chair. 'Your mum and dad know you're here?'

'Yeah, they know. I've written to them. They'll get the letter soon.'

*

Dear Mum

I have arrived and I have somewhere to stay. It's not as hot as you would think and there are lots of shady trees. I have a room in a lovely hostel and it has beautiful soft carpet on the floor in that peach colour you have always liked. My room-mate is nice. We are allowed to put posters on the wall, so I will buy some soon. I have made lots of friends. I have a job now as a receptionist for the local doctor. Everyone is really friendly. It is okay to give the girls my room. That will make more room for your new baby, when it comes. Say hi to Rick and the girls for me. Hope you are all well. I am getting a great suntan. I am eating so much, I will have to be careful I don't put on weight.

Love,

Rosa

*

Grace was peeling potatoes when Joseph walked into the kitchen. 'A letter came from Rosa today. She has a job. She seems okay,' she said.

Joseph reached into the fridge for a beer. He ripped back the silver tab and allowed the froth to seep through the hole before tipping it down his throat. 'A job. What crazy person gave that girl a job?'

'She sounds happy.' Grace put the peeled potatoes in a chipped green enamel colander and rinsed them under the tap.

'Happy. That girl is never happy. Did she ask how her father was? Her poor father. Did she think of him? Did she mention me in the letter?'

'She didn't exactly mention you. But the letter was for the whole family. Not just me. I know she thinks about you.'

'How do you know that? Has she been telling lies again? She needs to shut her lying mouth before I shut it for her. All that girl ever does is dream and lie. It's okay to be a dreamer, but a liar…that's another thing… If I ever told lies about my father, he would break my jaw, just like I should break hers. Break her fucking jaw…like this.' He raised a clenched fist, then reached inside the fridge for another beer.

*

'Did you go to school here?' Rosa said.

'Yeah. Went to St Monica's down near the Gap. Mum was out bush then. Got sent into town to school. And Gypsy was born after me. Different dads. Didn't grow up together. Authorities said it was for my own good. Hated school. Left when I was sixteen.'

'What do you do now?'

'Out at Heryl Springs, mustering. Don't get into town much.'

Archie was like no one she had ever met before. She began to feel like she was on a film set and Archie was the hero. He stretched his legs out a little further under the table and Rosa looked again at his boots. No man she had ever known had ever worn riding boots. Archie was a first in so many ways for Rosa.

'Have you ever been to the city?' she asked him.

'Yeah, once with school. Not big on cities. Too many people.'

Archie bought her another Marsala and Coke. 'Cigarette?' he said.

She took one from the pack and leant forward for him to light it.

124

She caught his gaze through the smoke. They sat in silence for a while, smoking and listening to the music, watching the dancers move and sway.

'Dance?' said Archie.

'Dance,' said Rosa.

He slipped his arm around her waist and pulled her close. She pressed her naked hand to his, and they danced, a long slow dance, thigh to thigh, heart to heart. The band played the last song, 'The House of the Rising Sun'.

Under the wide dark night sky, Archie walked with her back to the hostel. They reached the door of Room 10 just as the caretaker came around the corner.

'No blokes allowed in here. Specially, black ones. Out you get.' The caretaker motioned with his thumb towards the gate.

Archie smiled, his teeth bright, kissed Rosa on the cheek and was gone into the dark night.

But he was back the next day. Rosa was sitting on the doorstep of Room 10, smoking just after she had finished at Win's. Archie came around the corner of the building down the path towards her, with his confident, long-legged, easy stride. Just like Al Pacino, only sleeker, darker and cooler with his fine black hair tied in a ponytail, faded blue jeans, and those boots.

'Wanna come for a walk, Rosa?' he said.

'Sure thing,' she said, stubbing her cigarette. She jumped up and took his hand.

They walked towards the town, taking their time; they were in no hurry to go anywhere in particular. There was nowhere much to go, anyway. They stopped outside a stone church, and sat on the grass under the shade of a red gum.

'Do you call yourself a local?' said Rosa. She picked up a twig and scratched a pattern in the sparse dry grass.

'Suppose I am. I was born here. My mother was born in the creek.' His voice seemed softer, almost a whisper.

'In the creek?' Rosa waved a fly away from her face.

'Yeah, down there. She never goes there now. Fighting and grog down there,' Archie said.

He visited her the next day and the day after that and the day after that until the days became weeks and, before she knew it, she had known him for a month or more.

Archie had the letters L O V E tattooed on the four fingers of his right hand.

One warm afternoon when they were sitting under a gum tree they had both come to think of as theirs, Rosa asked him, 'How old were you when you had that done, Archie?'

'No one's ever asked me that before. They always ask why I had it done. '

She leaned against Archie's arm and took his hand in hers. 'Did you have anyone in mind when you had it done?'

'Nah. Not really. Not then. But you've come along now.'

Rosa laughed. She laughed a lot now, just like Gyspy. They sat for a long time not speaking, under their red gum in the late afternoon shade.

'Does the water ever flow in the creek?' said Rosa, breaking the silence.

'You sure do ask a lot of questions. Sometimes, when it floods in the summer. When a big rain comes.' He snapped a twig with his long fingers. 'If you see the river flow, you're not a tourist any more. They reckon you'll always come back. And you'll stay.'

'I wonder if I'll ever see it flow.'

Archie put his arm around her and pulled her close to him. 'Why'd you leave home?' he said.

'Wanted to travel…see the world, I guess. I'm an only child and Mum and Dad are pretty well off. I got tired of helping Mum in her dress shop. It was boring. I suppose I just wanted to find out what life is all about.'

'You sure picked a strange place to come if you wanted to see the world,' said Archie. He leant back against the tree trunk. 'Not too much happens here. Not too much changes either. You hungry?'

Rosa was always hungry. Archie jumped up, pulled her to her

feet and took her hand. They strolled to the bottom pub, where they had drank and danced the first night they met. Under a noisy air conditioner, they sat and drank cold beer, ate hot chips and smoked cigarettes. Words weren't necessary. His dark soft eyes and his presence were enough. She breathed him in and breathed him out.

After a while, they went out and sat together on the balcony, still not saying much. The pub was the tallest building in town and from the balcony there was a panoramic view of the entire township and the backdrop of ochre-coloured serpent-like ranges that encircled the town like an ancient guardian.

Long after the sun had gone down, he walked her back to the hostel. They stood out the front, leaning against the wire fence.

Archie gripped the fence and kicked the clay soil with his boot. He looked down and kicked the hard clay, again. Harder this time. 'Going back out to the station in a few days. Been in town too long, now. A man gets restless.'

Rosa's throat tightened. She hadn't expected this. She hadn't for one moment given any thought to him going back to the station, going back to his work. All she could say was 'Restless?'

Archie stroked her hair. She rested her head on his shoulder, close to him she felt his heart beating against her heart. The scene would be forever fixed in her memory. If only time would stand still, she would always be near him, he wouldn't go. But he was going. He was leaving.

'How long do you think it'll be before you come back into town?' said Rosa, trying not to cry. She didn't cry easily. Her father had made sure of that.

'Dunno. Don't know. Could be weeks. Could be days. Depends on the boss. When I turn up, I suppose. But we'll keep in touch, eh?'

'Keep in touch? But how? Will you come around and see me as soon as you get back?' Rosa's tears were flowing freely now.

She looked into those eyes. He kissed her tears. They stood together for a long time, not moving, not speaking.

His arms dropped before hers did. Archie pulled a worn-looking wallet from his back pocket and took out a twenty-dollar note. He took her hand and kissed the inside of Rosa's wrist and pressed the note into her palm. 'Don't you lose that, now. It's my last. You buy yourself some tucker and don't let that old bag Win push you round. All right?' He stroked her hair.

'Will you come around and see me as soon as you get back?' Rosa whispered.

'You'll be my first stop.' Archie turned and walked away, looked back once, and waved.

Rosa watched him in the moonlight until he turned the corner and was out of sight.

*

Only two weeks later, she got the news. She heard it from Win. Of all people, it had to be her. First thing in the morning, soon as she walked in the door.

'They found him bashed. Dead. Down in the creek.'

'Who? Who did they find?' said Rosa.

'Gyp's brother – what was his name? Archie. Yeah, that was it – Archie. But what do you expect. He was different from Gyp – she's just like us. Probably won't see her for a while, but. They'll have all their sorry business and stuff to get on with. Reckon there's a rain coming.'

Rosa walked over to the sink and filled it with water. It wasn't as if she had a script to read from. What was she supposed to say? She had only just met him. He was a stranger, but it was as if she had known him all her life, as if she had always been with him, as if she should be with him now.

'Bloody hell, girl. What's wrong with you? The sink's overflowing. And where's your apron?'

Rosa reached behind the door for an apron. 'Sorry.' She tied it around her waist as if she were sleepwalking.

Win came and stood next to her and stared. 'You look a bit pale, love. Time of the month or something, is it? Go and have a bit of a sit down for a while.'

She looked down on herself from above, again. She watched herself washing dishes, tears streaming down her face, pretending to be someone else, as if this had happened to someone else, as if she, Rosa, had been a character in a story.

'You're a waste of space today, girlie.' Win sent her home just after the lunchtime rush.

'Look after yourself, love,' Charlie called after her. 'You look like a ghost.'

*

Alone under the night sky.

Rosa sat on the doorstep of Room 10 staring up at the stars. She half-expected Archie to come striding around the corner any minute; that he would come and take her hand, pull her to her feet and kiss her. A few nights earlier, he had come to her in a dream. His face had been so clear, his cheekbones high and glossy, the expression in his eyes a mix of love and longing. A mosquito drew blood from her arm. She swatted it and watched a lump form on her skin. Thunder rolled and rumbled in the distance; lightning cracked and lit the velvet sky.

In her mind, Rosa could see him on the back of a chestnut horse – white shirt, cuffs rolled up, Akubra hat, straight back, riding proud and tall in a cloud of red dust. She closed her eyes and thought of the first time they had danced, a long slow dance, thigh to thigh, heart to heart. She thought of the last time she had seen him when he walked away from her and she had watched him until he turned the corner and was out of sight. But she hadn't known then it was the last time. No one can ever know when it is the last time.

The thunder rumbled closer; a forked lightning bolt split the sky. And then the rain came, pounding down, splashing on the parched ground at her feet.

25 April 2003

Dear Rose,

Today I read to Sister Anne from my journal. She keeps one herself. She told me not everything she writes is true. Sometimes she says it is easier to invent things than to write the truth. It's a kind of code, she says, for what might have happened, what should never have happened and maybe what didn't happen. I guess maybe my fiction is a little like that.

I find myself wondering if she ever experienced the love of a man. It would seem so sad to go through one's entire life not knowing the love of a man.

But there again, I guess there might be worse things. Never to be able to have a child might be worse. And I never had a child.

Iris

The Marriage Plot

Rain changes everything, especially in the outback. Three big rains came and went. Rosa stayed washing dishes and working for Win, wrote letters home to her mother telling her all about her job as a receptionist for the local doctor. And she yearned for Archie. Every night before she drifted off to sleep, she whispered his name. But one night she forgot to whisper his name.

Tom introduced himself to her, one day, in Win's Café. 'Where you from?' he asked her.

And she glanced over her shoulder and said, 'Where are you from?' not caring.

He began coming in to the cafe every time he was in town and he would always wait for Rosa to take his order. Everything about Tom was hard and crusty. He was only an inch taller than Rosa. His freckled skin always seemed to be sunburnt and when he took off his Akubra hat, his white scalp shone through his fox-coloured hair. Each time he came in, he asked her out and each time he asked, she said no. Then one Friday when he asked, she said yes.

So it became a bit of a routine; he took her to the pub whenever he was he was in town. He talked mainly to his mates and Rosa just tagged along. Better than staying at the hostel by herself, and Tom paid for all the drinks. Rosa would sit at the bar next to him while he and his mates talked and laughed about nothing much. You couldn't even call it a conversation, just town gossip, jokes and banter. Occasionally they would try and include Rosa. If they swore or told a foul joke, one of them usually said, 'Block your ears, love.' Usually, Tom was drunk by the end of the night; sometimes, he could barely stand up.

Tom worked out on his parents' cattle station – Heryl Springs –

five thousand square miles and two thousand head of cattle. He was Thelma and Doug Bigmann's only son.

'It's only a hundred miles out. Come out with me next week. I'll introduce you to Mum and Dad,' Tom said one night when he walked her back to the hostel, one night when he wasn't too drunk.

'Okay,' Rosa said. She didn't have to think about the invitation too hard. She had received a letter from her mother that morning.

Dear Rosa
How could you leave me here alone to deal with everything alone? Your father is getting worse and I need you.
Please come home, Rosa.
Love,
Mum

Tom picked her up from the hostel in his white ute and they drove out to the station on the dirt road that wound past the ochre-coloured ranges that stretched snake-like for as far as they could see. Tom sped along with his elbow out the open window. He seemed to have forgotten that Rosa was there.

She broke the silence. 'Did you ever know a stockman called Archie?'

'We've had a few called Archie. They come and go. Why do you ask?' Tom glanced sideways at her, and then fixed his gaze back on the road.

'No reason. Just knew a stockman by that name once.' Rosa looked ahead, the dust and pebbles flying. Her throat was tight and dry.

Dogs barked like crazy when they pulled up outside the homestead. Rosa had imagined that Tom's mother Thelma would be a shortish woman with grey hair and plump arms, the type of woman who looked like she might make good scones. Instead, Thelma looked like a version of Judy Garland and smelled of Chanel Number 5, or at least that's what Rosa thought it might be. She was wearing a slim-fitting black dress and large gold hoop earrings. Thelma seemed to totter rather than walk, as if her heels were too high or her skirt was too tight.

'Gin and tonic, dear?' Thelma asked.

Rosa had never had a gin and tonic before. 'Yes, thank you. My favourite drink,' she said.

Thelma led her out to the wisteria-covered veranda. Shakily, she motioned to Rosa to take a seat on one of the white cane chairs with soft green and white cushions. Rosa could smell horses, dust and cattle and she stared out in awe at the expanse of red earth in front of her, across to the holding yards where the large brown beasts stood together, and behind them a blazing fireball sun was setting on the horizon.

'I've never been to a station before.' Rosa sipped her drink and swirled the ice around in the heavy glass.

'Not too many city girls have,' said Thelma. 'It takes a while to get used to station life.'

Tom went inside and came back out with a stubbie. The dogs started barking again heralding Doug and his white ute, a replica of Tom's, with two more red heelers in the back. He took off his hat and wiped his brow with the back of his arm. He was a bit shorter than Tom and looked much older than Rosa had imagined. When he took his hat off, his skin looked more cracked than lined and what hair he had left was the same colour as Tom's.

Doug held out his hand. 'G'day, mate.'

Rosa wasn't sure if he was talking to her or Tom, but she shook his hand.

*

Months went by and Rosa just let Tom happen. She pretended she was interested in his station work, remembered to ask about Thelma and Doug, and Tom just became a habit: a habit that suited her purposes. Perhaps it suited Tom's purposes, too.

One warm night, after they had been out for tea at the pub, and he was relatively sober, Tom drove her home to the hostel. He pulled up out the front and jerked on the handbrake, turned to her and kissed

her, roughly. His lips were dry and split. He rammed his hand down
the front of her jeans and said, 'It'd be good to get married, Rosa. What
do you reckon?'

The first wedding she had ever attended was to be her own.

5 May 2003

Dear Rose,

It is so lovely to have the autumn sun on my face. Earlier, I sat on my veranda and began reading *Jane Eyre* again. Poor Jane. I wouldn't mind betting the loathsome wounded Rochester turned into a real bastard after they were married.

I used to believe the Cinderella tale, but I can't fall for it any more, not the ending anyway. The ugly sisters are around everywhere, in life and literature, but Prince Charming never was 'real', not even for Cinderella. I bet he turned out just like I reckon old Rochester did for Jane.

The marriage plot is indeed a plot. The other day I was reading that handfasting is something from the Middle Ages. But it doesn't matter what we call it – getting hitched…tying the knot – it means the same thing.

We all find our own chains, don't we? Bind ourselves to what we think is good for us. It's only when we realise it isn't good, we understand we are bound.

Arnold is acting strangely. He's refusing to get out of bed and then staying up all night watching the television without the sound. It might be related to his brain damage. I'm not sure. I will get the doctor to visit tomorrow.

Iris

Wedding Party

'I don't how I'm going to get this to sit right,' the hairdresser said. 'You've got hair like fishing wire, Rosa,' she laughed, and tapped her on the shoulder. 'But it'll be right on the night, won't it, hon?'

Lil was the only hairdresser in town. She could easily have been Win's daughter, with her drawn-on eyebrows and thin red lips.

'Your family coming to the wedding?' Lil let fly with the hairspray.

No. Better this way. She had posted them a letter a yesterday. Mail delivery was slow from the outback.

> Dear Mum and Dad,
>
> Just a short note to let you know I got married at the end of last month. It was only a simple affair in a backyard. You wouldn't have enjoyed it. It is so hot here. Please give the girls and Rick my love. My husband's name is Tom Bigmann. I will bring Tom down to meet you soon.
>
> Love
>
> Rosa

'I don't have any family to speak of, Lil,' she said. 'I was fostered out.'

'Oh, never mind, darl. You need some blush over that pale foundation,' Lil filled the soft brush with pink powder and circled it on Rosa's cheeks.

Rosa looked at herself in the mirror. I look like a clown, she thought. She had spent the night before her wedding in Room 10 at the hostel. Since she had been there, she had lost count of the different women who she had shared with. Most them were only staying a while and then they went home to their families. As soon as she had got to know them, they left to go home. She had become friendly with most of them, except for the first one, who took her whale and horse posters with her. 'Good luck with everything. I like you okay, Rosa, but I don't think you are a girl I could ever get close to,' she'd said while she pulled the posters down from the wall.

Not many of the people who were coming to the wedding were her friends. None of them really, except for Gypsy.

The hairdresser interrupted her thoughts. 'And what about you, matron of honour? You want any make-up or you going au naturel?'

'No make-up for me,' Gypsy said.

Rosa looked at her. She didn't need anything. She was perfect just the way she was. Her soft brown skin glistened against the pastel pink lace of the bridesmaid's dress.

'We've got time for a glass of champagne. I've got some out the back in Lil's fridge. How about you put your dress on, and we'll have a toast.'

Gypsy seemed not to have a care in the world. Well, why should she? It wasn't her who was getting married. Rosa felt her stomach knot, as if she had been punched.

Her dress was hanging up in Lil's back room, the room where the stained streaking caps and hair dyes and perming solutions were stored. The room smelled of ammonia. Rosa pulled the dress over her head. It was a little loose. She looked at herself in the fly-spotted mirror and for a moment she thought someone else had walked into the room. She put on the wide-brimmed picture hat and looked at herself again. She reminded herself of a doll she used to have.

'You coming out or what? Champagne's getting warm,' called Gypsy.

Rosa looked at herself one last time in the mirror and walked back into the salon. Lil and Gypsy both grinned at her. They all laughed when the cork hit the ceiling. The sparkling fizz was cold on the back of Rosa's throat.

'And look what the cat's dragged in, again,' said Gypsy.

Charlie pushed the door open. He looked like he had been scrubbed, his cheeks were so red.

One morning after the breakfast rush in the café had died down, Rosa had asked him, 'Charlie, have you ever given anyone away before?'

He'd flipped a grubby tea towel over his shoulder and began scraping bacon fat from the hotplate. 'No…no…probably not, except maybe my cousin who stole ten bucks from my money box when I was twelve…but no…'

Rosa laughed. 'No, I didn't mean that way, Charlie. I meant giving a bride away…giving me away.'

He stopped his scraping and looked at her. 'You…you getting married, Rosa? Who the hell to?'

'Tom. Tom Bigmann,' said Rosa, diving her hands deep into the washing-up water.

'Tom, from Heryl Springs? You marrying him?'

'Yeah. Guess I won't be washing dishes too much longer, either. Tom said he's going to buy me a flower shop so I can learn to be a florist, just like I always wanted to.' Rosa pulled her hands out of the water and walked over to Charlie and held out her ring. The washing detergent had made it sparkle even more.

'And you want me to give you away to them? They reckon their shit don't stink, that Bigmann mob.'

Rosa laughed. 'Who else would I ask?'

'Well… Suppose I'll have to get some new shoes.'

*

Rosa had never seen Charlie out of his stained cooking whites. Today he looked so clean, his face shiny and slapped with aftershave, his hired suit and new shoes. Those shoes would be pinching his feet. She'd never seem him wear anything but fat-splattered runners.

'Nice shoes, Charlie.' Rosa smiled at him.

Charlie walked over to Rosa and kissed her on the cheek. 'A shame your family can't see you today. Life will be different for you now, love. It's not that easy for a tourist sheila to become a local here.'

'Time to go, you two,' said Gypsy. 'Don't forget your bouquet.'

*

The wedding car slowed and stopped in front of the old stone church. The heel of Rosa's white platform shoe caught momentarily on the edge of the car, but she managed to steady herself as she stepped out into the mid-afternoon heat. A fly buzzed near her ear. She swatted it, but it made its way to the corner of her eye. The champagne's sweetness lingered on her lips, but it didn't stop her shaking. She gripped her trailing bouquet of roses, baby's breath and asparagus fern with both hands for fear of dropping it.

Gyspy, straight-backed, bronze and glistening, carried a bunch of long-stemmed daisies loosely at her side. Towering above Tom's two young nieces, blonde and pink, in lace dresses with broad ribbon sashes, Gypsy looked faintly awkward, yet strangely regal.

The church organ began its tremulous tune.

5 June 2003

Dear Rose,

I find myself thinking of when I first met Arnold and how life was when I first went to live with him on the station. I think that's where my love of writing stories began, scribbling in my notebook at the end of the day, sitting out on the homestead veranda, me drinking tea and him smoking.

Out on the station, there were times when I felt a long, long way from home, so far away from the dark mountain and the thick forests. So far away from my family.

But the thing about exile is, it gives you time. Time to construct settings, to invent characters, to put them under pressure, to resolve and not resolve their conflicts, to reveal and conceal their secrets. Exile has its blessings. But you can't make sense of everything through writing fiction.

Sometimes you have to tell the truth.

Iris

Promises

'Well, time to do what you came to do, honey. You go first. Don't want Tom to get mixed up with who he's marrying, do we now?' said Gypsy.

'Time to go, girl,' said Charlie. He took Rosa's arm, linked it through his and stroked her hand.

The hem of her long white lace dress dragged in the red dust on the stone steps. They began the slow walk down the aisle, past the rows of smiling faces, hats, floral dresses and white shirts and coloured ties – the Bigmanns' friends and Tom's mates – to the altar, where Tom stood waiting.

Rosa took her place alongside Tom. Behind the altar, the sun streamed through the leadlight window of green, yellow and rose coloured glass. The organ stopped playing and the minister began. The rings sat on an open Bible on a small table in front of the altar.

Tom's grip tightened around her hand. The smell of honeysuckle from the altar flowers flooded the hot thick air. She began to feel faint and leant against Tom's shoulder to steady herself. If she could have looked down on herself from above, she would have seen how like a yielding, bending daisy on a long stem she looked.

Gypsy moved forward and took Rosa's bouquet. Rosa and Tom began their wedding vows. Tom slipped the gold band on her slim finger and he kissed her. Her high heels made her a little taller than him and he had to stand on his toes. It was a short dry kiss. The congregation clapped. Dust danced on the streams of light bouncing on the white altar cloth.

This was it now. The promise was made. Tiny beads of sweat sat like pearls on the backs of her hands that hairdresser Lil had dusted with talcum powder 'to make them look translucent and flawless'.

The nervous scrawl was so unlike her usual neat school font as she signed her maiden name for the last time. She passed the pen to Tom without looking up. Suntanned, square and solid, his hands were already freckled from the harsh outback sun and the gold ring on his thick finger somehow looked so new and foreign, like it didn't belong.

Tom put his arm around Rosa's waist and led her towards Thelma and Doug. They both kissed her.

'Part of our family now, Rosa,' said Thelma. 'Shame your family couldn't be here, Rosa. But then…perhaps it's just as well…' Thelma's voice trailed off. She walked over to Doug and straightened his tie.

'Part of the family, now,' echoed Doug. 'Hope it won't be too long before you and Tom give us a grandson, or even two.' Doug laughed a laugh that was too loud.

Rosa smiled, wishing she could have answered Thelma and Doug in some way, but words were wedged in her throat.

'Okay, group shots now. Family first,' called a small man with a huge camera.

Thelma had arranged the photographer to come up from the city. 'Righto, now out to Lady's Gap,' called the small man. Did Rosa imagine she heard Thelma saying to him ever so quietly, 'See if you can get someone to powder Gypsy down a bit. A bit of pale foundation would do the trick.'

The wedding was an opportunity for Thelma to wear her Japanese pearls and her hand-tailored silk dress, and for Doug to wear the Italian suit she had insisted upon him buying. They owned Heryl Springs Station after all; they were the richest people for miles; they had worked hard; it was their land. Why shouldn't they invite half the town to the wedding?

Tom wanted the reception at the top pub. There were only two pubs in town – the top and the bottom. When they arrived, the prawn cocktails had already been set out on the bridal table. Rosa took her seat next to Tom. In front of her, moisture dripped from the chilled glass onto the white porcelain saucer, the iceberg lettuce leaves framing the soft coral centre. She picked up the little silver fork and began to eat, not because she was hungry but because that was what she was supposed to do. She took a few slow mouthfuls and pushed the dish aside.

The waiter poured Moët into the crystal glasses. Rosa drank deeply; she was thirsty. During the main course, a fish bone caught in her throat. She couldn't speak. But Tom didn't notice…too busy talking to his best man, Bazza, and Thelma and Doug.

Rosa swallowed hard but the fish bone was stuck fast. Somehow, when Charlie was making his speech, she forgot about the hard sharp thing piercing her throat for a minute and the bone dislodged. Poor Charlie, how's he ever going to get through this? thought Rosa. Charlie's face was red as he stood and mumbled about not having ever made a speech before. Then he went silent and it seemed like he had stage fright and was going to have to finish it there. But he took a swig of beer and began again.

'I remember Rosa when she first came to town. She was like a rose, pink and white, wilting in the heat. I didn't think she'd make the distance. But she's gotten used to it now. We might make a local of her yet. She can handle the heat. Let's just hope she'll be able to handle everything else that might come her way…'

The speeches over, it was time to dance. Tom, with a beer tankard on a chain around his neck, a present from the best man, led Rosa to the dance floor. He held her as close as the tankard would permit and they did a waltz of a kind to 'Unchained Melody'.

He breathed beer into her face. 'You can lose your wog name now, Rosa,' he whispered in her ear. 'Your name is the same as mine now.'

Yes, she would have to remember her new name now. No more was she Rosa Kabanosy; she was Rosa Bigmann now.

*

Perhaps it was because he was a migrant; perhaps it was because it was his male lineage; but for whatever reason, Joseph Kabanosy was very particular about his name. Rosa could remember him spelling it out to people.

He would be infuriated if a letter arrived and the family name was misspelt. 'Can't they spell my name right?' he would bellow.

Grace had suggested to him on more than one occasion that he should keep a scrapbook with all the envelopes where his name had been misspelled. But her father would never have the patience for anything like that. Rosa remembered saying once she had wished their name was something easy like Smith or Jones that would never be misspelt.

'What's wrong with your own name? You don't like your name?' said her father, slamming his fist on the table.

'Of course I like my name, Dad…it's just that people can't always spell it.'

'People. Which people? Stupid people.'

'No, Dad. Just people at school. They can't say it properly.'

'Oh, so you're ashamed, young lady? You're ashamed of your father. You scared they call you wog or something? You tell them I call them cunts. You come here and give your father a kiss and say you are sorry.'

Rosa ran out of the room into the garden and sat under the rose bush that always seemed to be in bloom and hid her face in her hands.

*

The band stopped playing in the middle of a song.

A tall, dark man stumbled through the door. He was wearing a stockman's hat and a white shirt. 'Hey, Gypsy…get a drink for me,' he called.

Doug and Thelma stayed seated but Tom's best man, Bazza, got up from his chair as if he was about to draw a pistol.

With his stockman's stride, he went over to the man and pushed him in the chest, hard. 'What do you think you're doing in here, you black cunt?'

The man fell against the bar and, pulling himself up, staggered out into the night.

Rosa walked over to Gypsy and said quietly, 'Will you help me tidy myself up, Gyp?'

'Gypsy, I don't know what to say about that.' Rosa looked at Gypsy in the mirror.

'Nothing you can say, sister. Let's get you straightened out.'

Rosa looked at her face in the bathroom mirror. Mascara and eyeliner had smudged around her eyes and the red lipstick had faded to a faint outline. I look like a drawing that needs colouring in, she thought.

Gypsy helped her take off her hat and ran a comb over her hair, still thick and hard with lacquer. She pulled out a dead leaf that had settled into one of Rosa's blonde curls. 'How did that get in there through your hat, girl?'

Rosa glanced at Gypsy's reflection in the mirror. No make-up. Her skin shone like honey. Gypsy needed no enhancement. If Rosa could have looked like anyone, she would have looked like Gypsy.

The band struck up again with 'Proud Mary'. When Rosa walked back out, Tom grabbed her and they began dancing again. Thelma had taken the tankard from around his neck. Rosa couldn't look at him when he danced in his stiff, stomping way. He danced as if he was still on the back of a horse. Rosa swayed to the music, wishing she could leave and go to their hotel room, the only bridal suite in town, but she wanted Tom to be a bit drunker.

Finally, Thelma and Doug told Tom it was time to leave. 'Time to take your bride home, son,' said Doug.

Gypsy kissed Rosa on the cheek. 'Good luck, sister.'

Charlie, who had been standing at the bar for most of the night, said to Tom, 'You look after this girl.'

'Oh, I will,' said Tom, straightening himself.

The door of the best room in the hotel was stiff and Tom stumbled as he pushed it open. He loosened his pink, paisley tie, threw off his coat and fell backwards onto the bed. 'Thank goodness that shit's all over,' he said, closing his eyes.

Rosa sat on the edge of the bed and undid the rows of pearl buttons on the cuffs of her sleeves. Then she twisted her arms and began undoing the buttons down her back. Twenty-four of them. 'This will be fun for your husband on your wedding night,' the dressmaker had said. Tom was outstretched across the bed, fully dressed and snoring.

She slipped into a white broderie anglaise nightdress. The soft folds fell from the bodice that shaped her small, firm breasts. She pulled back the covers and squeezed herself to the edge of the bed and turned on her side. Tom began snoring loudly now. Tears ran across her face onto the pillow.

Before she drifted off to sleep, Rosa whispered his name: 'Archie.'

Somewhere deep in the night, Tom had reached for her and planted his seed inside her. She had been half asleep, but she knew this was what a wife should do. And it didn't last long.

In the morning, she woke to see him dressing in jeans and a checked shirt.

'Come on, Rosa. Mum and Dad are expecting us out at the station today. No holidays on a station. Hurry up, love. Dad's killed a beast for us.' Tom tucked his shirt in and buckled his tan leather belt. 'We can have a honeymoon any time, eh.'

'Yes, we can have a honeymoon any time.' Rosa didn't mind about not having a honeymoon. She didn't marry him for a honeymoon.

'And darl, I can't wear this ring. It's dangerous when I'm working.' He handed it back to her. 'Keep it for me in that box of yours.'

Rosa twisted the gold band on her own finger round and round as if tightening a bottle top. The ring didn't fit her well – it was loose.

10 December 2003

Dear Rose,

I spent the morning in the garden with the roses – the first bloom is always beautiful. I love the double blooms, soft white, tinged with pink. Arnold said he wanted to trim the bush, to deadhead it. But I asked him not to, just yet.

'Iris, if you deadhead them in summer, the blooms will keep on coming. But you have to make the right cut so the wound drains properly. All the old growth has to go. If a bloom is spent, Iris, it is spent,' he told me.

Arnold is often remarkably lucid. He's always giving me these little gardening gems, but I am so loath to cut any flower even if it is dead. I prefer them to fall in their own way. Arnold would be too shy to say to me that flowers contain the sexuality of plants, which of course is the case.

I can see the blooms through the window in front of my writing desk. The sight of them makes me feel alive.

The other day, I was reading about the flowers of the desert. Apparently, the desert rose is well adapted to desert life. The small seeds have a hard seed coat which protects them from the harsh arid environment.

Iris

Hunger Is a Strange Beast

Like Charlie said, marriage to Tom sealed her status as a local in theory only. To be a real local took a lot more than a change of name. Marriage allowed her right of entry of a kind, but small towns, especially small outback towns, are careful who they let in. They have to see your cards first. Tom's cards had always been on the table.

Life was different now she had crossed the bridge from being a girl who lived at the hostel to being married to a station owner's son. No more having to worry about who her next room-mate would be, no more scraping together enough money for food, cigarettes and rent. She was married now, and she had a florist business and a home of her own. No more would she have to think about going home to help her mother; she had her own responsibilities now, and her mother would understand, surely?

*

Dear Mum,

I have a lovely house now and I am busy looking after Tom. I have given up my job at the doctor's and spend most of my time cooking for Tom and keeping the house clean. It gets very dusty here and I clean every day. And yes, a surprise. I am expecting a baby in May.

Hope you and the family are well.

Love,

Rosa

*

Thelma and Doug had bought the house in town for Tom when he and

Rosa got married. The wide veranda framing the outside of the house made it seem like a smaller version of the cattle station homestead. The house had four bedrooms. Thelma and Doug made sure of that. Plenty of bedrooms for children. Tom spent most of his time out on the station and only came in on weekends. Sometimes, if he was out on mustering, he didn't come into town for weeks.

'Don't know how I'm ever going to get you pregnant…you in town and me out on the station…just going to have to make these weekends count,' said Tom before he left one morning, when he had come into town. 'And make sure you eat something today. Mum said you look too thin. She reckons you need a bit more weight on you to get pregnant.'

Rosa could have gone with him to live at the station. Many times he had asked her to go, to be with him, with the horses, the dogs and the cattle in the heat and the dust.

'I can't live without my flowers, Tom. You know that,' she would tell him.

'Sometimes I wish I hadn't bought you that flower shop. You never think of anything else these days but bloody flowers, and those soppy poems you're always writing,' Tom said the last time he asked her to live out on the station and she had said no.

Rosa knew if she lived on the station they would all watch her, try to make her eat when she wasn't even hungry. And nobody sunbaked on a station.

Rosa rarely saw anyone she knew from her days at the hostel. Itinerants don't tend to buy flowers. Most of them had moved on, anyway. She didn't need friends any more, anyway. She had everything she needed. Rosa lay out in the sun every weekend, the hot rays blazing down on her back, changing her fair skin to a dark, brown tan. Her life, now, was working in the flower shop during the day and sunbaking at the weekend. And when she was lying in the sun, she forgot about being hungry.

Now she was married to Tom, Rosa had to leave behind the transient liminal space she used to share with those, who like her, didn't belong, who weren't planning on staying for too long. But Rosa was staying now and like Charlie had told her, 'You won't fit in here. You're not cut out to be a local.'

And it had been a long time since Rosa had seen Win. She had bumped into her in the street one day and they'd chatted briefly. 'Well, it's going to take more than a shop and a few flowers for you to fit in here, girl,' she'd said. Win had sold the café 'on account of her bad back' and she had heard Charlie had moved further north.

And Gypsy…well, she had to look after her mother now.

Somehow, Rosa spun on the periphery. Even though townsfolk came into her shop, said hello and bought flowers, when she looked at them and they looked at her, it was like looking into a mirror with no reflection.

One day a woman, a friend of Thelma's, came into the shop to order a wreath. 'Love, I've been in this shop for five minutes and the whole time I've been in here you haven't moved from in front of those flower buckets. You in a trance or something?' She was dressed in a mustard-coloured polyester dress and carried a white handbag on the crook of her arm. If she had been wearing a hat, she would have looked just like the Queen.

'Oh, sorry…I was just thinking about something.' Rosa had jumped.

'Well, how about you stop thinking about "something" and give me some service, love?' the woman said.

Rosa had been miles away thinking about a conversation between her parents she thought she might have overheard once. And it might have gone something like this:

Joseph, do you think Rosa sometimes makes things up? Imagines things?' her mother said.

'Spins a yarn? Gilds, what do they call it? The daisy. Gilds the daisy?'

'The lily is what you mean, Joseph. "Gilds the lily" is the expression. Well, not tells lies exactly. She doesn't seem to be able to tell fact from fiction.'

*'All that girl ever does is dream and lie. It's okay to be a dreamer, but a
liar – that's another thing.*

But maybe she imagined it. Maybe they never had that conversation
at all.

*

Sometimes, when Thelma was in from the station, she would stay
with Rosa 'to keep her company'. Rosa didn't need any company, and
especially not Thelma's. On her last visit, after dinner they sat out the
veranda drinking the white wine Thelma had ordered from the city.

Thelma sipped her wine slowly, twisting the stem of her glass between
her fingers. 'Rosa,' she began, 'Doug and I were wondering…if…well…
you have considered going to the doctor again. Consulting, you know, a
specialist to find out what the problem is. Tom can't wait to have a son. I
think you know that and it's been a while now. I can give you the name
of a doctor in the city. She has an excellent reputation.'

She would have been better off never having consulted the doctor.
But it was just a routine check to keep Thelma and Doug happy. The
doctor was older than she had imagined. Her dark skin was moist in
the folds, gold bracelets circled her wrists and her turquoise silk sari
enveloped her small frame. The examination was deft and quick.

'You can get dressed now.'

Rosa obeyed and sat down in a chair next to the desk.

The doctor pushed her gold spectacles up her nose and looked at
Rosa. 'With a body such as yours I think it will take you many, many
years to fall with a child.'

Rosa stared at the caste mark on the woman's forehead.

'In fact, to be blunt, I think you need to address your weight. Pretty
soon your periods will stop completely if you keep going this way.
You are dangerously underweight and even if you were not, for you
to conceive a child now without medical intervention would be very
difficult. Your womb is not in the correct position and I suspect you

151

may have other issues. I am so sorry to be a prophet of doom. You must start to eat. Eat. Your body must be in a state of natural balance for conception to occur, my dear. Fertility requires a certain internal harmony and poise. The cellular functioning of the body seeks and to a certain extent demands stability. You will never fall pregnant in the state you are in now.'

'How did you go with the doctor?' Tom had asked her when he came into town.

'Oh, fine. Nothing to worry about at all. The doctor said everything was fine, absolutely fine,' Rosa told him. 'I am perfectly normal.'

15 December 2003

153

Dear Rose,

I sometimes think I would have liked to be a florist. All the florists I have ever known have had a very keen eye for balance.

Arnold is occupied with weeding at the moment, which is a good thing because he is becoming more and more restless and at times gets very agitated. The garden seems to be the place where he is most at ease.

Earlier, when I took him out his cup of tea, I was surprised when he said to me, 'You used to be real skinny, Iris. Remember. Just skin and bone. But you aren't now.' And he laughed.

I must say I was a little bit shocked and annoyed. I said to him, 'You should know better than to comment on a woman's weight, Arnold.' I was going to make him some scones, but I won't be doing that now.

    Iris

Body Language

Grass grew sparsely in the heat, but the desert roses seemed to grow well alongside the house in the dry earth.

'You ought to pull those things out, Rosa. They're only weeds. They'll spread over the whole garden if you don't watch it,' Tom would often say.

He seemed to like the hard, bare earth. But flowers were a comfort to her, somehow reminding her that growth was possible in the desert.

As was often the case on Sunday morning, Tom had to meet his father in town to see a man about a dog or a horse, and then maybe have a drink after that. He had left early, but not until he had deposited his seed high inside her, the warm sticky desire he called love.

'Maybe this time we'll score a six, if we haven't already,' he whispered in her ear just before he left. 'Got to get Mum and Dad off my back, soon.'

'I'm only a few days late, Tom,' she said.

'I'll be back for dinner,' he said. He grabbed a bread roll from the kitchen on his way out.

Now the day was hers. It was in front of her like a blank page. While the air in the house was still cool, she made some buttered toast. Rosa threw half a piece in the rubbish and left the other half on a plate. Better leave evidence she had eaten. Tom would check when he returned. No calories in coffee, though. She turned away to make coffee and looked back to see a cockroach was making its way across the uneaten toast, its legs loaded with the greasy butter. Heavy with grease, it continued its slow, trailing walk across the kitchen bench.

The kitchen was long and dark. When she opened the louvre windows, she felt the hot air on her face. The overhead fan whirred and the radio crackled. There was no other noise. Apart from Rosa and the cockroach, the big house was empty. She wiped the long wooden table with a cloth, erasing the cockroach's trail. When Tom wasn't there, and that was most of the time, Rosa felt like the house was hers alone.

She would walk through the empty rooms, straightening the cotton bedspreads, switching on the fans and checking the vases of roses had enough water. There was only one room she didn't enter, the room where once the crying had never stopped. On and on, night and day, crying and crying. Tom never knew how bad it was because he was never there. Now, the door was always shut. Tom said they would use it again soon. He was sure it would be soon. It could happen anytime. He wanted to put flowers in there. But Rosa made sure the door was kept shut

'No, Tom. Flowers die. I don't want to have to collect the dead.'

When the dream came, it was always the same.

*

Someone opens the door. Pink gossamer-like curtains blow in the honeysuckle-scented breeze that wafts through the open window. A pink teddy bear with an eternal smile sits on top of the chest of drawers, the moonlight lights up the rag dolls and red hearts on the wallpaper and a cry, soft and muffled, comes from the empty cradle that gradually becomes quieter and quieter, less and less, until there is only silence.

*

In the outback, the summer sun could be relied upon to rise early. In the height of summer, you could be sure the temperature would be at least thirty degrees by ten o'clock; the days would be hot or hotter still. Her old beach towel spread out on the cracked dry earth in the back garden, Rosa lay on it, face down. The towel was one of the few things she brought with her in her suitcase when she left home. Just why she thought she would need a beach towel in the outback, she wasn't sure.

And why she hung on to it, when she could have easily bought herself
a brand-new one, she wasn't sure either. If she closed her eyes, she
could smell the trace of the sea and beach sand; she could see the waves
and the coastline. She remembered the summer days when she took
Delphine and Camille to the beach for the day. Sometimes Rick would
tag along with them, too, if his mates weren't around. She wondered
what they all looked like now, her two younger sisters and her brother.
Her mother hadn't sent any photos for ages. I hope she's not sick again,
Rosa thought. She hadn't had a letter in a while.

The hard clumps of dry kikuyu pressed against her bare thighs. She
spread her fingers, long and thin, grasping tufts of grass and noticed
the green stains under her nails from the fresh bunches she had been
arranging all week. Even in the outback you could order in seasonal
flowers. They would arrive in refrigerated boxes: delicate white baby's
breath, purple irises and soft pink orchids. But her favourite was, and
always had been, the roses. Red, hardy and tough with long graceful
stems balancing buds which would later become full blooms, like ballet
dancers in pirouette. And the perfume would take her somewhere far
away from the outback town with its whirring fans and air conditioners
and a supermarket that sold more grog than food.

Rosa shifted on the towel. She often lay in the same spot and it was
as if the earth had taken on the shape of her body, moulding to her. Tom
was always nagging her about smoking but she took no notice of him.
She pulled a Marlboro from the packet, lit up and opened her book to
the page with the turned-down corner. Reading *Jane Eyre* again as an
adult was a different experience than it had been when she'd studied the
book at school. Rosa was no longer the idealistic schoolgirl who believed
in happy endings. Bertha probably had voices in her head, Rosa thought.
Maybe that's why she set fire to the house. Bertha never had a child, but
Jane Eyre had one in the end. But regardless of happy endings, Rosa
knew Bertha and Jane were both prisoners of a different kind.

The afternoon stretched on into that silence that settles in extreme
heat. Reading could be tiring, tapping into someone else's thoughts,

someone else's life. Sometimes it's better just to think and imagine and feel your own pen scratching away on the page. What would Tom make of the last poem she had scribbled?

Remains

Pastel petals
strewn
on the ochre
earth
curled and parched
in the merciless
sun
and hot desert wind.

Desert roses
blazed
to ash
scattered
lovely no more
here no more
but for the seed

He wouldn't know what to make of it. Or he might have taken it personally and say it wasn't his job to water the flowers – he didn't have time for that. Anyway, he would never see it. Rosa turned on her back so that the sun would bake her front and back evenly. She ran her hands over her hips – still a bit more weight to go. She would have to be careful of Thelma. As if she needed to gain weight when she'd still got quite a bit to lose. Her back felt tight and burnt. She'd been lying in the sun most of the afternoon and must have dozed off.

Getting up from her towel and stretching as she stood up, she felt a wet patch between her legs. The blood had come thick and dark. Ten days late, but now the blood came. Would she tell Tom or would she wait for him to ask? Maybe she'd wait for him to ask. No, she had better tell him. She went inside and lay down on the bed and waited for him. She wanted him to see her tan and the weight she had lost.

She heard Tom push open the fly screen.

He stood in the doorway of the bedroom, his bulk filling the space. 'What's for tea, Rosa?' Tom smelled of beer. He always came home smelling of beer when he had been in town with his father.

'Are you hungry?' Rosa tried to remember what she had in the fridge.

'I said what's for tea?'

'Well…nothing yet.'

'What have you been doing here all day anyway? All you ever do is scribble in that stupid notebook and play with your flowers. What do you write about anyway? Why don't you ever want to eat? You look like a bloody skeleton.'

The alcohol was strong on Tom's breath.

'Tom…I am not…I thought I was…but I'm not…' Rosa had to tell him.

Tom stood for a minute next to the bed, motionless, as if in a still shot. 'So, you're not…'

'No…Tom…I'm sorry…so sorry…'

The door slammed behind him.

Rosa went to the scales and weighed herself. She looked at herself in the full-length mirror. Still a bit further to go yet – still too much padding around the hips. No tea tonight and no breakfast in the morning. She ran her hands over the fine downy hair that was beginning to sprout on her arms. At least now Tom had gone off she wouldn't need to cook any tea.

Lying in bed, waiting for Tom to come back, Rosa thought for some strange reason of Sister Angela. Sister Angela with her hooked nose and kind smile, her chalky smell and thick glasses. Why she had asked her, Rosa couldn't remember. Perhaps it had been when they were studying *Seven Little Australians*.

'How many children do you think you might have, Rosa?' Sister Teresa had asked her.

She recalled her answer, clearly. 'I don't think I will have any children, Sister. I never want to be married.'

'Why ever not, child? Is it the drudgery you are afraid of, dear?' Her eyes were intense behind her thick glasses.

'I don't want to be a prisoner, Sister.'

Rosa remembered Sister Teresa's face more clearly than her words.

'Rosa, my child, I am shocked. Do you think your dear mother is a prisoner? Surely you cannot think that?'

Rosa blushed to her white schoolgirl's collar. 'I'm not sure, Sister.'

Perhaps it was because of this conversation that Sister Angela had ripped up her essay in front of the entire English class, in her final year of school. Sister Agnes held up Rosa's essay as if it had been a filthy nappy.

*

Somewhere in the small hours, Rosa heard the back door bang and Tom slid into the bed next to her. He smelled of perfume and beer.

'Sorry, honey. Sorry,' he said, patting her. 'Maybe next time, honey. Maybe next time,' he said breathing beer into her face. And within seconds he was snoring.

The next morning, she got up early, long before Tom stirred. Barefoot, she floated down the passage, into the empty bedrooms, straightening the cotton bedspreads one by one, switching on the fans and checking that the vases of roses had enough water. All except for that one room.

In the kitchen, long and dark, she opened the louvre windows and felt the warm morning air on her face. The overhead fan whirred and she parted the beaded curtain at the back door and stepped out over the scorched pink petals spread across the brick-hard earth. You have to be a hard seed to survive in the desert.

29 December 2003

Dear Rose,

I'm finding myself thinking a lot about curses. I'm not sure if I do believe in curses. What are they? Black magic? Bad wishes? Maybe, in a way I do believe in them. Perhaps if you wish ill on a person long enough and hard enough it might come to pass. There again, there's the type of curse that results from a person's action, a bad action, an action that hurts or disrespects something that is sacred, a kind of moral trespass. If someone broke into St Margaret's and pissed all over the altar for a joke, would they be cursed? I'm not sure. They probably deserve to be. If you spit into the eye of the universe, then maybe you curse yourself, in a way. If you act with supreme disrespect, then it has to rebound somehow, surely?

And then of course there is guilt. Guilt is a curse in itself. Lady Macbeth, for example. What an interesting character she was. She killed herself in the end. I suppose you could ask if some powerful force outside herself caused her to become ill, forced her hand in taking her own life. Or was it that the guilt of her actions became too much to bear?

I remember hearing a discussion once on the radio about the fact that Lady Macbeth was most likely suffering from a bad case of post-natal depression. Not a lady with too many morals, you'd have to say, post-natal depression or not. In fact, I think the person implied that Macbeth's famous speech was, in fact, Lady Macbeth's suicide note. And she was a sleepwalker, too. That's not something I have ever done. Or if I have, Arnold has never mentioned it.

But some people just act with total arrogance, as if they have some divine right to do exactly as they wish. Not everyone suffers from guilt though. Maybe that's it. If you are incapable of guilt, then a curse will descend on you, because my theory is no one can escape the energy of their actions. It's just basic metaphysics.

    Iris

Stain

One sweltering Monday in March, Tom's thirtieth birthday present arrived on the northbound goods train: a brand-new sports car – silver hubcaps, black tyres, satin smooth and passion red duco – glistening like a mirage in the shimmering heat.

'The station's had a good year. A few good rains and good returns on the cattle. That's why it's a bit more than I would normally give you, son. But just don't be a James Dean,' his father said when he handed over the keys.

His parents loved and spoiled him. It wasn't that they were bad or even stupid people, they just couldn't seem to help themselves. Rosa knew, more than anything, they wanted him to have an heir. If only she could get pregnant and give Tom his son – his heir and their grandson – they would leave her to her flowers, poetry and sunbaking. One living boy child was all it would take. She thought she'd overheard Thelma talking to Tom about it one evening out at the station, after dinner when they were sitting out on the veranda having a customary drink.

'It's been nearly two years now and still no sign of another child. So strange she never even mentions the baby's name. It's as if she has forgotten the birth ever happened. Does she think she dreamt it?'

Rosa had listened and watched, straining from the shadows.

'You took a while to have me, Mum, by all accounts.' Tom put his hat back on and said, 'Just going to lock the dogs up, Mum.' Perhaps even Tom was getting tired of his parent's expectations.

Maybe one day soon, it would happen, especially now she was eating again, Rosa thought. Nearly ten years had passed since their wedding day. Time was slipping by and now Tom had turned thirty.

But the day the sports car arrived, nothing was further from Tom's mind than babies. He drove down the driveway, spinning the wheels in the gravel and honked the horn until Rosa came to the door. She stood holding the fly screen half open. The machine gleamed in the outback sun.

'Rosa…Rosa,' he yelled. 'Don't just stand there. Come here and look at her. She's a beauty. Have a look at the wheels on her.'

Rosa walked towards him, squinting in the bright sunlight.

He grabbed her hand and ran it slowly over the curves of the bonnet, the polished red enamel. 'Feel her. I love her. God, I love her. Feel that shapely body.'

The car was almost too hot to touch. She pulled her hand back. 'It's so hot, Tom. My hand is burning.'

He released her and, unexpectedly, he kissed her palm. He was filled with the happiness of someone who has just got what they always wanted. 'Jump in. Come for a spin.'

The black leather seat moulded to her body, encasing her slim frame.

'Fasten your seat belt, woman.' Tom turned the keys in the ignition. 'Okay, let's take her for a rip.'

He sped out past the Gap, on past the rolling snake-like hills, past the ghost gums, past the huge stone boulders. His sun-bleached hair blew back from his forehead, his hairline receding just like Doug's. His freckled hands were large compared to the rest him and he gripped the steering wheel hard, his shoulders arched under his white shirt. She looked at him side on. He seemed in another world, as if he had forgotten she was in the car – he drove as if she wasn't even there.

'Don't let me ever catch you sneaking her out for a drive, Rosa. She's mine,' he said when they returned.

'No, Tom. Of course I would never do that.'

*

163

Tom Bigmann, cattle station owner's son, popular local identity, now drove a brand new Porsche. He had his new baby. And he'd never been more popular with his mates.

Rosa had her shop, her flowers and her writing. That would have to do, for the time being. Maybe she would bloom in her own way, in her own time, in this harsh outback town. Through writing her poetry and plays, she could live within herself. She had everything she needed in her secret garden.

Even in her writing class at the community centre, she kept to herself. Hello, smile, goodbye. Most of the people there wanted to write bush ballads. Pleasant to everyone, close to no one. That was the safest way. Except maybe the teacher – Rob.

He liked her last poem, he liked it very much. 'Would you like to read it to the class?' he asked her.

> Apart
>
> It comes in waves.
> at first you take it
> like a body blow
> hunch your shoulders
> to take the force
> bend
> and then come up again to gasp
> for air
> clench your fists,
> nails into palms
> grit your teeth
> keep the words in
> shield your mind from spectres
> try to block them out.
> but when it comes
> the second wave is worse.
>
> Ignore the stiff ache
> in your throat
> swallow sobs,

sorrow unspoken
wake in the night
terror of silence
in a dream
sadness
twists and turns
a dagger in your chest
block your ears
when you hear that song
hold your breath
so you don't cry out loud
brace yourself
and your hollow heart
it could crack
cover your eyes
so you can't see them
together.

'But I thought you were married, Rosa. Recently married, and so young. You haven't parted, have you?' Rob said when she had finished reading.

'Yes, you're right, Rob. I am recently married and no, we haven't parted.'

'Then why would you write such a poem of grief?' said Rob.

'So I know how it will feel when it happens.'

*

It became a game, waiting for the next time she could take Tom's sports car out on the open road. The car keys hung on the hook by the hall table when he was gone. When the silence settled like a blanket in the afternoon heat, when even the neighbour's dog stopped barking, she'd back out of the driveway. He'd never know. He was miles away.

Once the car hit the open road, she pressed the accelerator and felt the power of the motor increase its speed in just seconds. She sped on past the twin ghost gums, through the Gap and past the twin boulders, the Rocks.

But she'd heard they were sacred – men's business, not for women's eyes. Whenever she passed the site, she made a conscious effort not to look. No, she always sped up when she drove past the stones. She turned up the music in the cassette deck – 'Born to Run' – feeling the thrill and dread of the loneliness of the deserted road ahead, imagining Tom's face if he ever found out that she had taken his baby, his beloved, for a spin.

She reached the dry creek bed, slowed down, turned around and pressed her foot to the floor again. With the windows down, the hot air scorched her face and her long hair flew behind her, lashing her neck like a whip.

Not a single car, a single person, until she reached the road leading back into town. The wheels crunched on gravel as she drove back into the driveway. She pressed her palm on the car bonnet. Hot. But plenty of time for the engine to cool.

*

Just why she had started eating again, she wasn't sure. Perhaps it might have had something to do with the evening of the cattlemen's association ball. The shoestring straps of the black silk gown had hung off her shoulders and she had to find some safety pins to hold it together.

Tom had been struggling with the knot in his tie and he turned and looked at her. 'You look absolutely fucking disgusting.' His face was contorted and flushed as he spoke. 'Your bones are sticking out and you look…you look bloody repulsive. I'm not taking you out to a ball looking like a scarecrow. Cover yourself up a bit more, can't you?'

If Tom ever did her a favour, it was that insult. Tom's revulsion somehow pulled Rosa back over the line she had been about to cross. Slowly she began eating again. It was not as if Tom even noticed in a positive way that she was becoming healthy again. He just stopped telling her how unattractive she looked and pinched her bottom occasionally.

But Tom was away more and more, and whenever he did come

into town, he spent most of his time out cavorting and boozing with his mates. Unlike the early days when Tom used to take her along with him, Rosa wasn't invited to card games, drinking sessions or the pub to listen to country and western bands that played loudly and badly.

'You could take me out somewhere once in a while,' she complained one night as Tom headed out the back door.

'You always want to go just when the party is getting started,' Tom snapped back at her.

'I just get tired these days…'

'You're always bloody tired. I'm only in town for a week, for Christ's sake, woman. A man's gotta have some fun.' He stood in the doorway for a second as if he was going to say something else.

'Go then, if you want to,' said Rosa.

'Yeah…well…shit…a man's got to relax some time.' He slammed the fly wire door and strode heavily down the gravel driveway.

Rosa was unable to sleep in the heat and she was sitting on the veranda just after midnight when Tom came staggering back down the driveway. He was swigging on a stubbie.

'Rosa, darl, you go on in. I'm just going to take my baby for a spin.'

'But Tom, you're as pissed as a newt. You can't drive…please…'

'Not going far. Don't worry. I'm just going to have a drink with Bazza. You go on in, Rosa. He's only round the corner.'

Bazza – that meant trouble – two wild boys in from the station. But she knew there was nothing she could do to stop them. He screeched out of the driveway and she stood and watched, hoping that he wasn't going far.

Somewhere around dawn, Tom slid into the bed next to Rosa. Paint. Even though she was half asleep, she could smell paint, for sure. She turned her back against him and wondered what on earth he would be painting in the early hours of the morning.

*

Rosa stood at the fence watering her desert roses.

Her neighbour waved and called, 'Hello, how are you?' and began walking towards her.

Mrs Blewitt only spoke to gossip or complain. The last time it was about Rosa's cat. 'That cat of yours had a Major Mitchell in your back yard the other day when you were at work. Did you know? It played with the poor thing for hours. Feathers everywhere. Cruel things, cats. Couldn't you keep it inside a bit more?'

No, this time she was smiling, so she must want to tell me some gossip, Rosa thought, hoping that it wouldn't take too long.

'You wouldn't read about it. Some dickheads have spray-painted the Rocks. Just like two big gold nuggets, they reckon. Supposed to be a sacred site. Blackfellas probably put a curse on whoever done it.'

'Spray-painted?' said Rosa. 'When?'

'Last night. Some idiot's idea of a joke I suppose. Tell you what, though. I wouldn't be them for quids, them that done it. No way. Kadaitcha business.'

Tom was still sleeping when Rosa went back inside. He had left his shirt strewn on the bedroom floor. Rosa picked it up. Paint. Gold paint – splattered on the sleeve.

*

When Tom was away, which was nearly most of the time, Rosa didn't miss him at all. But for some reason she had been thinking about him these last few days. Much more than usual. And most strangely, she had dreamt about him a few nights back. In her dream, she looked at a photograph of him but it wasn't him. He had become someone else she didn't recognise.

When the news came through, Rosa was checking the flower buckets in the shop. It didn't take long for the water to fester. Daily she would go around sniffing the buckets, trimming the stems and changing the water. When two policemen walked into the shop, she thought they were looking for someone. Yes, they were looking for her.

Thelma had telegraphed them from the station. Tom had been thrown from the horse. Badly concussed. Lost consciousness immediately. His head hit a rock. Left leg broken – badly. The Flying Doctor took him straight to the city. Possibility of paralysis. In intensive care. Rosa left on the next plane out. She met Thelma in the foyer at the hospital.

Thelma's face was ashen. 'I worried so much about that stupid sports car. I always thought that would get him. Never thought it'd be a horse. One of our best horses, too,' Thelma said in a choked voice that sounded like it belonged to someone else. 'Not sure what happened. No warning. Just threw him. Now look at him… My beautiful boy,' she whispered.

The two of them went up in the lift, not speaking, not looking at each other. They walked down the passage along the shiny green hospital tiles, past the trolleys stacked with crisp white linen and into Tom's private room.

Rosa walked over to his bedside. Thelma followed her. Tom was wired up to drips and his head was covered in bandages, his leg raised in a cast.

Doug was sitting in the chair next to the bed, hat on his lap. He looked smaller and years older than the last time Rosa had seen him. 'Surgeon's just been. Said that he'll probably recover, in time. He's going to need a lot of rehab. Going to have to live in the city. And he'll never ride again. Never ride again. May as well put a bullet to his head… This'll kill him.' Doug's voice broke and he covered his face with his hands.

Thelma stood, motionless in front of the hospital window with her back to them all.

*

Rosa wondered about the feathers she had found on the front doorstep just days before the accident. Maybe they weren't feathers. Maybe she was getting mixed up. Maybe what she had seen were the feather-like seeds from her desert rose. Mrs Blewitt had warned her to tie the seeds pods with wire to stop the seeds escaping when the pod burst. Could easily have been the seeds. Scattered. Could have come from anywhere. Or the cat might have killed a bird.

25 January 2004

Dear Rose,

I was telling Arnold today I have always suspected my father wanted more sons. In fact, I feel sure he might have been happier if we all had been boys. I think Jim would definitely have preferred to be the eldest boy and not my younger brother. I imagine, after I left, he told everyone he was the eldest. The eldest son of a war veteran…that would have been good for his tough-guy image. Dad left the newsagency to Jim; Bridie and Marie got the cash; and I got Mum's house, eventually. But there are many types of legacies.

I finally plucked up the courage to go into Dad's newsagency the other day. I was half expecting to see my father behind the counter. But of course, he's been dead for years. A young girl with blonde hair and a tattoo on her arm asked if she could help me. 'Too late for that,' I said. She laughed, sweet thing.

I knew it was a stupid thing to do, to call in to Jim's business expecting him to welcome me, his sister, back. He wasn't even there, but if he had been, I wonder if he would have acknowledged me. Possibly he wouldn't have even recognised me. The other day I was at Imelda's and when I walked into her entrance and I glanced into the hall mirror, I said to her that I didn't realise she had invited anyone else. Then I realised it was me.

I noticed that Jim was stocking books, something our father had never done. I had a quick look at some of the titles he was keeping – biographies, history, politics, that kind of thing. I think maybe he had always wanted to be a writer. I remember he had been very good at English when he was at school. He might have even won a prize. Yes, that's right – he came home one night, so proud, and told my father he had been given a certificate for the best essay for the year. And my father said, 'Essays are all very well, son, but you can get out there and mow the lawn tonight, and if there was any prize money you can give it to your mother.' What a thing to say to your son. 'Writing essays doesn't get the grass cut,' our father said to Jim. I remember feeling sorry for him.

And I have been thinking about it so much, this business of competing voices in families. Perhaps, if there are several writers in the family, they will always be in competition. Anyway, I don't imagine I will see Jim again unless I bump into him by accident, or there is another funeral and then, most likely, he will look the other way.

Iris

No More Roses

It wasn't that hard to pack up the house, but shutting the shop was another matter altogether. Rosa was going to miss her little oasis, her world of flowers, now that they had to leave town. She had even called her shop Oasis. Maybe she'd have another florist shop in the city, but it wouldn't be the same. A young woman and her mother had bought the business and planned to sell outback souvenirs and cut bunches from plastic buckets.

'We're going to change the entire concept,' the woman told Rosa. 'No more roses. Too expensive. Who wants roses anyway?'

Rosa took the silver-framed mirror, a present from Gyspy, from the wall and walked out the door and closed it for the last time. Nearly ten years had passed since she had come to live in the outback and now she was leaving and going back to where she came from all that time ago. Time was different in the outback.

She hated herself for thinking it – but she often did, especially when he had a bad day: Tom might as well have died. It might have been easier for all of them if he had, especially for her. He had many bad days, days when he barely spoke, couldn't remember anything and would just sit staring at the television whether it was turned on or not. Now, he shuffled and limped through the days facing a future of never again mustering cattle, of never again riding a horse under the scorching outback sun.

Rosa packed each room of the house herself, except the room where the door was always closed. She realised there wasn't anything in the house she valued, except for her writing journals and what was in little Alice's room, the room she never entered except in dreams. She wondered if the dreams would stop when they were in the new house in the city. Always the same. Soft gossamer-like curtains, a pink teddy bear with an eternal smile, an empty cradle and the silence.

Rosa asked the removalists to pack whatever was in that little room. 'I know there is not much in there, but I want it packed carefully and clearly marked – "Spare Room".' But some things you can't pack.

Gypsy came to visit her before she and Tom left. 'How you going to cope back in the big smoke, girl? Will it be good to be near your family again?'

'That remains to be seen, I guess, Gyp. I'm not sure how I will be received or even if I will be received at all.'

'But they are your blood, your family.' Gypsy looked radiant and ripe. She was expecting her first child.

Rosa stood close to her, breathing in the smell of sandalwood, absorbing her essence. If she could have been anyone, Rosa would have been Gypsy.

'Doesn't always mean a lot in some families, Gyp. All depends what's at stake,' said Rosa looking at Gypsy's belly. 'Will you call your baby Archie if it's a boy?' she said.

'What do you think, Rosa?' Gypsy said and smiled that smile of hers. She turned to Rosa and hugged her. 'Bye, now. And stay in touch. I guess I should say bye to Tom.'

Gypsy walked down the passage into the near empty lounge room. Tom was sitting in a chair with his stiff leg stretched out.

'Bye, Tom. Hope you get better soon.'

Tom didn't move or reply. Gypsy walked towards the back door and turned and waved to Rosa. For a moment, Rosa saw Archie again, his slim graceful body waving goodbye.

29 April 2004

Dear Rose,

Last night, thinking out aloud, I said to Arnold that maybe I should send them all – Jim, Bridie and Marie – a copy of the manuscript before I publish my novel.

I thought he would ignore me as usual but then out of the blue, he piped up and said, 'Well, I'm not sure what you expect them to say.' He had turned to look at me before he spoke, which was strange in itself. These days he rarely looks at me at all.

I wonder what would happen if they did read my manuscript. I can imagine Bridie saying, 'What really pisses me off is that her fiction is her truth. Her fiction makes it all true on the page. It's her version of us, not the real version. And she gets to publish it, other people read it. Books on library shelves last forever, you know. Grandchildren could read it. That would be her legacy, not ours.'

I can hear Mum's ghost saying, 'But if we aren't like the characters in the book and we know it, and other people know it, why would we worry she is writing about us? Just because she writes about a mother, doesn't mean she's writing about me. I mean, everyone has a mother. And a father. And usually a brother or sister too.' Mum, ever the peacemaker.

And Jim would interrupt. 'I warned her about writing that shit. Especially the shit about Dad. But she went right on and did it.' Then Marie would chip in, 'Yes, well, I have read it and I hate it but if we confront her about it she'd probably just say something wanky.'

And my father's ghost, would say, 'I said a long time ago she would be a big problem for someone one day, that girl. Got a big problem inside her that one – dark and savage.'

Iris

Unpacking

No more dark kitchen with opaque louvres, noisy air conditioner or red and blue plastic strip curtain at the back door to keep the flies out. Now, here in her light-filled suburban kitchen with crystals hanging in the window, refracted light bounced off the walls. Here, jasmine grew prolifically and when she opened the French doors she could reach and cut a sprig. Marjoram and basil flourished in the herb garden and the clay pot outside the back door offered sweet little red tomatoes all through the summer months. Rosa's home town with its four seasons – sometimes all in one day – stiff sea breezes and fresh milk was familiar to her, but it was a foreign territory to Tom.

So much had changed for Tom, and Tom had changed so much. The only time Rosa had seen any sign of the old Tom was when one of his old mates had come to visit. Perhaps he was still there somewhere inside his shell. Perhaps there was never much of him anyway.

Slowly they settled into a routine which, if not joyful, was bearable. Sometimes, it seemed as if they had never lived in the outback at all. No more dry, cracked earth; no more scorching herself in the fierce summer sun. Seedlings sprouted easily in the rich dark soil and Rosa had a garden full of roses and trees whose leaves turned golden in the autumn. Now, she wore a big floppy hat and one of Tom's old shirts to protect herself from the sun's rays even in the winter months. His leg, stiff and useless, stretched out in front of him, Tom would sit and watch her work from the veranda. Some days were better for him than others. Occasionally, he would call out instructions but most of the time he sat staring out into nowhere in particular.

Returning to the town where she was born, to where she began her days all those years ago, unleashed in Rosa a torrent of memories

– memories and recollections of unfinished business that peppered her thoughts: night and day. Writing had become her friend and witness; writing had overtaken her passion for flowers. There was so much of earlier life that needed tidying up, so much that needed to be put back in place.

Visiting her mother's grave, for example. Yellow roses were her mother's favourite, so Rosa picked all that remained on the bush and, with her florist's skill, she removed the thick thorns with the blade of her secateurs. She arranged the roses with a few white daisy stems and bay leaf branches. Mum would have liked them, she thought, and wrapped the bunch in pink tissue paper and tied grey gauze ribbon in a soft bow. It was early autumn and the breeze was warm and the brown, fallen leaves crunched under her feet as she walked with the flowers towards her mother's grave. A small headstone: 'Grace Kabanosy – wife and mother – loved by all'. Cradling the bouquet as it were a baby, Rosa sank to her knees and laid the bouquet down on the marble slab. She made the sign of the cross and her loud, hoarse sobs cut through still afternoon the air. A burnished red leaf floated down on her head, unnoticed, and settled in her dark curly hair.

When she arrived home, Tom said, 'You look like you've seen a ghost.'

Did it help to turn memories into a fiction? Rosa wasn't sure.

*

Act Two: Scene 2

Mother is unrolling reams of pink crêpe paper and there is a large pincushion with pins on the kitchen table. Dark Rosaleen is practising her lines for the school play in which she has been cast as Briar Rose.

MOTHER: Stay still now. We've got to get this right. (She drapes the crepe paper around Dark Rosaleen's waist, pinning the paper to the shape of her small body.)

DARK ROSALEEN: Oh, Mama, it's going to look so beautiful. And I am going to marry the prince. (*She smooths the skirt with her hands.*)

MOTHER: Turn around now so I can pleat the back.

DARK ROSALEEN: (*Turns and faces the kitchen door.*) Don't prick me with a pin, Mama. (*Laughs.*)

FATHER: (*Walks in, work boots in hand.*) How are you my beautiful one? (*Reaches over and strokes Dark Rosaleen's face.*) Your skin is like silk.

MOTHER: (*Speaking through a mouthful of pins.*) Hello, husband dearest. How was your day?

FATHER: You look like an old crow and you smell of onions. (Walks to the fridge, takes out a beer and leaves the stage.)

MOTHER: (*Roughly rips the dress off Dark Rosaleen.*) Don't think that you will be wearing that. No stage play for you. You need to know your place. (*Throws the paper costume into the fireplace where a log fire is burning.*)

DARK ROSALEEN: Oh no, Mama. You have scratched me with the pins. Oh please, Mama. My Briar Rose dress… I will never be able to marry the prince now. (*Head in hands, sobs and runs off stage.*)

MOTHER: Indeed you won't, daughter. There will be no prince for you. (*She stands in front of the fireplace and watches the costume burn.*)

*

The autumn sunshine came and went and the fallen leaves became mulch at the base of the apple trees at the bottom of the garden. The days became short and the nights long. Tom spent the evenings watching the television without the sound. The fire blazed and cracked in the fireplace. And Rosa wrote. A scene kept returning to her.

When she and Tom had first returned from the outback, they had spent Christmas with her family. It was the first Christmas she had spent with them since she had left all those years before and the last time she had seen her father, Joseph Kabanosy. Sometimes, when it came, she would shelve the memory, put it away in a box in her mind, arrange some flowers in a vase, but sometimes it just wouldn't be put away and she had to relive it, write it.

*

Act One: Scene 3

Shadows of DARK ROSALEEN and PRINCESS are in the kitchen chopping fruit for a fruit salad as an alternative to the plum pudding. It is DARK ROSALEEN'S idea. The atmosphere is tense. It is the first Christmas they have been alone together in a long while. There is a large bowl of fruit on the kitchen bench. All characters, except for the narrator, appear as shadows and voices behind the shadow curtain.

PRINCESS: What's wrong with having my plum pudding? You are the only one complaining.

DARK ROSALEEN: I'll do it then, if you like. I'll make the fruit salad.

PRINCESS: (*Puts the knife down.*) Sure. Go for it. You're the only one who is going to eat it anyway. (*Starts to walk out of the kitchen.*)

DARK ROSALEEN: (*Peeling an apple with a knife.*) You've never contacted me once since I have been back, and you never contacted me once while I was away.

PRINCESS: Oh, really. Did it ever occur to you how you upset the whole family? Pa nearly went mad with worry. And all because you wanted to be thin and brown. I had to watch Ma and Pa stress and fret about you. You went away for so long with scarcely a word. At first they thought you were going to die. They didn't know what was going to become of you when you went so far away. Then you didn't invite them to your wedding and you didn't even come to Mum's funeral. Your own mother.

DARK ROSALEEN: Do you think I did it on purpose? Do you think it was fun? I wasn't well. My baby girl had just died. There's so much you don't know.

179

PRINCESS: You *could* help it, Rosaleen – you and your selfish self-indulgence. And you've got the gall to whinge that I didn't visit you. Well, I'm sorry if that hurt you. You were locked away, weren't you?
DARK ROSALEEN: (*Yelling.*) You bitch! You mean, lousy, fucking bitch. (*Rosaleen still holds the apple with the green peel trailing to her elbow.*)
Father, wearing a hand-knitted brown cardigan, enters from the side door coming in from the garden, carrying a watermelon. Princess begins to cry.
FATHER: What's going on in here? Rosaleen, I heard you yelling from out in the garden. You want the world to hear you and your problems? What have you done to your sister? (*FATHER walks over to PRINCESS and puts his arm around her. He points to DARK ROSALEEN.*) There, my Princesses, don't be upset. Not on Christmas Day. You, you and your fucking dramas. Dragging the family name through the dirt. Get out, skeleton. Get out and don't come back. (*Stabs the air with his finger.*)
FATHER'S SON: (*Walks towards Rosaleen and jabs her in the chest.*) 'Get out…get out and don't come back.
Lights dim. Stage is clear. Chorus voices come from off the stage.
VOICE ONE: Well, every family has a mad woman in the attic, I guess.
VOICE TWO: Who?
VOICE ONE: Well…you know who…
NARRATOR: (*Walks to the front of the curtain.*) Well, isn't Dark Rosaleen a troublemaker? You get one in every family. No prizes for guessing who the lunatic is in this family.

*

Tom had been sitting in the lounge room watching television, or maybe sleeping, completely unaware of the drama unfolding in the kitchen that Christmas morning. He was heavily drugged, recovering from his accident, and was aware of very little that went on around him. But Rosa's family had always been a complete mystery to him anyway, something he had preferred to stay out of completely. 'They are a fucking weird lot, your family, Rosa,' he'd said that day they left her father's house for the last time.

Shortly after that dreadful Christmas Day, Joseph Kabanosy died. Rosa heard that he passed away in the arms of his girls. In Rosa's mind, her sisters dissolved into one form, one entity: Princess.

Tom didn't go to Joseph's funeral. Or the wake. Rosa had faced her father's death alone.

25 May 2004

Dear Rose,

This memory game is a tough one sometimes. I sometimes wonder if you can remember how you actually felt when you loved someone, the details of those feelings. Do you actually still love them, even though it might be years ago?

Emotional memory is such a strange thing – nothing to do with facts at all. It's a little like fiction – it stays with you regardless of whether it actually happened or not.

Dreams are the same. Nightmares are just as terrifying as reality. Sad, crying dreams are just as distressing as real events.

I was saying to Sister Anne the other day that it is so hard to draw the line between dreams and memories. What is the difference really, especially if you are writing fiction? She asked me about my characters and I had to think for a minute how I construct their emotional world. I told her I have felt the emotions of all my characters at various times, in different ways in my lifetime, but not necessarily within the same context of the experiences of my characters. Maybe in quite different circumstances, but I have felt the same emotions nonetheless.

Sister Anne seemed to understand. She said, 'Yes, it seems the older we get, the larger our emotional repertoire becomes.'

Her reply surprised me a little. I guess I didn't expect her to understand. I said to her that all artists use their own emotional world as raw material for their work and she just looked at me as if I was preaching to the converted.

Then she asked me, 'Do you find that you seek drama in your own life, manufacture it even?'

I had to reply honestly because she is my friend as well as confidante.

So I said, 'I think I would have to say that I relish new emotional experiences. I file them away and add them to my inventory for future use.'

Sister Anne said that she felt that she had lived long enough to have experienced most of the Shakespearian emotions at some stage or other. I had to wonder if she had experienced sexual passion and love, but I strongly suspect she had. Of course, I didn't ask.

She seemed in a very philosophical mood today. She said to me in an usually quiet voice, while she was making the ginger tea, she wondered if a person could be so detached from their own experience of life that they simply process it and transform it into art.

Very astute of her. She must know, as I do, that there is a shadowy space in-between the experience and memory. Some people would call it a place of lies.

Iris

Truth Is For Philosophers

Rosa sat at her desk writing, as had become her early morning habit. Outside the front door was a rosebush that seemed always in bloom. Its blood-red blossoms hung over an arbour that bent and struggled with the weight of the wild thorny branches, the tight heavy buds. Often, she would pick the flowers and arrange them in a crystal vase on her desk. She scratched in her journal the fractured memory of her dream, the dream that came so often and had visited her again that night and was still with her.

The curtains are open but the window is opaque. I can't see the rosebush now, only imagine how it would be.

Tom's rough voice made her jump. 'Rosa, your brother's on the phone.'

'Brother? Which brother?'

'I thought you only had one.' Tom limped back down the hallway.

Rick's voice sounded strange on the phone. It had been so long since they had spoken. He wanted to meet with her, to catch up, he said. Certainly they had some catching up to do. They should meet at New Black, he said.

Rosa was so stunned to hear from him, she just agreed. Yes, she would see him there tomorrow. Yes, at 10 a.m. 'What is it you want to see me about?'

The phone line went dead. He had hung up before he heard her question.

Tom had been standing in the hallway listening. 'Well, that's a turn-up for the books,' he said.

Rosa knew the restaurant – stylish, shiny and expensive. She sat waiting at a table in the corner. Chairs scraped hard on the white tiles and the clatter of the cappuccino machine competed with the lounge music and chatter. Expensive perfume, brand-name sunglasses placed on the table tops, designer bags hanging over the backs of chairs: she was a long way from Win's Café now. Rosa gazed out of the window, and it occurred to her that maybe he might not turn up. Perhaps he might have changed his mind, or maybe she had the wrong café. Had he even contacted her at all? Had she just imagined it? Her palms were clammy. Even though she had seen him at their father's funeral, she hadn't spoken to him and he hadn't spoken to her. It was as if she had been muted by some kind of invisible wall that had evolved between them. Rick had just looked right through her. It was one of those strange unspoken things that happen between people sometimes, especially in families.

What had stopped her from going right up to him and saying hello? She wasn't sure. At the funeral, Rick's face had seemed veiled, as if he had become someone else. Camille and Delphine had claimed their usual positions. But, after all, it made sense to hold their father's wake at Camille's place because she had the biggest house, with the most beautiful view and the most expensive furniture. 'The girls', as her mother had always called her sisters, had sat together at his funeral, like a chorus in a Greek tragedy. Rosa had never been included as one of 'the girls' in her parents' conversations. Rosa had sat on her own. She didn't recognise many of the people who had spread out over Camille's manicured lawn. Except for Spyros. She did recognise him. Spyros, Rick's old childhood friend. Spyros who had lived in the house over the back.

'Your old man was a character all right, Rosa,' Spyros had said, cornering her next to Camille's lemon tree.

'Do you still live with your parents, Spyros?' said Rosa, remembering how his parents had spoiled him and attended to his every whim. She could never understand what he and Rick had in common, apart from the fact that they lived in the same neighbourhood.

Yeah, no, he did. His parents had seen the death notice. They'd said Rick would like to see him, that he should go and pay his respects.

'You're not married, then?' Rosa asked him, not thinking for a moment that he would be.

Yeah, no, he'd been married once, but it didn't work out. Yeah, no, it was cheap and easy living with the olds.

Rosa remembered their father had said, years ago, 'He's stupid, that boy. Not too much between his big ears. His parents think he's some kind of Greek god, but he's thick as a lamp post. Sandwich short of a sauce bottle, isn't that what they say? And don't you ever let me catch him sniffing around you, Bones.'

Joseph probably wouldn't have wanted him at his funeral. But he was Rick's friend and, in the old days, maybe his only friend. Having him at the wake had been like having a bit of living family history there – a sort of endorsement to those years. Thick as he might have been, he'd been there when Rick was young, when they all were young: the fat Greek kid who lived over the back fence. For some reason, their father's wake had seemed like it was Rick's show – he seemed to take centre stage.

'Hey, Rick, he sure could be an old bastard – your old man – sometimes, that's for sure,' Spyros had said loudly, in that almost-yelling way he had of speaking and laughing at the same time.

'Mate, we never gave your old man any cheek, Rick. No fuckin' way.'

Camille was handing around smoked salmon crackers and Camembert cheese. 'Oh, come on now, Spyros. Our dad was all puff and wind. You know that. He was always beautiful to us girls,' she'd said. 'Here, have another canapé.' Camille passed him the silver platter.

He took two and stuffed them into his mouth at once.

'Canapé'? Rosa thought that there had once a time when Camille would have said, 'Have a cheese bickie.' Had she taken elocution lessons?

Rick was drinking from a bottle of ouzo that Spyros had brought along. Rosa remembered that Rick's face had been flushed, even though she couldn't recall his features. He had been talking and laughing in a manner that for him, Rick, was strange. Loud, excited, wound-up. A mad kind of grief. Someone, most probably Camille, had turned the music up loud and Rick and Spyros had started dancing to Greek music. Rick had always liked pretending he was Greek. Spyros and Rick had had their arms around each other, dancing and laughing, tossing their jackets high in the air and passing the ouzo bottle one to the other. Delphine tired of 'the game' and went to join Camille in the kitchen. Rosa remembered that she had drunk at least one bottle of champagne herself, but it didn't seem to have any effect on her. Perhaps champagne is best kept for celebrations.

Camille had now turned on the festive lights, and the backyard looked like it was decked out more for a party than a wake. Most of the guests had left; maybe they could see what was coming. The music got louder and faster and Rick and Spyros danced and laughed until they fell down together on the grass, wiping the tears of laughter from their faces.

'Hey. Rick,' said Spyros, 'remember the night your old man belted you nearly fuckin' senseless? You know, when you crashed his car. You was about sixteen. Remember…remember that? Mate, I thought that he was going to fuckin' kill you.' Spyros punched Rick in the shoulder laughing. 'Mate, Jesus, how could you ever forget? My mum nearly called the cops. We watched it over the fence. You had a massive back eye, remember? Reckon he could of broke your nose, too. You looked like a twisted sandshoe for weeks. Bloody oath, you looked funny, mate. Remember that?' Spyros laughed.

Rick covered his face with his hands and sank to his knees. He let out a low moan and then a deep rasping sound like a branch snapping from a tree.

Rosa recalled that Rick never drank coffee, or at least he never had when they lived at home. Years in the army might have changed that, though. She wondered if he'd notice the grey regrowth she hadn't had time to touch up, or the extra kilos that had crept on around her middle. She tried to remember what he looked like. Would she recognise him? She took out her notebook and tried to write a few more lines, but she couldn't concentrate. She glanced at her watch, regretting that she had arrived so early. Too many thoughts of the past, some of which they shared; a past which included two sisters who idolised him and despised her. Rosa always suspected that he saw himself as her elder brother rather than her younger one, that he saw himself as the head of the family now their father had died – the eldest sibling, even though he wasn't.

Rosa looked again at the oversized clock on the glossy, white wall of the coffee shop. The morning-tea crowd from the government office opposite waited patiently in line at the counter.

The waitress stopped at Rosa's side. 'Are you ready to order?'

She looked again at the clock and realised that she had been sitting there for at least thirty minutes or more. She was just about to tell the waitress that she was still waiting, when the door swung open. For a moment, she thought it was her father.

'My brother is here now,' Rosa said, stood up and walked towards him.

They embraced with the strange uncertain embrace of people who knew each other intimately once. He had lost all his hair and any boyish trace of him was gone, completely gone. The young waitress stood dutifully by the table. Rick ordered a pot of tea for two and a pot of hot water. Rosa only ever drank coffee.

Rick poured the tea for Rosa and hot water for himself. His hands were muscular and his nails were clean. He took his mobile phone out of his pocket and placed it on the table, adjusting it so that it was exactly parallel to the edge. Alongside the phone he set a silver key ring with just two keys on it. Rosa caught a whiff of expensive cologne and she noticed he wore a heavy, silver chain around his neck. The back of his shirt collar was up around his neck. Rosa wasn't sure if it was part of his look or not, so she didn't say anything. Better to let sleeping dogs…

'How long has it been, Rick?'

Rosa looked at him across the table, searching his face for something of the boy who used to hide in cupboards and jump out at her, who would put a rotten peach on her chair. His skin was tight now, tanned and clear, but his forehead was deeply lined. He looked both old and young. She thought his eyes had changed. Not the soft, flecked, hazel eyes that she remembered. Now they had a hard, ruthless expression, but maybe it was just alertness. The whites of his eyes were so white, not a hint of red. Maybe that was what made them look hard.

'Been a while, darl.'

'Are you in town for long?' Rosa patted her hair and smoothed the sides of her skirt.

'Only as long as I need to be. Maybe a couple more days. Just got a few loose ends to tie up about a house I used to own here. Don't really want to hang around any longer than I have to.'

'So, why did you call me? I mean…after all these years…'

'Why not? You're my sister, aren't you? And I haven't seen you for years. The girls said that you are writing a book.'

So word travels, even in cities, Rosa thought. Someone must have told Camille and Delphine that she was a writer now.

'So you've caught up with them, then, our sisters?'

'Yeah, no, I have. I'm staying at Camille's house while I'm in town. What's your book about, Rosa?'

'It's a play, actually. It's about…now, that's a question…what's it about? It's about home…I guess…about what home means to people.'

'Our home?'

'No. Not really. Kind of, I suppose. Has Camille been talking to you about my play?'

'Just interested, Rosa, that's all. We're just interested,' Rick adjusted his wallet and keys. He drank the last of his hot water, turned the cup upside down in the saucer and pushed it to the centre of the table.

'Do you like the army?'

'Pays the bills, darl. Sure as hell pays the bills.'

There was more to this meeting than just a friendly chat, Rosa knew that. She knew the way her family operated. But she couldn't help feeling an echo of the affection she had felt for him, her younger brother, when they lived at home.

'You know, Rick, I reckon Dad would have really missed you when you left.'

'Yeah. He would've missed having someone to knock around.'

'Was it that bad?' Rosa knew that it was.

'I left, didn't I? And I didn't come back. Anyway, you left before I did?' He readjusted his phone and keys as he spoke. He kept reaching to his side pocket as if to check that something was there.

Rosa had heard that some soldiers suffer great anxiety when they are separated from their weapons.

'Ever think about the old place, Rick?' Rosa leaned forward, resting her chin on her hands.

'You mean the old dump. Nah, not ever, really. Too much else to think about. And now Mum and Dad are both gone, well…' Rick's gaze was intense. His eyes seemed to be set on a point somewhere in the middle of her forehead.

'There's two kinds of home, I reckon,' said Rosa. 'The one you live in and the one that lives inside you.'

'How do you figure that?' Rick beckoned the waitress.

She took the cups and teapot away.

'I just figure it, that's all. I've been thinking about it a lot…because of the play, I guess. I just reckon you can leave an unhappy home but most of it goes with you.'

'Oh, come on, Rosa. The past is the past. People can change things.'

'No. We just know those things again, in another place.'

Rick laughed a hard sort of laugh. 'Rosa, you make me smile. You have always been such a philosopher. So how's that book of yours coming along? Are you going to publish it?'

'You mean my play. Well, you know how the rest of the family feel about my writing and my plays.'

'Are you writing about them? Are you writing about the old man?'

'Of course I'm not…but of course I am. You have to be a writer to understand about that.' Rosa immediately regretted what she'd said.

'So you don't reckon an army sergeant thinks about stuff like that?'

'I don't know, Rick. Do you?'

The waitress set down clean cups and fresh tea and hot water in front of them.

He laughed again. More loudly this time. 'I think about lots of things, Rosa. Maybe I just don't talk about them like you do. You always were the brains of the family. Maybe I've just had to get on with it. Maybe I haven't had the time to pontificate and philosophise about stuff like you have. Maybe I've seen too much action to think about things too much. All I know is, I want to tell my own story and so does everyone else. We don't want it told for us.'

Rosa looked out the glass doors. Life was scurrying past in shopping bags, buses and briefcases. Brains, huh? Did her brains get her anywhere? Her so-called brains got her into a lot of trouble. Sometimes silence is the easiest path, she thought. She traced the figure eight with her fingertip in the spilt sugar.

'So Rick, you reckon you don't ever think about the old place?'

'No, Rosa, I don't. I just told you that. Worse still, I don't even remember much about home. I just was there for the time I had to be and I got out when I could. Never really think about it. All I need these days are my keys and my phone. And there's not much you can't buy.'

A silence fell between them.

'True story?' Rosa said.

'No, suppose not. Just don't want to remember all that shit. Guess I've just moved on big-time.'

The waitress slipped the account on the table.

Rick stood up, put his hands on the table and leaned towards her. Again she caught a whiff of his cologne, but this time it was tinged with the smell of fresh perspiration.

'Rosa, when you were a kid, you were always making things up – telling lies. It's time to cut out the lying. Oh, and I see you've got your fucking notebook with you. Are you going to use this as a scene in your play? Give it up, Rosa. Leave home. The past is the past, Rosa. Leave it there.'

Rosa felt the colour rise in her face. It was a blush, but not of embarrassment. 'Rick, I'm not trying to hurt anyone, I'm just trying to…'

'Just you remember what I said…'

'Oh, Rick…I don't think you understand about art.'

'Maybe not, but I understand about bullshit. I know what the truth is.'

'Well, truth is for philosophers, Rick. Lies are for poets, lovers and thieves.'

He tossed a twenty-dollar note on the table. A single autumn leaf blew in with the chilly breeze of his departure. Rosa picked up the leaf and put it inside her notebook, turned the page and began to write.

25 July 2004

Dear Rose,

I suppose it had to happen sometime. I would have liked to discuss it with Arnold but he has been so distant lately, as if he is drifting out somewhere. Seeing them again had such an impact on me that I haven't been able to speak it or write it until now. Must be over a month ago, now, that it happened. I think I will feel better about it if I put it down on paper.

It was such a sparkling morning, even though it was, and still is, winter. The sky was a clear and cloudless blue and the river shone like glass. I decided to leave Arnold for a bit and go for a walk around the botanic gardens. I walked past the convict stone wall and on to the Japanese gardens and then I stood for a while watching the ducks swimming between the pastel-coloured water lilies on the pond. How natural and right it all seemed for them to be swimming in their little family groups on this crystal morning. I walked across the red wooden bridge, thinking to find a park bench to sit on for a while.

And then there they were, just a couple of metres away from me: my two sisters, Bridie and Marie. They were sitting together on a picnic blanket drinking takeaway coffee. Funny that I should remember that small detail, the brown polystyrene cups. I froze. For a moment, I was unable to move as if I was watching myself from the branch of the Wollemi pine tree that I sat beneath. I'll never know if they recognised me or not, but when I looked back at them, they had quickly packed up their blanket and were walking away together towards the car park. I'll never know, will I?

It's been years since I have seen either of them, and even longer since they have spoken to me. I keep getting these opposing voices.

Arguing with myself. Imagining what Bridie and Marie would have said after they got up and left.

'What does she expect? There was no need to take such a dramatic stance. She could have smiled and waved. She didn't have to stand there, fixed in the moment,' Bridie would say in that huffy way of hers.

'Maybe she wanted to hold on to the experience. Maybe she doesn't want to let it go, the sense of exile, I mean,' Marie might say. 'As I remember, she always was the most sympathetic one of the two.'

'Oh, don't tell me – she needed it for her art? Iris, the tortured artist. Iris, the exiled one.'

Perhaps they might say those things, perhaps they might not. Perhaps they were not even there. But I can't deny that exile is a great vantage point for seeing many things.

When I returned home, I didn't mention it to Arnold. If I had, he would have said that I was making up stories. Again.

Iris

Family Circle

Writing now had become her compensation, her reason for being. Some might say it was a barren existence, but Rosa survived as she had always survived, living within herself, encased in her imaginings. But she never worked on Fridays. Fridays were for walking and thinking. Walking was a chance to get away from her desk, to unwind, to see things from a different point of view. Often, on her walks, something about a character would come to her. She would realise that she had taken the character in the wrong direction, or the plot needed a certain event or other.

This Friday was no different from any other and Rosa began her circular walk around the lake. She'd left Tom at home in front of the TV with the sound off, and she expected him still to be there when she returned.

The scent of pine was strong after the rain, and small birds darted amongst the pines. She set out down the track, the rhythm of her steps matching the unfolding of her thoughts. She stopped for a moment next to a waterfall to watch the clear fast-flowing water. A little duckling was struggling to get back up the waterfall. It must have been swept downstream in the rain and been separated from its family, Rosa thought. She watched as the duckling frantically tried to get back up the waterfall. Then, seemingly in some kind of desperate logic, it swam over to a small rock which had a tiny fall of water running down its side – a miniature waterfall. With ease, the duckling climbed up to the top and looked around. If only life was that easy, Rosa thought. Just choose the next easy option and claim success. But the duckling would eventually realise it was still on its own. Why didn't it just swim downstream, on the current, not try so hard to swim against the tide? It might do well on its own and there would be plenty of food for it after all this rain. Maybe it could join another group. But the urge to be with its own group, its own family, must have been a primal instinct.

Rosa continued walking and hoped that she hadn't been talking to herself out loud again.

Tom had been picking her up on it lately. 'Who are you talking to, Rosa?' he'd suddenly say when she wasn't aware she had said anything.

She wondered if he was playing games with her.

Rosa continued down the track, thinking about the bird. That little ducking would do anything to be with its family. Had it been exiled from the clan? Was it a misfit? Rosa knew she was a misfit. Her father, when he was alive, always called her sisters Princess. To him, it seemed that they, Delphine and Camille, needed no distinction. He seldom, if ever, called Rosa by name. He called her Bones. But why should it matter now? Her father was dead now and she would never be his princess, nor did she want to be.

Rosa sometimes wondered if she sought exile or if it sought her. Many times she had discussed this with her counsellor. Rosa had been seeing her for some time now, ever since she returned. She recalled their last conversation.

*

'Well, perhaps fiction and poetry make all things possible. Everything can be revised, rewritten on the page. Things don't have to stay as they are.'

'Rosa, do you think that we have a choice whether we can live our lives as fact or fiction?'

'Yes, I believe we have that choice. We choose our own reality.'

'Do you think writers believe that their writing makes them immortal, Rosa?'

'Like the gods, you mean?'

'Well, yes, a little. Perhaps what I am asking is about giving eternal life to an experience.'

'Yes, maybe, but all stories have their versions. Time changes everything.'

'How do you feel about the passing of time, Rosa?'

'Lost time, you mean?'

'No, Rosa. Just time that has gone.'

'Well, whatever we have seen, wherever we have been, whatever we have done is always with us, don't you think? Even though time passes, it is always with us. I think the tracks of our past follow us.'

The sessions always ended with the counsellor handing Rosa a barley sugar from a Wedgwood bowl.

*

Midpoint on her routine walk, Rosa always stopped at Nirvana for coffee. Sometimes, she would meet a writing friend there, but usually she was alone. These days, Rosa did most things alone. The café smelled of garlic and basil, and Pachelbel's Canon in D major played softly. She looked at the huge wholemeal and apricot muffins dusted with icing sugar and bursting out of their paper cases. She could smell the sweet doughy warmth of them and could almost taste the tart softness of the cooked apricot as she stood there, fooling herself that she might have one.

A woman with long dreadlocks brought her coffee to her. Rosa noticed the brown squareness of her hands, the smoothness and gloss of her skin, the silver rings which adorned her thick fingers and the bracelets that jangled on her wrists. Rosa mentally filed away the details of the image.

At her favourite table with a view over the water, she took a slow deliberate mouthful of the coffee and thought of the muffin she didn't have. She had begun denying herself again, because it gave her a sense of control when everything else seemed out her control.

Flipping through the pages of her notebook, she read over some of her work. Some of the scenes were proving difficult. In fact, the whole play was proving difficult. There's a sense of vindication in writing your pain and turning it into someone else's, even if only on the page, she thought. But she was struggling with this play. She imagined the review.

This play is missing something. The playwright has attempted a script which is somewhere between Cinderella *and* The Ugly Duckling. *It is clear that the heroine in the story is ostracised from the rest of the family. The frustrating part is that we never find out why. It just isn't clear. Unfortunately, the audience is left wondering and it just doesn't work. This play is unresolved, unfinished. A failure, in fact.*

The strong black coffee was hot at the back of her throat and she gazed across at the lake. One thing you can rely on is that people, in general, have limited imaginations, Rosa mused. Often, you have to spell it out for people.

She looked around the crowded café. Observation was second nature to her now: a snippet of a conversation, a flick of the head, a particular way of wearing a scarf, snatches and fragments of life, anything that could bring a character to life was hers for the taking.

Her eyes rested on an elderly couple in the corner. To Rosa, momentarily, they looked like twins. Perhaps they were. But sitting across from each other, they appeared too disconnected to be twins. Husband and wife, more likely, a man and a woman married for many years. The woman had a vacant gaze, no frown line, and a downturned mouth which, to Rosa, was more suggestive of sadness than of uninterest. And the man's head was bowed. He may just have been weary. Of his wife, or of life in general? Or perhaps he just didn't like the coffee.

At the table opposite the sad tired-looking couple, a young mother was giving a little boy the froth off the top of her cappuccino with a spoon. She held one hand under his chin while he licked the spoon. What a treat for him. It was probably the chocolate he liked best. Mother and son seemed so close and bonded. A single mother, most likely, Rosa thought.

In the corner, at the table under a large reproduction of Renoir's *Luncheon of the Boating Party*, two young people held hands across the table. Their coffee was untouched. Lovers for sure, Rosa thought. He could easily be a poet – he looks like the young Keats. And she looks like she would fit in a Pre-Raphaelite picture with her long flowing auburn hair and pale skin. An artist, for sure. Too far away to hear their hushed voices, Rosa imagined what the lovers were saying. She scribbled in her notebook. Their conversation would probably go something like this:

'I don't think I would ever make a nature writer. I mean…I appreciate the beauty of the natural world…somehow I find it boring to write about it. I mean, really, nature just is. Writers should leave it be,' said the young poet.

'But what about artists? Do you think that they shouldn't paint the landscape?' asked the artist.

'Well, I have always liked Matisse – I prefer decorative interiors, still life, reclining nudes…that kind of thing,' he replied.

'Don't you think reclining nudes are nature?'

'Of course, but you know what I mean…trees, mountains and things… this lovely lake. I don't really know the natural world. I'm just more of a human nature writer, I guess. And all my poems are set in interiors, always bound by the three walls of the stage.'

Or maybe they would just talk about what they watched on TV last night, with him not paying any real attention at all and wondering when they might have sex again. Perhaps he wasn't a poet at all, but an apprentice hairdresser and she might have worked in a fashion boutique or a supermarket even.

Rosa watched the young man put an apricot muffin to his mouth and bite on it, softly, leaving a trace of white icing sugar on is mouth. The Pre-Raphaelite girl leant across and wiped it with her serviette.

'Coffee okay?' the waitress asked.

Rosa nodded, smiled and gazed again across the glass-like lake. She wrote a few more lines in her notebook and returned to drinking her coffee. And then her hands holding coffee froze in front of her face. Could it really be them? The two of them, together? Graceful and contained, they glided like swans towards a table.

Rosa had rehearsed this scene in her head so often, because

somehow she had known that one day it would happen. She had often wondered what she would do at such a moment, what she would say, what she would feel. No amount of rehearsal could have prepared her for this scene, she knew that now. She felt the spotlight flood over her and for a second or two all around her was dark.

When Rosa was younger, old ladies at bus stops would say, 'Are these your younger sisters, dear? Not like them are you, dear?'

Boys at school would ask, 'How come you don't look like your sisters? What went wrong?'

It would be easy to say that the root of her problems with her sisters was her own jealousy, her own envy, her own vanity. Perhaps that was it. Maybe she should have confronted this aspect of herself and asked for their forgiveness. But was this what it was about? And she had caused so much worry for their parents. After all, it was she who had walked out on the family. Who could blame her sisters, really? She could walk over, try and talk to them. Had they seen her now?

The two women leant forward and spoke to each other, almost forehead to forehead.

Like a tableau, Rosa sat there still, unmoving. Had it been a scene from a stage play, the lights would have dimmed and the curtains would have closed. Rosa continued to stare at the table and felt rather than heard the shuffling of chairs, the tossing of coins on the table, the closing of the door. It all happened so quickly that Rosa wasn't even sure it had actually happened. Perhaps she had imagined it all.

The waitress walked past her table and said, 'You look a bit pale. Did you see a ghost?'

Eventually, she must have finished her coffee because her cup was empty when she left.

Rosa began walking around the lake again, barely aware of the sun burning her scalp when she stopped and stood again at the waterfall. Would she see the duckling joyfully reunited with its family? No. The duckling was gone: swept away on in the stream that was still running clear and fast, under the stone bridge, winding into the green forest.

20 August 2004

Dear Rose,

Sometimes, I imagine conversations. I don't know where they come from. Arguing with myself?

I went to see Sister Anne today. It is always such a relief to talk to her. She made me a cup of ginger tea and gave me a slice of cream sponge. But there are times with her when I wonder who is counselling who.

'What have you been writing about this week?' she asked me.

So I told her I was writing about women and captivity and a woman who stuck with a man, despite his philandering, his drinking, his not caring, his accident, his brain damage.

Sister Anne asked me why she did that. And that is a hard question to answer because it has so many aspects to it. So I replied that maybe it was because he was wounded.

Then she asked me, 'Does she think she can heal him, save him, change him?'

I told her, I didn't think that was the reason.

'Why doesn't she leave? She could, if she is still young,' Sister Anne kept on at me. Of course, she had no knowledge of marriage and of men.

I told her that she must remember the character had no home – she could never have gone back home to her parents' home. If she had, she would have been returning to jail.

'Marrying a man to escape an intolerable situation only to end up in a far worse situation, a different kind of captivity, is pretty standard literary fodder,' I said to her.

I was amazed how intrigued she seemed by the subject.

She didn't answer straight away. She thought for a while and then she said, 'Yes, dear, joining a convent is a little like that.'

I had never looked at it like that.

Iris

Spilt Salt

It was hard to know why she bothered, really. When she bought it, the black silk nightdress, Rosa thought how different it was to the pure virginal broderie anglaise number she had worn on her wedding night. She hadn't even thought about being sexy in those days. Just took it for granted. Now it had to be worked at, contrived: smoke and mirrors, an illusion of what the years had stolen.

When she tried the nightdress on in the soft light of the small friendly boutique, the salesgirl said, 'It looks lovely on you. So…you know…'

But now, in the hard lights of the hotel bathroom, in the unrelenting mirror, she saw an ageing woman with breasts that drooped and a pot belly that looked almost pregnant beneath the soft silky folds. The low cut of the garment revealed her chest, which had once been white and supple but was now red, wrinkled and spotted with pigmentation. She wished now that she'd bought the longer one because of the blue varicose vein that ran the length of her calf. Close up in the mirror, she noticed that her eyebrows looked straggly and grey, and tried to pull a few out with her tweezers. As she did so, she saw the shaving rash under her arms. She pressed some lip gloss across her lips and snapped the bathroom light off.

Earlier in the day, she and Tom had walked along the beach. His limp made it difficult to walk too far. As they walked, she drifted off into her own thoughts, watching her own feet in the sand, hearing only the sound of the waves and squeals of the seagulls overhead. Finally, they sat down next to each other on a rock. She stared out to sea.

She felt his arm reach around her, his lips on her cheek, his whispering in her ear, 'I love you, Rosa.'

Maybe she had just imagined it. Perhaps it had happened some time long ago, in another place, and not that afternoon on the beach, the day of their thirtieth wedding anniversary.

Now, as she lay in the bed next to him, he smelled sour. She couldn't quite remember how long it had been that she had been offended by the smell of him. She wondered if her smell bothered him. She'd read somewhere that when people love each other they liked each other's smell. Now she was repelled by his chipped fingernails embedded with oil from tinkering with his cars, and his cigarette-stained teeth. She hated the way his toenails sometimes scratched her when they lay together. Inwardly, she would scream when he didn't close the toilet door. The torrential sound would echo all the way down the hallway, particularly if he had been drinking beer. Funny how little irritations grow over time.

She lay still until she heard his breath get louder and finally felt the silence that comes with the sleep of another. Now, in her mind's eye, she looked down on herself and Tom together in the bed. Her lying in the dark in her new silk nightdress and him turned away from her. They were just going through the motions really, doing what they felt couples were supposed to do on their wedding anniversary. Or maybe Tom wasn't all that aware and it was Rosa who was going through the motions by herself. Tom had forgotten so much, so many things. And Tom didn't remember, she was sure, the pink teddy bear, the smell of the honeysuckle, the soft muffled cry. Tom had forgotten. They had never spoken of it. Not once since they moved to the city.

Rosa slept little that anniversary night in the queen-sized bed but he seemed to sleep well.

They had breakfast that morning in the hotel dining room in silence. He read the paper, or tried to at least. Glasses on the end of his nose, he shook the outstretched paper before he turned the pages. For a moment, he reminded her of a man who used to catch the bus every morning when she was on her way to school. In her mind, Rosa used to call him Ted. Ted would always be dressed in a crumpled pinstriped suit, an unironed shirt, and a loose grubby-looking tie. As he read each page, Ted would tear the middle and go on to the next until the entire newspaper was ripped. He must have gained some satisfaction from ripping the pages.

'Why don't you rip the pages, Tom?'

He didn't even look up. He often didn't hear what she said.

They seemed to be surrounded by honeymoon couples. It was almost as if they had been planted there by the fates as a kind of cautionary tale, drawing attention to the very fine line that exists between comedy and tragedy; love and contemptuous familiarity. How long was too long? she wondered. How long does a person stay in a relationship that isn't working before it becomes damaging to the soul; before two people become middle-aged caricatures of their former selves?

And the drive home from their weekend away was silent. Rosa doubted that Tom was ever troubled by silence. It was kind of essential for fishing, so for him not speaking was nothing more than habit.

Eventually he did speak. 'I've got another fishing trip coming up next week, Rosa,' he said.

'Oh,' she said, 'that will be nice for you, Tom. It will be a break for you from my constant chatter.'

He said nothing. It was as if he only heard the words he himself spoke and that he was incapable of hearing hers. Could it have been part of the brain damage?

Rosa thought about the lines of her most recent poem. She had struggled with this one at first, replacing words and rearranging the lines, but she felt it was close now.

Anniversary Letter

Another bottle of red is opened, crystal
glasses are refilled, but they both know
that it's a mistake, because only the rough stuff is left.
Their friends have all gone home now,
and they are left alone,
staring down at the tainted tablecloth,
no longer stiff starched and white.
Making patterns with fingertips in spilt salt,

leaning away from each other,
forcing smiles with grape-stained teeth,
like vampires sated.
The evening drifts towards dawn.
The ghost of good times hovers and they try to laugh
about a remembered something or other,
and the waiter, polishing cutlery, yawns loudly.
They always were the last to leave.

How would Tom would react if he read it? But little chance of that. He only ever read the sports pages. Never a book. Never asked her about her writing.

Not long ago, Rosa had been at a garage sale rummaging through the stack of self-help books, an old woman stood next to her, turned and said, 'Marriage is all about endurance, love. Don't give up. I did. And now I'm sorry.'

Perhaps the comment was something to do with the book Rosa was holding in her hand: *Love and Marriage*. But she couldn't help but wonder why the old lady had chosen her, a perfect stranger, as her confidante. Did she, Rosa, have the appearance of a long-suffering wife? Had it become engrained in the set of her lips, the expression of her mouth?

You leave your marriage when there is nothing left. Not when you are arguing. Where there is nothing left at all. When all is completely lost. Had she read this in a book somewhere or heard it in a film or a radio play, or just dreamt it? However she had come to know it, she knew it was true.

*

When Tom's next fishing trip came round, Rosa watched him pile his tackle in the back his ute. He would be gone for a month. Perhaps the trip might take Tom out of himself, Rosa hoped. His old mate, Bazza, had come down from the station. Rosa had heard that doctors had treated a serious melanoma on his face just shortly after Tom's accident.

While they were packing the ute, Bazza kept his head on an angle to hide his disfigurement. But she saw the full horror of it when he looked up at her and said, 'Don't worry, I'll look after him.'

She tried to hide her shock at the sight of the red scar that travelled from his temple down his face in into his neck. 'Thank you…thank you, Bazza, have a good time…'

He had been such a handsome man once, but now… She handed Tom his peanut butter sandwiches and thermos of coffee.

He brushed her cheek with his dry lips out of habit. 'See you in three weeks,' he said, waving without looking at her.

'Four…four weeks…' she said.

She knew that he would come back, that he would always come back, that he would never leave. She, Rosa, would have to be the one to go.

Packing was easier than she thought. She had heard of people who have good friends who come over and help them leave their husbands, but Rosa packed alone. In many ways, she had been packing for a long time.

The wedding pictures were in an album that hadn't been opened for so long that the pages had stuck together. She remembered her bouquet – pink rosebuds, daisies, and three small lilies. She remembered the hairdresser, Lillian, teasing and spraying her unruly locks into submission. How warm the outback sun had been that day. And she had worn white. She stared down at the photograph and remembered the white lace train that had dragged in the red dust. It was strange. She had expected her bridesmaid, Gypsy, to hold her train for her. She didn't.

Rosa had been packing for ten days now and she was almost finished the morning she decided to ring the removalist. The boxes were stacked in the lounge room, waiting for her. It was now only a matter of making the phone call and packing her clothes into suitcases. She had been on the brink of signing a lease on a town house for rent. When she inspected it, it was sparkling white and clean. Sterile. No cobwebs. No Tom.

'I'd like to arrange for a removalist to come, please.'

She looked at the corkboard hanging in the kitchen with all her appointments and 'things to do'. Pick up Tom's dry-cleaning. Collect Tom's script from the chemist. Order the Christmas ham. All the little details that added up to her life, gave her purpose. She wouldn't even need a trolley in the supermarket any more. One of those plastic carry baskets would do the job. The trolley was part of her role: to buy the food, to plan the meals, to create a home for two. This would be no more. Was she robbing herself of something? Not love. No, that was gone; but a type of life that you can't have alone?

'When would you like the goods to be picked up?'

She heard the dog barking next door, signalling that the postman had come.

'When…?'

'Yes, when would you like the goods picked up?'

Perhaps it was too soon. Perhaps she just needed to sort out a few more things. Maybe there were still the food cupboards to sort through.

'Look…maybe…I'm not sure…sorry…I'll ring back tomorrow,' said Rosa and put the phone down.

She didn't call back the next day, or the day after that. She went shopping at the supermarket and filled her trolley. When she got home, it took her half an hour to unpack the bags. She felt her sense of purpose returning. She got caught up in writing her plays and poetry. The last poem she had written needed more work. She'd changed her mind about it. It wasn't quite there. It was missing something.

The night before Tom was due to return, she lay awake. Her thoughts overtook her desire for sleep. She imagined how she would write the scene. A middle-aged woman lies in bed thinking about her failed marriage. The monologue would be interesting:

I have stayed with him with him for a long time, stuck with him, despite everything he did. Why did I do that? Was it because he was wounded and I thought that I could heal him? Change him? What a fool's errand that is, to think you can ever change anyone. At least I have learned that lesson.

Well, Rosa was doing what she always did, changing everything into fiction. At least she hadn't lost that. But she had lost her wedding ring and she had never replaced it. Her ring that had long since slipped away down a loose floorboard, or had wedged into a dusty skirting board; or was tossed out with the potato peelings on a night when she was rushing to make tea; or was swallowed by a vacuum cleaner in a strange motel room somewhere on a long-forgotten holiday.

Sleep just wouldn't come, so she got up and went to her bookcase and pulled out one of her favourite comfort books, *Leaves of Grass*, flicking the pages, stopping and reading bits here and there.

She reached for her notebook. She could make it work out for her and Tom. Make everything right. Fiction and poetry make all things possible. She would write as she wished it would be.

*

Act Three, Scene 3

ROSA is putting the last of her clothes in a suitcase when TOM walks in to the bedroom after returning early from a fishing trip.

TOM: I've just seen a removalist van pull out of our driveway, Rosa. What's going on?

ROSA: I'm leaving you, Tom. I can't stand it any longer.

Tom sinks slowly down onto the bed. He sits with his head bowed, covering his face with his hand. Silence.

ROSA: Look, I'm sorry… I should have given you more warning but it's over Tom, you must know that.

Tom sits with his head in his hands. Silence.

ROSA: You won't starve, if that's what you're worried about. I've left lots of meals in the freezer.

Tom remains motionless with his head in his hands. Silence.

ROSA: (*Stands next to Tom and reaches out to touch his shoulder.*) Tom, are you okay? (*The lights dim and the set fades to black. The spotlight remains on TOM seated and ROSA standing, her hand on TOM's shoulder.*) Are you okay, Tom?

*Tom takes his hands from his face reaches into his breast pocket and pulls
out a small silver ring. He takes ROSA's hand from his shoulder and slips
the ring on her finger.*
ROSA: (*Gasps loudly.*) Tom… (*Gasps again.*) My wedding ring… I
thought it was lost…
*Silence. ROSA and TOM maintain their freeze position. Silence. Spotlight
dims slowly to black. Curtain.*

*

Rosa heard the ute pull up in the driveway. She heard the men's voices,
the low rumble, the crunching steps in the loose stones, the thud of
boots flung on the back porch.

'See you, mate. I'll drop the fish around tomorrow,' called Bazza.

Rosa walked out to the back porch where Tom was unpacking his
tackle. 'Hello, Tom. How was your trip?'

Her husband looked up for a second, but didn't reply and walked
back into the house.

20 November 2004

Dear Rose,

I wonder if I have, to some degree, relished the role of the tortured artist. It was almost as if that was the role I chose for myself, as if I wanted to be misunderstood by my family, to set myself apart, to give myself the part of the tragic heroine.

Oh well, at least it is spring again. The roses are blooming and the bumblebees seem to be doing their work. The jasmine is more prolific than ever.

Even Arnold seems to have perked up a little bit. He sat out in the sun with me this morning for a little while.

I said to him that sometimes I feel like a piece of torn-off paper, ragged at the edges and incomplete.

'You've lost me there, Iris,' he said.

Iris

Things Don't Always Go As Expected

It was Tom who left in the end.

The next fishing trip came around sooner than she had expected. Once again, Tom packed up his white ute with his tackle and Bazza had come down again from the north to go with him. How long was he going to be gone for, Rosa wanted to know. Tom wasn't sure. Maybe a bit longer than last time. And Tom didn't want her to make any peanut butter sandwiches. They made him feel sick.

Well, she hadn't anticipated this time alone again so soon, but she had plenty to work on. A theatre company in the city were reading her script and she had ideas she wanted to develop for the next one. Anyway, she had been alone so many times before.

It had been close to dinner time when Bazza knocked on the door ten days after they had left for the fishing trip.

'Bazza,' Rosa said, 'I hadn't expected to see you. Where is Tom? Isn't he with you?' Rosa held the door open and looked across the lawn at Bazza's parked car, expecting to see Tom sitting in there.

'Can I come in for a minute?' Bazza asked. He walked through the open doorway, down the hallway and stood in front of the log fire that Rosa had just lit.

'Nice fire… Tom asked me to come and tell you something.' He turned the disfigured side of his face away from her and straightened the collar of his shirt.

'Tell me what? Where is he?'

'He…he…just wanted me to let you know…to let you…know that he won't be coming back.' He looked straight at her now.

'Won't be coming back?' Rosa gasped, momentarily surprised at her own reaction. 'What do you mean he won't be back?'

'That's what I mean. He won't be back. He asked me to come and tell you. Rosa, he hates it here, he wants to be free. He's coming back up north. Don't worry about his stuff. He said he'll arrange for it to be sent up and you can keep the house. He's got plenty of money and Doug's still alive. Don't worry about him, Rosa. He'll be okay. Sorry to be the bearing of bad tidings.'

'But why? Why now? There must be a reason.' The shock of abandonment came like a punch from behind.

Bazza no longer tried to hide his scars. She searched Bazza's face for a glimmer of a smile, thinking for a second that it might be a joke.

'He just said…you and him…just can't do it together any more. Just can't make a go of it together. Simple as that. Sorry I have to be the one to tell you. But he just couldn't face you…sorry.'

Rosa sank into the chair next to the fire. 'So that's it then.'

'I guess so. Like I said, don't worry about his stuff…he'll take care of it.'

She stared up at his mutilated face. The plastic surgeons must have done the best they could, but the lower part of one side of his face was missing and Rosa was sure that one of his eyes was glass.

As if he read her mind, he said, 'Sorry. I know I'm hard to look at.'

'Oh, no. That's not it… I'm just so stunned that he couldn't tell me himself.' Rosa walked over to the drinks cabinet, took out a glass and began mixing a gin and tonic. She didn't measure the gin.

'You're not that old, Rosa. You can't be any more than fifty or so. You can still start again. It's not your fault. And Tom's nearly sixty. You wouldn't want to go on living the rest of your life with a ghost, surely?'

Rosa watched him walk down the hallway and fade slowly away. She sat down in front of the fire, wondering how she could have not seen Tom's departure coming. She had always thought the decision was hers to make. A smell of burning and the shrill sound of the smoke alarm shook her from her thoughts. The chicken soup she had been warming was ruined, but she had lost her appetite, completely. She snatched it off the stove and put it outside the back door. Sitting down again by the log fire, she watched it till it went out. Sleep was the only thing that might help. She made her way to the bedroom and lay in the dark chilly room. And the dream came.

*

The door of the room opens just as it always had done. The curtains float in the scented breeze that drifts through the open window. A pink mosquito net drapes over the empty cradle. The tinkling sound of a baby's rattle breaks the silence, then that same muffled cry, then nothing.

*

When she woke the next morning, she knew she was alone now. Tom had gone for good.

'Surely, he hasn't met someone else,' Rosa said out loud, her thoughts racing. 'Surely not?' But it wasn't unheard of for men to return to someone from their past. Perhaps that was what had happened. But who? Rosa tried to think who might possibly be interested in Tom.

She recalled a real estate salesman had once told her that if you had a liking for a house, there was someone else out there who would too. There is always someone who might want what you have, especially if you don't want it any more, he'd said. She had always thought that if he did find someone else to take her place, she would feel relieved. But she realised now that that no amount of writing fiction in which emotions are imagined or projected will prepare you for how you will really feel when something actually happens outside the pages of a book.

Rosa thought about a conversation she had heard somewhere in the distant past.

'Well, be careful what you write about. Writing can be a bit like wishing, you know. It just might happen.'

'Yes, be careful what you write about. Writing can be a bit like dreaming, you know. It can be frightening.'

214

The days drifted by and Rosa kept on writing her play. Writing was the only thing that kept her from being overtaken by the panic of loneliness. She stopped lighting the fire at night-time and when she had finished writing for the day, she would lie on the bed in the dark silence.

It had been a long time since she had thought about Archie. A long time. Even longer since she had dreamed about him. But lying in the cold, she was thinking about him now. She imagined herself back in the hostel, in the room that she shared with a girl with hair dyed blonde so harshly it looked like fairy floss. A soft knock on the door and her heart would have turned over. She would have sensed him before she saw him. And she could feel his presence, his love, enveloping her now.

5 March 2005

Dear Rose,

Since I have been taking the new tablets, my dreams have become much more vivid. I must try to write them down more. I used to share a room with a girl when I lived in a hostel years ago and every night she would wake up in the night crying. Loudly. I had to ask to change rooms in the end. All I cared about then was getting a decent night's sleep. But now I wonder why she dreamed like that, what could have happened to her? Why did she suffer so? I will never know now.

Sometimes I think writing fiction is like being party to a waking dream. I'm not sure what Sister Anne would think of that. But I feel I must find a way to give my characters peace.

I don't go to the writer's group any more. I felt like an imposter there, somehow. One of them, I think they call him Ernest, said there was probably only a limited market for my work in its present form. He said I need to ask myself who my readers are and redraft, and rewrite particularly for that audience. Not sure about that strategy. I mean, did Van Gogh ever ask himself who his viewers were? Not that I am any Van Gogh, but I think that a work has to be true to itself. In the end, they stopped asking me to go, which was a kind of relief.

Arnold isn't getting any better. He doesn't even work in the garden any more. He still wanders off sometimes. The doctor came today and gave him an injection. He said I will have to find somewhere for him soon. I think I will miss him, especially on windy nights. How I hate the wind.

Iris

Dancing In the Moonlight

Rosa stepped out of the taxi and her stiletto heel caught on the edge of the car. She steadied herself and walked carefully to her front door. Cigarette smoke, the perfume, the alcohol breath – she brought her opening night home with her. She had sat close to the front in the theatre. It was a small theatre, so it didn't seem to matter that it was only half full – well, at least a third anyway. The lighting had been perfect, but the acting had not been as she had expected. To her, the characters seemed like fakes, like imitations of the ones in the script she had written. But the theatre company seemed pleased at the end of the show. The director, Neville, was glowing. The local newspaper had been there and she and Neville had given a brief interview. *The Glass Slipper* – two years of work for fifteen minutes of fame, Rosa thought.

She searched in her bag for her keys. The house was empty of course, in darkness except for the porch light. Who did she expect to be there, waiting with flowers and champagne? Not Tom. Not any of her family. No one. Rosa managed to open the door. She would celebrate, though; she had to celebrate her success, even if she was alone. It was the end of winter, August, and for some reason it was warm, balmy almost. Perhaps that was because it had been raining heavily the day before.

She took a bottle of champagne from the fridge and chose her favourite crystal glass from the cupboard. The glass had once been part of a set. The others had long since disappeared or been broken. One faithful glass remained. Solo.

She made her way to the back porch and lit three perfumed candles – sandalwood – and popped the cork. The champagne tasted good, the bubbles spilled over the crystal glass. She looked up at the indigo sky.

The stars were bright, but it was the moon that drew her. The waxing crescent. An August moon. A Scott Fitzgerald moon. But Rosa felt that it was hers, her own, its soft beams raining directly on her. Dancing a slow, solitary dance on the balcony under the natural spotlight, she almost wished she was naked. Under the moonlight, she raised the crystal glass to her lips and took another sip.

She took off her stilettos and began to move slowly, singing softly to herself the lines of 'I'll Be Your Lover Now'. She drank again from her crystal glass. As she danced, she felt the moonbeams anointing her, blessing her with a gossamer glow. The shape of the dark cypress tree, haloed in the light of the moon, seemed to sway with her. The shape of a bat hung from one of the branches. Before he left, Tom had threatened so often to chop the cypress down, but it was safe from him now. She tried to remember when she had last danced under the moonlight. Perhaps she never had.

*

It seemed like she had been dancing for hours when she finally said goodnight to the moon and came inside. She caught sight of herself in her dressing table mirror. Smudged mascara, laddered black stockings, hair falling from her silver clip. Of course, none of her family had been there for her opening night. It seemed silly even to think they might have been. Her family had been absent for most of her life, if she really thought about it. After that conversation with Rick, she thought that at least one of them might have shown up, if only out of curiosity. Listening to Rick it sounded like they were all convinced that she had been writing about them, about the family. Yes, the play was dark in parts. But what family doesn't have its dark secrets? Or myths? She could hear Rick saying that nobody had authority to turn fantasy into fact. Why not? 'That's what art is all about' would have been her response him.

*

She threw off her dress, tossed her jewellery on the bedside cabinet and crawled under the blankets. Sleep for Rosa did not always come easily. Tonight, sleep came like death, hard and heavy. But somewhere deep in the night Rosa heard a familiar cry. Loud and demanding. Shrill. Piercing. Rosa watched herself rolling around in the bed, covering her ears with her hands. The cry went on and on until eventually it tailed off to a muffled sob. Rosa felt a soft breath close to her face, fine downy hair in the crook of her neck, smelled the sweet smell of milk. She woke and her arm reached out across the bed, searching.

Once, Rosa had told her counsellor that sometimes she dreamt she was dreaming.

'Dreams within dreams are not uncommon in creative types. Dreaming you are dreaming is a little like writing about writing, don't you think?' her counsellor had said.

Rosa wasn't sure if that was the case. 'Maybe that might be so. Shakespeare made much of sleep. His plays abound with sleep scenes and the torments of insomnia, and dreams.'

'Why do you think you find dreams so fascinating, Rosa?'

She couldn't answer that. Sleep itself fascinated her. Perhaps it was because she sometimes had vivid dreams that stayed with her for days and even years.

But she didn't sleepwalk. Tom had never mentioned it if she did.

The bed was cold and she had woken too early. She wasn't ready for the day to begin yet.

7 June 2005

Dear Rose,

Autumn went by so quickly. Can it get much colder? I don't remember this house being so cold when I lived here, when I was a kid. But maybe it was.

The roses aren't looking too good, but then we've had so little rain. I passed Imelda in the street today and she ignored me. It has been the coldest winter I can remember. Too cold even to write. The shed is leaking and the wood is wet. I won't be able to light the fire for days. Today, a magpie hit the window and cracked the glass. I picked the last rose today. I put it in a jar next to my bed.

The police brought Arnold home again today. He is beginning to be like an old dog who wanders off and gets lost.

Iris

Flowers

Two months had gone by since the play had finished and, three days ago, Rosa celebrated her fiftieth birthday. Alone. And she had started smoking again. The cat had run away, but not because of the smoke. She had only forgotten to feed it a few times, but now it been gone for days. Rain had set in. Perhaps Fluffy would come back when the weather improved. The white Persian tomcat had gone walkabout before and eventually it always returned, its coat muddied and knotted and its ears torn and battle-scarred. She never knew where it went.

Apart from raindrops making a hard repetitive sound in the bucket in a corner of the kitchen, the house was silent. Since the opening night, her phone had scarcely rung.

The director of the play, Neville, had called to let her know only seven people attended the last session and most of those were volunteers and students. But, he told her, he wasn't worried. His career as a director was progressing well, but he had decided to be more selective about the plays he directed in future. 'The reviews have been scathing at best, defamatory at worst, darling,' he'd said but he told her he was comforted that most of the criticism was directed at the script. He'd give her a call sometime when he returned from Sydney, but he was going to be gone for a while.

Rosa Bigmann should stick to writing greeting cards if she is going to present this sordid sentimental tripe, attempting to masquerade as dark drama, to the general public…or she could try writing a book about bumblebees. *The Glass Slipper* should never be seen on stage again.

Other writers she had known had been overwhelmed by bad

reviews, but she never thought she would be. Since the play had closed, her world had become quiet. Tom was no longer there to punctuate her days with his needs. Even during the day, a cold draught blew in under the doors. Too weary to light the fire, she stayed in bed most of the day. It was cheaper anyway, saved the wood. Sometimes sleeping, sometimes not, sometimes dreaming, sometimes not. Rosa was discovering that living alone can be a risky business; days can morph into weeks; and if you go for days without speaking to anyone, you can begin to doubt your own existence.

The shrill ring of doorbell jolted her out of her daze.

'Who could this be?' she said, aloud. Tying the sash on her silk robe she padded barefoot to the door. 'Flowers…irises…could these be from Tom? Why now? The play finished weeks ago,' Rosa spoke aloud to herself, again.

'Thanks,' she said to the faceless delivery person, taking the flowers. They were surprisingly heavy. Once they are cut, flowers are dead. Dead things always weigh heavy until they decay.

'Sign here, please.'

Her florist's eye took note of the arrangement. Roses. Red and pink. Nice tall stems, surrounded by greenery. But the baby's-breath, gypsophila, was out of place. It offended her artistic sense of balance – it just didn't sit right in the arrangement. Must have been a mistake to include it. She opened the envelope and took out the card. She stood statue-like. Her mouth went dry. It wasn't the original newspaper cutting, it was a copy. She had almost forgotten. No, not forgotten. When she looked into the bassinet all those years ago, there had been a pink blanket. That was all. Just a pink blanket. No baby crying and crying who wouldn't be still, who wouldn't be silent, who couldn't be silent. Just a soft pink blanket, edged with satin ribbon; only a soft blanket which, when she picked it up and held it to her face, smelled of baby powder, milk and her own perfume. She read the photocopy of a newspaper clipping attached to the card. Her hands trembled.

Alice Bigmann
Blessed little one
A short but innocent life
RIP

Rosa wrapped her silk gown close to her and got back into bed. She closed her eyes.

When she opened her eyes, both hands of the clock were on twelve. She didn't know if was midday or midnight.

Rosa fumbled for the light on the bedside table. How many hours had she lain there, sometimes sleeping, sometimes not, sometimes dreaming, sometimes not? She noticed her Hollywood stilettos in the corner of the lounge room looking like they had been kicked off by someone without a care. The shoes looked like they belonged to someone else. Rosa felt her stomach rumble. When had she eaten last? But she didn't feel like eating. Again, she didn't bother to light the fire. She sat down in the lounge room, cool moonlight shining through the window. She felt the sick silence descend on her.

It was gone now, this scene, this dream. Only the roses remained. Killed by the knife that cut them. Fresh flowers are always dead on arrival. She found a tall vase and filled it with cold water from the tap and placed the vase on the dining table, dead centre. She thought there had been baby's-breath. Perhaps she imagined it. What had happened to the newspaper cutting and the card? She must have put it in a safe place. Ah, there it was hiding amongst the irises. It read, 'To Nadine, Congratulations on graduating as a fully-fledged nurse. You will be amazing. Fondest love, Nana.' The delivery boy must have got things mixed up. Come to think of it, the young girl next door was called Nadine.

She looked around her. Her crystals hung from the window architrave. She bought a new one each year. Her books were stacked in odd piles all around the room, grouped in no particular way. Suddenly the ordinariness of her existence seemed almost utopian. The softness of her couch, the pattern on her Indian rug, the fly-specked mirror over her fireplace. Nothing moved unless she moved it. Nothing changed unless she changed it. These small ordinary things cocooned her with familiarity and predictability. And all this, this existence, this life, her life, to be threatened by flowers.

*

JACK: She went ahead with the play.
PRINCESS: Surely not, after all we said.
JACK: Well, she has. The review is in paper this morning. I read it first thing. It's playing for the rest of the week.
PRINCESS: And dragging our family's name through the mud with it. I'm going to send her some flowers.
JACK: I guess we have always known that Rosa is slightly unhinged.
KABANOSY'S GHOST: Slightly? You must be joking. She's crazy, that one. Always has been. Very dark that girl. A girl with a dark psychology.
PRINCESS: Poor Tom.
JACK: He doesn't know what she did either.
MOTHER'S GHOST: I think he forgot most things after the accident.
PRINCESS: I think Rosa has forgotten. Let's send her some flowers.

*

Days went by without her even opening the curtains or going to the letter box. The milk in the fridge had gone sour and she had used the last of the dry wood. She tried to think what day it was. It didn't matter. It felt like Sunday. How heavy and slow she felt. When had she showered last?

At some point, there had been a knock on the door, quite a persistent knock. She lay under the blankets not moving until it was quiet again. She heard familiar voices trailing off.

'She must have gone away. The letter box hasn't been cleared. Let's try again in a few days.'

The old wooden gate snapped shut.

224

The previous day seemed like a year ago. She looked at the clock. Six o'clock. That would have been tea time once for her and Tom. But Tom was long gone. Alice used to cry at teatime. Cry and cry. She hadn't written anything in nearly two months. Perhaps she'd never write anything again. If she could have raised the energy, she might have finished editing the next play that she was working on. It had been lying untouched for weeks in a cardboard box under her bed. Why bother? It would never be performed. It could never be performed. It was a shadow play and shadows need light to be seen. Light was fading fast.

2 July 2005

Dear Rose,

They took Arnold away today.

Iris

It Was All Quite Simple

Rosa sat shivering on the edge of her rumpled bed. She rested her feet on the bare boards that were scratched and knotted. Not even a hint of carpet. No, there never was any carpet. Nests of fluff and lint lay softly in the corners of the cold room, hinting at what had gone before. Her life was leaving its own dust: fragments of conversation, bits of expectation, traces of fear and dread, relics of dreams, and tears uncried.

The red and white petrol can was out in the shed. That would help her get the fire started. She floated out in the soft misty rain to the shed in her broderie anglaise nightdress that hung in folds from underneath her breasts and she reached up to the cobwebbed shelf and took down the can. Padding back softly back across the damp lawn, she carried the petrol back inside the house and walked down the passage into her bedroom. A match or two was all she needed, once she had tipped the petrol over the bedclothes. She walked over to the wardrobe and pulled out her faded pink chenille dressing gown and slipped her arms through the loose sleeves. After she had splashed the last of the petrol in the wardrobe, another match was all it took to get the fire roaring.

On the way to the bathroom, she pulled the smoke alarm off the kitchen wall and threw it out into the garden through the French doors. All she needed now was a nice warm bath. Water poured from the taps, and she sprinkled sandalwood oil into the rapidly filling bath.

Rosa turned off the taps just in time – it had begun to overflow. No need to undress. She slipped into the bath, feeling the warmth of the water on her skin and slid further down the porcelain tub and let her long hair hang in the water. The blow-dryer was already plugged in. She closed her eyes and she could see him: white shirt, cuffs rolled up, Akubra hat, straight back, riding proud and tall in a cloud of red dust. Rosa reached over and turned on the hairdryer. She began drying her hair and let it fall.

14 April 2006

Dear Rose,

A sad day. And it is windy again. Went to the Stations of the Cross at St Margaret's earlier. The priest said he thought that Good Friday might be a lonely day for many people. I think he's right.

I felt lonely when I stood in line at the fish shop and asked for one piece of flake.

'Just one?' the silly little shop assistant said, as if to rub it in.

'Just one,' I replied.

When Arnold was here, we would have a bowl of fresh prawns together on the porch on Good Friday. The last time we did that, I think I drank way too much. Might have called him some names. I think he forgave me, because he never spoke of it the following day.

He just said, 'Time we deadheaded some of those roses, Iris.'

I miss Arnold. Never thought I would say that. The roses are going to seed now.

He hardly ever spoke in the last few months, but now the house is so quiet without him. How strange it is to be, finally, all alone. I hope they feed him properly. I couldn't even write today. The day they took Arnold, I stood on the veranda and watched him as they put him into the car. He looked like a child in the back of the car. He was wearing the striped beanie I had bought him for his birthday.

The nursing sister said, 'Don't worry, dear. You can visit as often as you like.'

So easy for them to say. It is like visiting a stranger. Arnold, the Arnold I knew, has already gone. He just slipped away one day when I wasn't looking and an old man's body remained. That's all.

At least I will have the final part of my novel to keep me busy. I need to decide how much to reveal, and how much to conceal. It's always strange to come to the end of a novel. Like a kind of death when it's all done, all over.

Iris

Ashes

Someone called the fire brigade, of course. Most likely the woman who lived opposite and who cleaned her vertical blinds with soft cloth and detergent everyday had noticed the smoke. The blaze only burnt the front section of the house. A young fireman found Rosa's body. It was just as well that she didn't undress before she got into the bath, because the young man had never seen a dead body before and for the first one to be old and naked would seem too shocking. He knelt on one knee next to the bath as if in genuflection. But he wasn't genuflecting of course. What cause would he have to do so? He was just doing his job. Taking the victim's pulse, checking for life where clearly there was none.

'Looks like some woman might have done herself in here,' he yelled out to his colleagues.

A large figure in a yellow suit and mask came stomping down the hall. He put his head in the bathroom door. 'Oh, shit,' he said. 'Poor, old biddy. Thank Christ she left her clothes on. Better not touch anything. I'll call the cops. And an ambulance.'

The young man wiped a tear from his face.

'First time, mate? Don't worry, you'll get used to it,' said the man, lifting his mask.

Of course, the authorities notified Rosa's family. The funeral notices were arranged, and Rosa was laid to rest early, one cold morning on the first day of spring.

*

'At least Mum and Dad aren't here to witness it,' said Rick.

The director, Neville, had turned up for the wake – such as it was. But he didn't have that debonair stage-like aura about him that he so often did. Dressed in a dark suit and tie, he looked more like an undertaker than a character from a literary classic.

Rick opened a bottle of champagne.

'Hope it doesn't seem in bad taste to be drinking champagne,' said Delphine.

'No, I don't think Rosa would mind. She loved a glass herself,' said Camille.

Rick handed Neville a glass of champagne. He took a sip and stood next to him. Rick was wearing a casual jacket for the occasion and an open-neck shirt. The same height and similar build, Rick and Neville looked like versions of the same person.

'You seem to be just about Rosa's only friend, mate. We never did get to the bottom of whether there was a note or not, did we?' Rick addressed them all, as if he had been talking about a film he had watched or a book he had read.

Delphine and Camille exchanged a glance.

'Well, apparently there might have been some kind of charred note found in the kitchen. Very difficult to decipher. It may have said she didn't want any flowers. So Delphine and I made sure there were no flowers,' said Camille.

'Did she leave a will, do you know?' asked Rick, checking his phone.

Camille and Delphine both said in unison, 'I don't know.'

Neville drained the dregs of his champagne and handed his empty glass to Rick for a refill. 'I think you'll find her story was pretty well all she left behind.'

5 July 2006

Dear Rose,

I have just woken from the strangest dream. In my dream, Arnold was here sitting on the edge of my bed. He was young again. He had his Akubra hat in his hands and his blue eyes looked at me with love.

He said to me, 'Did we have a child once, Iris? A little girl? A baby girl?' He was holding a pink blanket in his hands. 'Just tell me, Iris. I need to know her name. I have forgotten. We had a baby, together, Iris. I know we did. I remember her dimpled little hands? Please tell me, Iris. What happened?'

I hope I never have that dream again. I wish it wasn't windy tonight. When Arnold was here, I could just call out to him and he would say, 'Put the dog inside, Iris, and go to bed.' But there is no Arnold any more. There is no one any more.

Iris

Remains

It fell to Delphine, Camille and Rick to sort through Rosa's effects. It was the first time any of them had ever visited her home, the first time they had ever stood in her light-filled kitchen with crystals hanging in the window and refracted light bouncing off the walls.

'I never realised Rosa liked gardening,' said Delphine, looking through the open French doors. 'Such a beautiful herb garden.' She reached for a sprig of basil leaves and crushed them between her fingers and put it to her face.

'Better get on with the job. Let's try and get finished as soon as we can, girls,' said Rick.

Obediently, Delphine and Camille began sorting through a box of charred papers: Rosa's notes, writing she had been working on. Much of it had been water-damaged.

Delphine lifted out what appeared to be a typed manuscript and shook it to remove the fine ash. 'Some of it's still intact.'

'It was probably the last thing she was working on before she died,' said Rick.

'Yes. We're lucky that it didn't fall into the wrong hands,' said Camille.

Delphine picked up the box and took it over to Rosa's old chaise longue. They all sat down together, Camille in the middle. With heads bent, they read through Rosa's work, passing the singed sheets of paper, the remains, one to the other.

'This isn't what was performed, is it?' said Rick.

'No, this seems to be more recent. You can see the editing marks – Rosa's handwriting. Perhaps it wasn't far from completion,' said Delphine.

'Well, let's see what this one is about. It's about our family, for sure,' said Rick. 'I told her not to write it. But it'll never see the light of day now. I'll make sure of that.'

'Yes, I know what you mean. Her writing has such a ring of familiarity about it. Like it has happened, but it hasn't. I mean this scene, for example. Who is Princess? She seems like someone we should know,' said Camille.

They bent their heads and read that page which was blackened and mottled at the edges like a pirate's treasure map. They sat together on the chaise longue on Rosa's back porch, the same porch where she had danced in the moonlight only months earlier. But they, her sisters and brother, weren't to know that. Delphine sat in the middle and Rick and Camille sat on either side of her as they read through the remains. An observer might have commented that they seemed relaxed, like a group of people fondly poring over old family pictures.

Rick took the damaged document from Delphine's hands and turned the pages and read some of the lines out loud.

'MOTHER: Do you think that Rosa sometimes makes things up? Imagines things?

'FATHER: Spins a yarn. Gilds, what do they call it…gilds the flower? No.

'MOTHER: The lily is what you mean, Father. "Gilds the lily" is the expression. Well, not tells lies, exactly. Just can't tell fact from fiction.

'FATHER: Exactly, she tells lies. All that girl ever does is dream and lie. It's okay to be a dreamer, but a liar…that's another thing… If I ever told lies about my father, he would break my jaw, just like I should break hers. Break her fucking jaw…like this (raises a clenched fist).

'Do you think she based the old man in this scene on Dad?' Rick asked.

'But our parents would never have had that conversation, that's for sure. Not about one of their children,' said Camille. 'Mum and Dad never spoke about Rosa like that after she left. Maybe Rosa thought they did,' said Camille.

'Yeah, maybe she was just a fucking liar,' said Rick.

'Seems like Rosa had a thing about being silenced or something,' said Delphine, flicking through the damaged pages.

'She wasn't treated any differently from any of us. Maybe she has just made this whole thing up. Maybe it has no relation to her own life. Maybe it's just fiction,' said Camille.

'Oh,' said Delphine, holding up one of the pages, 'I can't believe she has written this. I can't believe it…not now that he is dead… He should be left to rest in peace.'

'Well, read it out,' said Camille.

Delphine folded the papers and put them in her bag. 'Let's do this another day,' she said.

'What did she call the play?' said Rick.

A Shadow Play: Dark Rosaleen

Act One: Scene 3

DARK ROSALEEN and PRINCESS are shadows behind the curtain. DARK ROSALEEN is seated at kitchen table and PRINCESS is standing in a doorway, holding a suitcase.

DARK ROSALEEN: He should have been locked up for what he did, if you really face it.

PRINCESS: Who?

DARK ROSALEEN: You know who.

PRINCESS: You're demented. Seriously demented.

DARK ROSALEEN: So I'm demented if I tell the truth, am I?

PRINCESS: Truth. Truth? You're not telling the truth. You're full of lies. How could you even begin to say that about him?

DARK ROSALEEN: Please don't go off in this way – especially at night. You only have a few things in that suitcase, and it is so cold and dark outside. We should be able to talk about this. I will worry about you.

PRINCESS: You don't need to worry about me. I will survive like you survived. Do you think you are the only survivor in this family?

Lights dim. Stage is clear. Chorus voices come from off the stage. Dim lights behind the shadow curtain.

VOICE ONE: Well, it's hard to know the truth of the matter but clearly something was swept under the carpet.

VOICE TWO: That's if there was a carpet.

NARRATOR: (*Walks to the front of the curtain.*) That's the thing with surfaces – if you look underneath, you never know what you will find.

The spotlight dims.

A Day in August

Dear Rose,

It's has been hard finishing this novel. Hard to let it all go. But now it is done. The phone hasn't rung in weeks. I think I forgot to pay the bill. The rose in the vase next to my bed has died; the water has begun to smell. I wonder what day it is. It doesn't matter. Feels like Sunday. It'll be my birthday soon. Nobody will remember this one. Doesn't matter now. I feel so heavy and slow. Yesterday, someone knocked on the door, quite a persistent knock. I just lay under the blankets, not moving until it was quiet again. I could hear them talking.

'The letter box hasn't been cleared. Let's try again in a few days.'

And then my old wooden gate snapped shut. I looked out of the window. The women looked like my two sisters, but I must have been imagining things.

I am hungry. There's no food in the house, because I haven't been up to going out to the shops. I remember feeling hungry many times when I stayed with Auntie Jean and Uncle Ron. It's probably not fair to blame them, because they had other children to feed.

'No eating between meals in this house,' Auntie Jean would say. 'And don't let me catch you going near that pantry cupboard again. It's your own fault that you are in this condition. And your poor mother, God bless her, she's so ashamed. You're only fourteen. Girls like you…well… Try and stand up straight and hold your stomach in. The nuns will find it a good home and then you can go back and finish school. Let's hope you have learned your lesson. And try and wear longer skirts.'

Did the nuns find her a good home, I wonder? I only saw her for a few seconds. I remember pleading with the nun, who probably wasn't much older than I was, 'Please, please let me call her Rose.'

It's so cold now, but I will have to go out just one last time to take the package to Mr Bridport. I've finally found some string and I used brown paper that had been stuck at the back of cupboard for years. Arnold always held on to things – 'Never know when you might need that, Iris,' he'd say. And he was right about the brown paper. But I won't need much of anything any more.

My hair feels so greasy. I think I will have a bath as soon as I return. I guess I'll never know now how you, my beautiful Rose, fared.

Iris

PS: Now my work is done, I ask myself how I am going to get away with all these terrible and vicious lies. But in the end, ashes-to-ashes is the final scene for all of us. Dead women, like faded printed flowers on peeling wallpaper in old, forgotten houses tell no tales, but like flowers when they die, they leave their seeds behind.

Epilogue

Dead women tell tales.

It had been months now. Mia was beginning to feel she was being held captive by this manuscript, enmeshed in it somehow. She looked at the clock. Hours had slipped by, and the house had fallen silent. She couldn't remember if George had said goodnight or not, but he would be snoring by now. What a burden this job had been. Not so much the commas, spelling and punctuation but the woman herself, and the load she seemed to carry.

Worst of all was the final page, the handwritten letter, scratched on the back of a paper bag in red pen. It was impossible to know if it was an afterthought for the novel, or if it were a feverish letter. Again, Mia put on her glasses to read Iris's faint handwriting. No, she would not be including the letter in the novel. She had made the decision. Definitely not.

Mia had stacked copies of Iris's work, now edited with all the dashes placed and the 'i's dotted, ready to be sent off to publishers. What a relief it was to be sending the work out for the consideration of someone else, to be either accepted or rejected, but no longer Mia's millstone.

Sometimes, Mia felt as if she could have known Iris at some stage, and then in another sense it was as if she never really existed – that she was just a character in a story. Perhaps most troubling of all was a sense of yearning in Iris's writing, a longing for something distant and unnamed that no amount of editing could rectify.

Lately, Mia would wake to the sound of wind and to the sound of someone crying. When she opened her eyes fully, there was no wind outside, but her face would be wet and she could taste the salt of her own tears. And visions of Iris would come to Mia when she was sleeping. Not actually a dream but more of an image, a still, a portrait. And even sometimes when she wasn't sleeping, the scene would come to her. Iris in her tattered silk kimono, long grey hair flowing down her back. Iris standing in front of a mirror that did not reflect her face, only the view through the open window: wild roses covering an arbour sagging under the weight of the tangled briar and its tight heavy buds, white cockatoos high in the sky and Iris, red petals at her feet, holding the ripe womb of a rosehip, ready to burst, ready to let its seed go.

The last day

My Dearest Rose,

This is a letter that should say so much more, but I'm hoping that all will be said in my manuscript I am leaving for you, my own beautiful child.

Please forgive my imaginings, my dreaming, Rose, but it is all I have of you. You see, it is how I have coped. Perhaps you may never receive the package I wrapped so carefully in brown paper and string, smoothed out the creases and wished it well on its journey.

But I know, as you too must know by now, that in life, endings are never neat. They are ragged, untidy things that are the beginnings of something else.

So perhaps it is wrong and foolish of me to try to tie the loose ends in such a tidy manner. It's just that I want it to be that way and if I write it, perhaps it will be. What I don't know, I make up. Sometimes I think my whole life has been a fiction.

Perhaps this is all very selfish of me to have written to you in this way because if you do ever read my words, you will probably discover things you would prefer not to know. But no mother could have loved her daughter more than I have loved you, my dearest Rose.

From the bottom of my soul,

Iris

Your loving mother

Rose Songs

Rose Song 1

Branches once so strong, thorny, wild, sap-filled have become spindly, black and thin; now lush, green foliage is brown and brittle. Blooms are rare and only last a day or so before the petals give up and fall to the hard earth beneath. A solitary red rose appears without my ever having sighted the bud, as if it arrived fully formed just for me. I slash it at the throat. Steel blades of the secateurs sever the stem. A gust of wind blows and the blood-red petals fall, softly, touching the back of my hand as if in sad farewell. My roses. I blame myself. I have abandoned them, so why should they not abandon me? They are going to seed.

Rose Song 2

Tattered lace curtains blow in the wind that whistles through the open window. Walls are hospital green and grey shadows fall across the bed. Petals drop silently (although nothing can be completely silent) from the over-blown blooms in the chipped vase on top of the locked closet, making a mandala, a wish. But it's hard to recall the carpet.

Rose Song 3

Blood-red blossoms hang over the arbour that bends and struggles with the weight of tight heavy buds. Afraid, I enter the house. I can't see the rosebush now, but I know it is red and weeping, helpless in the rain, with thorns raised towards the sky. My feet settle on the faded, tattered carpet. For a long time, I was not sure if there ever was carpet, and now it's the carpet that haunts me the most.

Acknowledgements

The act of writing a novel does not take place in a vacuum, but amidst the everyday happenings of ordinary existence and interactions with other people: strangers, acquaintances, colleagues, mentors, close friends and family. To all the many people along the way who have supported me in the completion of this work, I say thank you. Those people who stand by you during the creative process leave their mark on your work and, in a sense, become part of it. In particular, I thank Dr Sue Gillett for her wonderful guidance and friendship.

Earlier versions of parts of this novel have been published as follows: 'Scene Thirteen', *Offset*, 2013; 'Not All Legacies Are an Act of Generosity', *Hecate*, 2014'; 'Anniversary Dinner', 'Remains', 'Apart', 'Untitled' & 'Interior View', Picaro Press, 2016. 'Rose Songs 1, 2 & 3' was exhibited as part of Co.Lab, 2017. The short story 'Hard Seed', on which this novel was based, was awarded the Katharine Susannah Prichard First Prize for short fiction in 2015. The chapter 'Strangers' was also commended.

La Trobe University and its Disciplinary Research Program in English, Theatre and Drama have generously funded the writing of this novel.

This novel is wholly a work of fiction. Characters, names, businesses, places, events and incidents are products of the author's creative imagination, or (if real) used in a fictitious manner. Any resemblance or similitude to actual persons, living or dead, or historic events is entirely coincidental.

www.ingramcontent.com/pod-product-compliance
Lightning Source LLC
Chambersburg PA
CBHW061612100726
47898CB00002B/623